JULIA GETS A LIFE

Lynne Barrett-Lee

Published by Accent Press Ltd – 2007
ISBN 1905170408 / 9781905170401
Copyright © Lynne Barrett-Lee 2007

Printed and bound in the UK

Cover Design by Anna Torborg

The publisher acknowledges the financial support
of the Welsh Books Council

For Peter, with all my love

Author's Note

Back in 1998, when this novel was first written, both Julia and myself lacked a number of things, without which life today would seem bizarre. Mobile phones, for example. An internet connection. Any notion that the city of Cardiff might soon become such a hip and happening place. Thus most of what follows is very much of its time, and so would not easily accommodate too much authorial tinkering. That said, in the interests of connecting with today, I've put to bed both Julia's Teletubbies and Max's ubiquitous yo-yo, and replaced them with Tweenies and a Nintendo VS. Neither pleases me in quite the same way, but then one's maternal history is invariably wedded to the cultural markers of its day. Conversely, marital strife - happily - is timeless...

Lynne Barrett-Lee June 2007

Chapter 1

I ALWAYS START WITH a list.

Today's list is written on the back of an old card. It reads:

Clothes/shoes etc.
Books – biogs. *Not* novels
Car/engineering mags
Wooden coat-hangers
Dumbbells
Trouser press

I keep cards (I keep most things), though not efficiently so. Like anything paper-based that is unsuitable for immediate binning, I tend to shove them anywhere I can find a suitable nook. This one I plucked from a wodge on my bedside table, that was stuffed between *Flat Stomach, Now!* and *Wild Swans*.

Inside the card there is a poem. It goes:

Roses are red,
Violets are blue,
What more could I need,
When I've someone like you?

Though real flowers were never much of a thing with him, Richard did do cards. Rubbish cards, mainly (this one is a montage of hearts, flowers, ribbons and what look like mouse droppings but are presumably buds, all buried under a crusty overspill of pearlised glitter), but personalised in his own sentimental, if rather prosaic, style. And there's more. It says, *To my wonderful wife on our anniversary. Love you always. Kiss, kiss kiss.* It's old, this one. From three, maybe four years back. But not longer, I estimate, because it was four years ago that we had the new carpet.

I know my list now so I rip it and bin it.

The thing about spring cleaning your bedroom is that it is tangibly different from cleaning, say, a kitchen. When you clear out a kitchen it's simply a case of pulling everything out, chucking away anything that looks like it might be a useful addition to a biology lab, scrubbing off all the crusty bits, and then lobbing it all back. But with your bedroom it's all start, stop, inspect, peruse, recall, smile wistfully, regret, start again, stop again etc., etc.

And filth, quite frankly, when you're as slovenly as I am. For me spring cleaning is simply the conjunction of two entirely unrelated words: something that occurs when you're flicking a duster and it just happens to be April.

Today though, I am spring cleaning proper. As well as the vacuum and a rag made of old pants (my mum's speciality), I have cans of polish, bin bags, a selection of cardboard boxes, labels and Sellotape, and carrier bags. I considered bringing up a cheese sandwich in a lunch box to keep me on task, but I couldn't because we've run out of bread.

Which is a remarkably apt illustration of the quality of my housewifery skills generally. As I cast about me now I note that my bedroom is beginning to look rather like an extension of me – well-intentioned, but tending towards disarray. This is because my possessions have all begun individual Triffid-like pilgrimages into previously uncharted regions. The top of the chest of drawers, for instance, was once home to just a lamp (horrible, wedding present), a photograph (of Richard and the children, by me) and a variable quantity of loose change. But now it looks more like Widow Twanky's lost property corner: a sea of balled socks and odd socks, tights and frayed knickers, with two empty wine glasses coming up for air.

Good God, my junk is *everywhere*. I really must get my head together and dump some. Except that the slattern in me has already sussed that I'm about to have a whole load more storage available, so my forays into strict and sensible space management seriously lack commitment.

I move around to the floor under the other bedside table and transfer what feels like a hundredweight of *What Car* and *New Civil Engineer* into a cardboard box which I carefully label *Mags*. Then I pull out the drawer and inspect its neat contents: a hardback biography, a blister pack of aspirins, a *Rennie:* just one, with its wrapper intact. No cards in here, I note. No scraps of paper. No paper clips, shirt buttons, dry cleaning tickets. No nothing that makes him seem human and real. It's so *sad*.

He's leaving today. I should write *him* a poem.

Daisies are dismal
Chrysanthemums stink
Have you back, dick-brain?
What do you think?

I have a five minute cry and then finish the packing.

Chapter 2

BUT IN THE MAIN I have licked the crying thing now. (Though I should have known that going through the debris of the last fifteen years would set me off. I would have wept if I'd found the button off my old Jasper Conran jacket.)

And Richard was not *leaving*, as such, because he actually left eleven weeks back. It was just his stuff that he was moving out. And not *leaving*, as such, because he was in fact propelled. By me. On a Thursday – or the small hours of Friday, if we're going to be precise. The night of the Cefn Melin Primary School Family Disco.

'Do I have to go to this?' he had asked me, plaintively. 'I've got a project meeting with the Council on Friday. And it's at 8.30 in the morning. Please. I could do without this.'

'But you promised to run the bar.' I gave him the familiar recap. He had. A week earlier, with a good two or three witnesses. I generally relied upon witnesses these days. Since the contract for the hotel Richard is building became part of our lives, a big part of his had been put out to tender; to be snapped up by builders and quarrymen and surveyors, while the hotel that Richard's firm were bringing into being heaved its sluggish way out of Cardiff Bay.

Move on then, to our house, a few hours later, where much of the backbone of PTA Fund-raising were assembled, many half-cut, on our sofas and floor. You can picture the scene. Moira Bugle, on the carpet, on her bottom, trying to make some sort of sense of the CD player.

'Haven't you got any *records*?' and so on. And 'They don't seem to care about *words* any more. And all this boomy stuff makes my teeth rattle. I'm sorry, but give me Ivor Novello or that John Denver any day...'

'They're both dead...'

'Well how about Tom Jones, lovely? Or those new ones. Now they *are* nice boys. Robson and Jerome. Julia, how about by there? Do you have any...no, I supposed not. Be a love, Derek, and help haul me up. '

And Rhiannon De Laney. How best to describe the bitch to you? Bitch works for me, of course. But if I'm being ruthlessly objective (and I'm sure there's a library book upstairs that would urge me to be so, as part of the healing process) I'd have to place her in the above-average-looking to beautiful category, but only if you like that sort of thing. Tall: she has those backwards flamingo type folding legs, thin, reddish/brunettish big hair, big nose (plus hook), big eyebrows, big lips. In fact, *gross* lips, like slugs. She wears lipstick *always* and she does that brown line round the edge which looks really stupid. In fact, there was an article in one of the Sunday supplements – *Depth*, perhaps? – that said brown lines are really uncool now. It showed lots of pictures of uncool celebs (mostly ropey soap stars with perma-tans) and pointed out how naff they looked. Hah! I'm so pleased. Hah!

Though on the down side, I rang my friend Colin last week, and he says guys actually quite like big lips because it puts them in mind of big…and also made them think the woman would be good at performing a Monica Lewinsky. Which is a touch depressing. My lips are only averagely thick, and I've heard collagen lip injections are the most painful thing a woman can undergo after giving birth and passing kidney stones.

Anyway, you get the picture. Big, brazen and looks like she's begging for it, is how Moira's Derek once described Rhiannon, though obviously well out of Moira's hearing. So she was always going to be trouble. And she is available. She is Cefn Melin's token single mother. Not that she fits the bill conceptually. For starters, she has a brand new teeny-weeny two bed townhouse, on the first phase of the new development just outside the village. It has a wrought iron knocker and a floodlit mini-rockery, and she parks her pastel hatchback on the herringbone drive. Rhiannon was once, it seems, married to a local businessman, but threw him out after some sort of scandal with a typist. So *she* says. As she would. There is one child, Angharad, who is six and seems to sport cream broderie anglaise trimmed socks with *everything*. The bootleg trouser must be a thorn in her side.

By day Rhiannon houseworks and networks around North Cardiff's under-fives haunts doing her *Seedlings* book parties. By night, she is, of course, a witch.

So why on earth did I agree so readily when she offered to stay and help clear up? Was I mad? *Am* I mad? Not at all. Just the victim of my own indignation. I can remember thinking at the time 'bloody right, she *can* stay and help clear up for a change. I'm sick and tired of her drifting along to everyone else's house after school fund-raising events and then wafting around the living room so the men

5

can all look up her skirt. And then leaving all the mess for everyone else to deal with. Especially given that the nearest we've ever got to an invite to her house was a (book party, naturally) coffee morning (ten to eleven-thirty) with only one sort of biscuit and serious pressure to sign up for an encyclopaedia on CD Rom. Yes, I can remember thinking all of that. I even made sure I was the one who got the rubber gloves.

How silly I was. This was clearing up as foreplay.

So then we move on to Richard's return. He, naturally, had been required to walk Rhiannon home: a round trip of thirty minutes, perhaps. But as I had gone to bed already, I hadn't any firm idea of how long he'd been gone. It was late, we were all tired and we'd all had rather more to drink than we'd intended. I came back down simply because he seemed to be taking an inordinately long time to come up to bed. The normal pattern of sounds hadn't happened. No bolt, no fridge opening, no glass being clinked as he poured out some juice. No flick of the light switch or rustle of the paper. I'd called out to him but had received no reply. I crossed the landing. He was down in the hall, staring at his reflection in the mirror. He was as still as a photograph, stiff and waxen.

'What are you doing?'

He started. 'Oh! I...er...didn't hear you. I...'

'Come on, come to bed...'

'I'm just going to sit down here for a while. I'm...'

At which point, he stopped speaking.

There is nothing so acute as the sense of foreboding. The man at the foot of the stairs suddenly looked no longer like Richard; and things, as they say, were not as they should have been. Knowing even then that there was something unpleasant about to unfold, I padded barefoot down the stairs and followed him into the kitchen. Then I said,

'Are you all right?'

'Yes, I'm fine.' He was facing the window, his back to me. But I could see his expression reflected in the glass. I didn't like what I saw.

'Are you sure?' I asked.

'*Yes!*' Slightly aggressive. 'I mean, no. No, I'm not.' And then he turned around and I knew he was going to tell me something bad.

*   *   *

6

Which is exactly what he did. He told me that he had just been to bed with Rhiannon De Laney, and that he didn't know what had possessed him, and that it was the most awful thing he had ever done, and that he was sorry and that he loved me and that he didn't know how he would cope with the rest of his life if I left him, and that he deserved for me to leave him and that he desperately hoped I would forgive him. That's about the gist of it, anyway. His exact words were difficult to pick out, because I was yelling at him throughout.

Eventually I went so wild that he became rather exasperated with me, I think. I don't know quite what he expected my reaction to be – do men hope their wives will turn into their mothers in these situations, and be calm and understanding and make cocoa, perhaps?

He kept trying to shush me and eventually said, quite sternly, 'Julia, we are grown-ups; we have children sleeping upstairs. Please try to hold yourself together.'

There have been few occasions in my life when I have wanted to throw something at somebody. We had a row once that resulted in a full English breakfast being flipped up to the ceiling. The bean splats were still in place when we moved, three years later. But it was Richard who threw it up there, not me. At this point, though, I can clearly recall scanning the kitchen for appropriate items. My bud vase? Too delicate. My flambé dish? Too loud. The washing up bowl? Full of washing up (which was *another* thing). I finally settled, bizarrely, on one of my Ikea seat pads – silent, unbreakable, on elastic (so re-usable) and, if aimed correctly, it could pack quite a punch, and perhaps a small gouge from the tab on the zip. And boy, did I want to hurt him. I plucked it, matador style, from the chair, and slammed it at his face with all the force I could muster.

We had by now reached the point where in all those forties Doris Day/Rock Hudson-style movies the man, (smiling sardonically, naturally) gently but firmly takes hold of the woman's flailing wrists and gathers her to him in a fond embrace. This was real life, though, so Richard just ducked. And said 'for Christ's sake, Julia, pack it in'.

I replied, 'No (thwack), I (thwack) bloody (big thwack) won't.'

He left soon after. Took his car keys, his coat and his mobile phone and without looking back, he galumphed up the path.

I tidied the (already quite tidy) house on autopilot. Some of the most thorough cleans I've done in my life have been in the aftermath of a blazing row. It's such a productive use of time that would otherwise be spent in pointless pursuits such as sitting with a mug of cold coffee saying why why why and suchlike. Instead, cushions got plumped, knick-knacks got straightened, and a million and one small items of debris – from woodlice to gravel to shards of stale Pringle – were plucked from the hall and the stairs and the living room and deposited in the bin in the kitchen, which I then emptied and scrubbed and sprayed with germ-busting spray.

I ran the dishwasher, laundered a half load of socks, gave the kitchen skirting boards a scrub with an old Mr Men toothbrush, then did them again with Richard's as well. I considered the writing of a small, pithy note, half wrote it in my head and then abandoned the idea. He had gone, like I'd asked him to. Back to Rhiannon's? And this time we both knew it was serious.

I sat in the kitchen for a good hour, undecided as to whether I felt vindicated in my zero tolerance stance, or simply frightened that he'd taken any notice of it. My stomach, confused and bewildered, convulsed, as picture upon picture of them flashed up to taunt me. Part of me wanted to dial his mobile and make up. Another part carried on silently fuming. The bastard. The *bastard*. How could he do something like that? At three thirty-seven, the bastard part won. I locked the doors, drew every bolt I could think of, and, flicking the light switch, I walked up the stairs and trod the few yards to our bedroom.

Then I climbed on the bed, lay face down on the duvet and cried pretty vigorously for two whole hours. But quietly, as grown-ups with children must do.

I woke at seven, still dressed, with a dead arm and a headache, and reality seeped and then deluged my consciousness. I went downstairs to find a Post-it note (one of mine, from the car, no doubt) that he'd slipped through the letterbox, having, I assumed, failed to get in. It said,

'*God, I'm so sorry. Please call me asap. I'm at the Pontprennau Road Inn. I don't know how to* – I turned it over. It was a very small Post-it note – *begin to tell you how sorry I am. Please call.*'

And he hadn't signed it. Which was so unlike him. Or not, I suppose, given that I did not, as far as I knew, have any outstanding feuds with the milkman or the man who delivered household gadgets. I clutched the note, alert to the small sounds of my children surfacing. Then I crumpled it, hard, in the heel of my hand and launched it, inexpertly, binwards. Which, I have to say, was actually quite unlike me.

Chapter 3

'WHAT'S NEEDED HERE IS a cooling-off period, and a chance to reassess your respective situations more objectively than you're able to in the heat of the moment.'

Which was all sound advice. The morning after I locked the doors on Richard, I held it together – just. As Richard generally left before the children came down, there was nothing, bar my own ravaged countenance, to alert them to the fact of their father's dreadful betrayal. I made them both sandwiches, laid out their breakfast and pretended it had been a whizz of a PTA do. Max, having been party to much of it, was scathing as only an eleven-year-old could be.

'When I'm old, I just won't be seen *dead* doing what you do. *No* way.' He launched a volley of Coco Pops at his bowl. 'In fact, parents shouldn't be allowed to dance at these things. Should they, Em?'

No, I thought wretchedly. They bloody shouldn't. Emma, older, and (in matters of ambience) wiser, ignored him, and instead, said, 'Are you alright, Mum? You look like the pits.'

'I feel it,' I said, conscious of her hand on my shoulder and the tears that were threatening to plop onto her toast. 'All this manic…er…partying. But I'll be okay. Really.'

Her look said quite unequivocally that she didn't believe me, but with what I immediately recognised as an instinct for self-preservation, she put a lid on her anxieties and my own backed-up hysteria, and sat down instead with her brother to eat. We muddled on gamely till the clock crawled to eight-thirty. I waited a further quarter of an hour before phoning Lily and unleashing the flood.

Lily has to be almost the most important female person in my life. She was our Au Pair for two years when we first moved to Wales and Emma and Max were tiny. I, suddenly displaced, and thus in a fit of possibly misplaced enthusiasm (or nappy-refusal, more like), was attempting to relaunch my fledgling photographic career. Okay, so all I actually did was a part-time job at Time Of Your Life Family Photo Studio and a bit of advertising freelancing, but without Lily I would have been crafting a straight-jacket for myself out of old muslins. Being French, and essentially stroppy, she was a right pain to live with (gravy? What is gravy? Oh, Mon Dieu! It is vile!)

but she was efficient and loyal and made brilliant quiches, and never complained when I had to work late. I missed her dreadfully when she returned to Bordeaux, but happily, within months, she was back, with a real job. Teaching French A level to francophile adults at the Continuing Ed. Dept at the University.

'Exactly,' she said now, waggling a finger at the television and scooping her thick coffee hair to one side. But the advice wasn't actually for me. I had called in sick (a *first*) and we were sitting at my kitchen table; me feverishly removing Emma's mauve 'disco chick' nail polish, while Lily, pragmatically (friend's crisis notwithstanding) kept half an eye on the Reggie Smartass Show. The words of wisdom were not addressed to my marital traumas, but to a middle-aged woman with bad facial thread veins who was engaged in some sort of battle with her neighbour (an aggressive hag in a nylon shirt-waister dress, who kept going 'Pah! Blewdy roobish!'). It was apparently over her right to herd yaks, or something equally life-enhancing. I normally enjoyed a kind of low-life pleasure on the odd occasion I got to watch these shows. There is something deeply therapeutic about comparing the smooth manageability of your own existence with people who write to television stations and take part in mid morning spleen-venting sessions.

Today, though, my brain kept returning to the astonishing fact that my husband had gone and had sex with someone other than me. And that was really, honestly, my principal reaction. Astonishment. We *had* a sex life. Had a rather good sex life, as far as I could tell. No one really knows what sort of sex life anyone else is having, I suppose, but we seemed to be chugging along inside all the usual parameters; he enjoyed it, I enjoyed it, it seemed to happen quite regularly and naturally. So what the hell did he think he was doing? Just how much sex did Richard need?

A new concept gripped me. Was this even *about* sex? Or about something else I had failed to provide? But what? My mind flipped through our marital log book. It hadn't been one long uneventful cruise down the motorway, but such pit-stops as we'd had had been generally productive; we functioned in all things, I'd thought, as a team. What now?

Lily arched one of her dense Gallic eyebrows. Then shook her head.

'This is what happens,' she told me. 'You married too young, I think. And he is English.'

'Half English. And so what?'

11

'And so expect the worst, I think.'

'Why?' Why indeed? Was there something I'd missed here?

'Hmm,' she said. 'Anyway, you are both bored as well.'

'I'm not!'

'You are. You are always going on.'

'Going on?'

She flicked up some fingers. 'Will Young, Liam Neeson, that man who does the nature programme–'

'Bill *Oddie*?'

'Oh, I don't know. The one in the jungle. Makes boats.'

'*Bushcraft*, you mean. That's not Bill Oddie. It's Ray Mears.'

She slapped a hand down on the table. 'There! You see?'

'But that's not the same, Lily. Not the same at all. That's normal. This is –'

'And that woman was *available*. And if Ray Mears was available, would you not –'

'No, I wouldn't! Because I'm married. You don't –'

'Well Richard *did*. Actually, I think I would kill him,' she decided. 'So what now? *Will* you kill him? Or tell him to come home and stop being silly when he rings?

'*If* he rings' I corrected, exasperated. There'd been the Post-it, of course, but so far the phone had been silent. And I bloody well wasn't going to ring him. Which was another thing. *Why* hadn't Richard rung? Why wasn't he on the doorstep right now grovelling at me? Or proffering petrol station flowers or something? But then I realised I didn't really have any yardsticks for infidelity. This wasn't a row. Wasn't something that held much scope for debate. I could jump about on my bit of moral high ground all I liked, but it would be a hollow victory – he wasn't about to argue, was he?

So then why wasn't he simply asking me to forgive him? Did he really think I was going to ring *him*? Surely not. And was the Post-it the best he could manage by way of apology? If it had been me, I would have been round like a shot. I would have grovelled, big time. I sipped at the cup of disgusting coffee that Lily placed in front of me and made faces at the old bitch in the Crimplene.

Richard telephoned only moments after Lily had gone. Had he been in the hedge, perhaps?

'We need to talk,' he said. Then, 'Oh, God, I'm so *sorry*, Julia.'

'Stop saying "oh, God, I'm so sorry",' I said.

I didn't like the 'Julia'. It made me feel cold. I was never Julia; he'd always called me darling or Ju. Being called Julia was spooky and horrible. Nevertheless, I agreed that he drive round, and that we should talk and that most importantly (his suggestion) we should conduct our summit meeting in good time so as to be all sorted out (as if) before the children got home from school.

Because we were either going to fight, or I was going to cry some more. Or both. But though neither sounded particularly appealing, there was still the small glow that was my innocence and his guilt. I cleared away Lily's lunch and washed up the dishes. I would have him back, of course. It would be ridiculous not to.

Coolish, calmish and almost collected, I ushered him in at a quarter past two.

At two-sixteen I immediately regretted my earlier compulsion to clear everything up. I took up my usual hostilities position (sinkside) but had nothing to do there other than flap a dishcloth around.

'So,' Richard said, hands in jeans pockets, rocking slightly in the kitchen doorway. He looked vulnerable, boyish and yet so handsome and masculine – male in a way I hadn't recently connected with. Someone another woman might set her sexual sights on. Separate from me. It was frightening.

'Did you go to work in those clothes?' I asked him. Had he been to work at all, in fact?

'Of course I bloody did. What else was I supposed to do? I've got a bloody hotel to get built, haven't I?'

He looked ready to give me a left hook as he said this, but then made a small adjustment to his face and said, 'I've taken the rest of the day off.'

'Oh,' I said. Then, 'Do you want a cup of tea?'

'No. I don't want a cup of tea.'

He yanked out a chair – plus the very same seat pad I'd hammered his face with – and sat down abruptly. I put the kettle on.

'So,' he said again. 'Where do we go from here?'

Which I thought was quite laughable as an opening line, except I didn't know then what he was going to say next. For one gut-wrenching moment, I thought he was going to tell me he wanted to leave *me*. Which was something that had never crossed my mind up until this point. But no, that couldn't possibly be the case, could it?

'Where?' I said, eventually. 'You tell me.'

13

'Julia, you've got to believe me when I tell you I am so, so, *so* sorry about what I've done.' He put both his hands up. 'I have no excuses. I'm not about to make any. I am truly sorry. You believe that, don't you?'

I swallowed the lump that was beginning to form in my gullet. Crying so *early!* Drat, bloody drat.

'I'm sure you are,' I said, leaning against the draining board and folding my arms across my chest. I sounded, I knew, like a wool shop proprietress in the *People's Friend*. 'But it's a bit late for that, isn't it? I bet you were feeling sorry while you were screwing her, weren't you (he had the grace to hang his head and nod a bit at this), but it didn't stop you, did it? How could you? How *could* you? What's wrong with me?'

He rose from the chair then seemed to think better of it. 'Nothing, *nothing*. Nothing at all,' he said. 'I love you. You know how much I love you. I can't believe I did it. I can't believe I've been so stupid...'

'I can.' All of a sudden I really could, too. I could see Rhiannon witch-face bitch-features standing in her cream lounge by her cream sofa swaying very slightly to the low-volume twanging of her insipid CD collection, saying, 'C'mon, Richard, let's have a quick smooch to this'. And I could see Richard's willy going *ping!* – could actually *see* it – and saying 'Yeah, c'mon, Richard, go for it, mate. Where's the harm?'

'I know,' he said. 'What can I say? I can't believe...'

Then I got cross. Bang! Just like that.

'Believe it! You've done it! You've had sex with Rhiannon De Laney! You've ruined everything. I hate you. I really hate you. And d'you know what? Mainly I can't stand the thought of you anywhere near me because you've put your (I flapped a hand in the general direction)...your...ugh!...inside that bitch. It's disgusting, and I...'

And then I had to stop speaking because I started crying properly. Richard now leapt up and crossed the kitchen in two strides. He put his arms around me, tight enough so that I couldn't push him away without kneeing him in the groin first.

Strangely, I didn't mind him holding me like this. I was upset and it seemed quite natural for him to do it. I felt safe cocooned within his bristly embrace. And I guess at that point I had every intention of holding things together. We were a family. We would sort everything out. But then he put a sledgehammer through all the cracks I'd planned to paper over. He said, 'Julia, I *have* to tell you something else. Something important.' And he held me tighter.

I held my breath.

'This is…this isn't…I mean…look. I'm so sorry…' That again. 'Julia, I've had sex with Rhiannon before.'

I inserted my knee into the ensuing silence and Richard exploded backwards across the room.

'You bastard!' Richard couldn't answer for groaning. 'You absolute *bastard*. How many times before?'

'Only once,' he squeaked finally, from the safety of the other end of the kitchen. 'Honestly, only the once. It was…'

'Don't even bother to tell me. I know exactly when it was.'

I lunged for the teapot and started making tea, vigorously, while Richard, still clutching himself, sat back on his chair.

'The Christmas fancy dress party,' he continued, ignoring me. You remember – I had to walk her home then. She came on to me, Julia. Really came on to me…'

So I'd been right. Two months back. I'd known something was up. I'd thought – how ridiculously naive can you be? – that he was behaving sheepishly because he'd kissed her. Just that. The whole hog, obviously. Full on the lips, with tongues. Which was certainly out of order, but I'd decided to forget it. Rhiannon fancied him. But then I fancied Caitlin Goodrich's husband. Everyone was being out of order that night.

'Nothing to do with you feeling her behind every ten minutes for most of the evening, then?' I grabbed two mugs from the mug tree and they banged together, hard. When I looked, one was chipped. One of my favourite ones, too.

'You know what it's like. It was just harmless fun. I had no idea that she was going to…'

I slapped at the kettle switch. 'Oh, I see. So it wasn't your fault at all then. She raped you, did she? Locked you in her prissy little starter home and pulled your pants off, did she?'

He exhaled. 'Now you're being stupid…'

'Don't you dare call me that!'

'I'm sorry…look, I'm just trying to explain what happened.' He stood up again. 'It was a mistake. I felt awful about it. Look, I don't even like her much…'

'Oh, that's even better! So you just thought you'd utilise her equipment, did you?'

15

'Look, you know she's always had a bit of a thing for me. It's hard being a man. It's…'

'Oh! You're so gross! I can't believe you are actually standing there and saying all this with a straight face.'

He sat down again. 'I just want to…'

'Do you want tea?'

'No.'

'Too bad, then.'

I slammed down a mug on the table beside him. A little sploshed out on the back of his hand. He winced, and, at that point, so pleased with his reaction, I almost tipped the whole lot over his head. Which was scary, in retrospect.

I moved back to the sink and took several deep breaths.

'So how many times?'

'Just two. I told you.'

'But how many would it have been if…'

'For Christ's sake, Julia. I just told you, didn't I? I confessed. I owned up because I couldn't stand what I'd done. I had to tell you. This wasn't some sort of sordid affair…'

'Sordid sounds just about right to me.'

I sipped at my tea and listened to the pulse in my temples. I noted the past tense he was using, which was good. And also that I believed him when he told me he had only had sex with her twice. But then the enormity of him lying to me for the past two months sank in. And then he'd done it again.

'Why did you do it again, Richard?'

My voice held that particular note of icy calm so beloved of thriller movies and usually attributed to the psychopathic counter-espionage bad guy. It wasn't lost on Richard. He stopped and thought before answering.

'It happened because I let it happen. But I didn't want to walk Rhiannon home in the first place. *You* know that. I told you I didn't. When everyone started to leave, I said "can anyone drop Rhiannon off?" And she said "don't worry, I'll stay and help you clear up. I can get home on my own. I'm not a baby." And *you* said, "good, we could do with some help". And I said "no, go on. You go." And you both said no. And I thought "shit" because I knew I would have to walk her home. How could I not? How could I let a woman walk home on her own at one in the morning? You even said so yourself. I knew she'd start doing…you know… I nearly told you then, but I…'

16

I had to break into this heart-sinking catalogue of disasters. I'd be feeling sorry for him next.

'Doing what? Getting her breasts out?'

He nodded vigorously. 'Almost. Yes, almost.'

'Oh, come on. No one's that blatant.'

'She is! She started saying about last time, and how she hadn't had such great sex in years and all that sort of thing, and how she kept remembering...'

'Don't tell me. How much she...no! This is making me want to be sick! You did it once, which was bad enough. And then you lied to me for two months. And then you did it again. *You did it again,* Richard. *You* did it. You make me sick.'

The words seemed to swirl in the air between us, my anger and distress now a palpable thing. Our gazes cut through it for several long seconds. Then Richard put his head in his hands, just like they do in films. And his shoulders moved very slightly. He was crying.

I stood and watched him cry for a good minute. Strangely, I no longer wanted to. Then I said, 'I'd like you to go upstairs and get some stuff. Then I think you should leave.'

'But Julia...'

'You wanted to know where we were going? Well you can go where you like. I don't want you any more.'

17

Chapter 4

IT WAS JUST LIKE being pregnant again. Night after night of horrible, fearful, gut-churning indecision. Hour upon hour in a chasm of dread. What about the children? What about money? What about the holiday in France we had planned? What about the house? What about the *mortgage*? And what about Richard? Where would he live? What *about* the children? Why on earth did he *do* this? And what was *I* doing? What about *us*?

Richard had decamped to a place called Malachite Street: a flat in a house near the centre of Cardiff, which, by the sound of it, had long since been stripped of its dignity, through years, probably decades, of student excesses and Anaglypta abuse. He had (after requesting his mail be re-directed) pointedly made mention of its temporary nature. I wasn't sure if by temporary he meant him or it. My four a.m. horrors would often be visited by visions of him, curled against a flea-ridden bolster, while freight trains from the valleys thundered thoughtfully by.

What to do? What to *do*?

The first list I made, post the crisis, was this:

Reasons to have Richard back

He's said he won't do it again
He still loves me (huh?)
The children
Utter financial apocalypse
Like being married (consider)
Still love him (probably, once cooled off)

Reasons to leave Richard

He might do it again
Infidelity symptom of big flaw in marriage
Always said I would if unfaithful
Hate him

But, eleven weeks into our 'estrangement', as Richard's mother, had she still been alive, would have put it, I've made some changes to my lists. Under 'Reasons to have Richard back', I now have:

He said he won't do it again (not sure I believe)
He said he still loves me (do believe)
The children (though adapting – getting lots of cash/presents from Father)
Complete and utter financial apocalypse
Love him (query)

Conversely, under reasons *not* to have him back, as well as drawer space and freedom to re-decorate in orange if I so wish (which *is* a factor) I now have:

He might do it again
Infidelity symptom of big flaw in male willpower
Always said I wouldn't (though not relevant – have read book that says so)
Like being single
Coping with re-visit of mince-based cuisine (just)
Not sure how feel about him *really*

Those last two are giving me some pause for thought, being a totally unexpected development, and related to a funny thing which happened to me the other day while I was waiting for Max outside school.

I don't get up to school much these days because I am an unwelcome fixture by the school gates at the best of times, and particularly so since I have become a tragic heroine/cause for concern/figure of fun etc. But the twin inconveniences of rain and cricket training finishing simultaneously with the start of *Neighbours* (even Max cannot run *that* fast) mean that I have been permitted a once-weekly loiter. In fact, I quite like it, because all the infant mothers who know me only as that woman who's husband went off with Rhiannon De Laney are long gone to prepare their kids fish finger suppers, and I am assured of meeting only those older stalwarts who have been associated with the school for as many years as I and who are not adverse to saying 'That bitch Rhiannon – who does she think she is?' etc. Which is all very encouraging.

But the funny thing was this. I found myself leering at Howard Ringrose, who as well as being my friend, is Max's teacher, head of PE and also God of Year Six.

I have known Howard for a long time. Though he has been God of Year Six for a couple of years now, he has previously been God of years Five and Four and some years back he was even God of Reception – though in this incarnation, it has to be said, he was probably more cuddly-teddy-bear-figure-in-tracksuit than sex-deity, and attracted twigs, drawings, things made out of eggshells and so on from most of the class, regardless of gender, instead of the love tokens of orange Aeros that the female contingent of his class buy him now.

But the whole *God* thing is pretty much part of the landscape. Mothers once noted for their adhesion to car seats during the three-thirty chaos, have blossomed into perfectly groomed gate-hangers after catching sight of his shins, and it's generally agreed that there is a small contingent of the after-school rugby club every year that are not there wholly due to a love of mud and scrums.

And we've always been pretty friendly. I've sold raffle tickets with him, manned cake stalls with him, sympathised about the National Curriculum with him. In short, we *got on*. And though I was fully able to appreciate his physical advantages, it never really occurred to me to fix him in my mind during a routine weekday quickie with Richard. Honestly. But now I've been leering at him.

And I mean leering. Not just admiring any more, from a philosophical standpoint, but actually *leering*, in a blokey type way. Now I know women have been known to do that sort of thing (I've been to see the Chippendales, and if I was one I'd leave the theatre with a stout saucepan over my genitals) but there is now a tangible difference in the quality of my appreciation of Howard. It has become sort of breathless and wistful.

Not a big thing, spelt out, perhaps, but to me it seemed to crystallise all the niggling little doubts I keep having every time I set myself up to have Richard back. I *really* am not sure I want him any more. As opposed to earlier, when I was saying I didn't want him any more just because I hated him, which is completely different and more to do with his betrayal. Isn't that dreadful? I'm really not sure if I still want to be married to him.

I've given this a lot of thought just lately and I'm no nearer being in touch with my inner child than I was before I read the book that told me to go and find her. Lily told me she thinks it's more to do with sex. She thinks a part of me resents the fact that Richard has had sex with someone else and I haven't, and that I need to get even with him – level the playing field, kind of – before I can decide what to do with the rest of my life. Which is interesting, because accepted opinion seems to be more along the lines of two wrongs don't make a right and suchlike, and that it will only make me feel worse. But surely that presupposes that one is *only* having sex with a third party in order to redress the balance? I actually *really* quite fancy Howard Ringrose. Come to think of it, I also actually rather fancy Emma's best friend's dad, *and* the postman *and* the guy who mans the car park booth at work. So the tit-for-tat rule doesn't apply, does it? I shall have to see what else I can find in the library.

Things To Do (shopping):

Find more books about female libido/sexuality with special reference to extra-marital case histories etc.
Buy Lady Chatterley's Lover (finally!) or similarly rude book

Of course, it may simply be that I'm not getting any sex. It's all well and good sighing knowingly at girly get-togethers along the lines of 'oh, men! Never satisfied! How I long to be able to go to bed with a Curly Wurly and a cup of hot chocolate! Ho Hum!' but the truth is, you do begin to miss it. I did, naturally, spend the first few weeks in a sexual limbo. I was far too busy feeling betrayed and unattractive and pathetic to even think about sex (except as related to the breakdown of my marriage in conjunction with what I'd like to do to Rhiannon De Laney given half a chance). But since the rediscovery of myself as a sexual being, I must admit I've thought of little else.

Perhaps I should go and find some.

Chapter 5

OKAY. SO WE'RE TWELVE and a half weeks post-marital-bliss now (as opposed to just post-marital, which would only occur at such time as we (I) decide that a divorce is the-best-way-forward). I am very gratified that I am able to say the D word without blanching, though I must confess to having certain misgivings about the whole post-ness of life generally. It sometimes seems that it is no more than a series of stages to be got through, culminating in dying and then having your body chopped up (according to circumstance, naturally). So far, I have been post-pubescent, post-graduate, post-nuptial, post-partum and post-natal.

Which, as well as post-marital (if applicable), leaves postmodernist, post-feminist, post-menopausal (Eeek!), Post-Office (and Post-Office savings account) i.e. *old,* and post-mortem.

But thinking such dismal and unedifying thoughts is just a reaction to stress and boredom. And something to use up the time that I would, under normal circumstances, fill with having sex. (None on horizon as yet.) It's also the time of year when Time-Of-Your-Life does its annual in-store snap-fest of under fives, so I am spending a tedious amount of time in traffic jams/unfamiliar underground staff car parks/consultations with floor managers who don't want to dismantle seasonal displays of nappy boxes to accommodate us/conversations with shoppers about where the toilets are. All this to find the face that will launch some rash cream or other, and drum up a substantial amount of business for my employer. God, I hate my work sometimes. I wish I was famous and rich and could go back to the simple joys of shooting brooding treescapes and clusters of scowling adolescents.

Today, we're based at *Planet Kid,* a new and, it has to be said, fairly groovy baby and kids store in the soft underbelly of Cardiff's retailing fringe. *Planet Kid*, the local paper said when it opened, is the last word in state-of-the-art retail outlets, having five kinds of toilet, computerised shoe fitting and electronic tagging for small escapees. In fact, such is its popularity that a species of human quite outside my comprehension queued to get in *from dawn* on opening day.

We've been allocated a spot in the middle of a kind of causeway, from which shoppers can plunge down ramps into a number of themed purchasing areas. But this is also the only route to Chews (the café), News (the information desk), Blues (the place to hang out while your child – as it most certainly will – is having a tantrum) and Loos (five kinds) – and though it feels a little like we've set up shop on the hard shoulder of the M4, it at least means every single person in the store will probably pass it at some point, during our ten to four stint.

I'm here with Rani – a definite plus-point. Rani has worked at Time-Of-Your-Life for almost as long as I have. Her real job is acting as secretary cum receptionist cum babe, but in truth she is the linchpin of the whole operation. On sorties like these it is Rani who organises the paperwork, deals with the money, negotiates advantageous deals with store managers and drags people away from their retail therapy with a spot of 'Oh, what an *amazingly* lovely baby – I can't *believe* you haven't considered professional modelling for her' inducement garbage. Never fails.

Except that it's Monday morning and there are precious few people around to accost. So we decide we both need a fortifying *Bob the Builder* bun, and Rani heads off to Chews to acquire them.

And it's then that I see her. Or, rather, I don't *actually* see her, at first. What I see is Caryl Phelps (baby Oscar, plus four-year-old, Emmy, married to a local tree surgeon stroke garden designer) cruising an underwear stand. I don't know Caryl Phelps *that* well, but certainly well enough to accost her. I'm just about to try and attract her attention when a familiar arrangement of bouncing auburn curls, cream blur clothing ensemble and lip-liner, slides up alongside her to compare knicker crotch durability or something.

Help, help, help, help, help!!!! What do I do? What do I say? There is a brick in the pit of my stomach, the likes of which I have not felt since I was twelve and lobbed a conker through our next door neighbour's cloakroom window. How *pathetic*. But what *do* you do in this situation? What do you *do*? And why does this have to happen while Rani is buying us cakes?

But they don't see me for the moment (thank you, God) so I have time to collect my thoughts. Which are:

What clothes am I wearing?
What shoes am I wearing?
What make-up am I wearing?
Which earrings did I put on this morning?

23

Should I zip to the loo and put blusher/eyeliner/more mascara on?

Have any flakes of nail varnish dropped off?

How many days post-hairwash am I? Eeek! Three!

Is there time to plunge my head into a basin, wash my fringe and blow-dry it under the warm-air dryer?

Might there be lipstick on my teeth?

And: Bitch, bitch, bitch. Oh God. Bitch

How dare she come in *Planet Kid*! How *dare* she! And how dare she have Caryl Phelps as a friend still. And how dare Caryl Phelps still associate with her! She should be ostracised in the whole of Wales and told to shove her *Seedlings* books up her cream g-string. She should be made to feature in an exposé in the Cefn Melin newsletter, or put in some stocks by the war memorial. She should be beaten about the head with rotting fish and have a baguette stuffed up each nostril. She should be...

'Julia! Hi!'

Eeek! Caryl Phelps!

'I didn't know you worked in here.'

'I don't. I work for Time-Of-Your-Life. We're running our annual...' Where is she? Where *is* she? '...portrait competition. Face2Face...'

'Of course. *Now* I remember. You're a photographer, aren't you? How glamorous!'

This? *Glamorous?*

'Not really. It's...'

'I was just saying to Rhiannon how lovely it'll be once mine are both at school – I can't wait. Isn't that dreadful? I don't mean it, of course, but sometimes...'

Oh, shut *up,* you twittering woman. Where's...oh, Christ! I get it! She doesn't know!

Caryl Phelps does not know that Rhiannon has shagged Richard. Caryl Phelps does not know that I have chucked him out. Caryl Phelps does not know that Rhiannon is my biggest enemy in all the world bar slugs and that as soon as she comes within ten feet of me I am liable to scream or cry or shake or have a hot flush – in fact any or all available adrenalin-induced reactions and that, mainly, I might just punch her face in.

'I know. But I *do* know what you mean. It's hard work with babies, isn't it? Non-stop nappies and feeds and crying and trying to force rusks down them and...har, har, har. Do you want to enter Oscar?'

'Oh, I don't know. He's just gone off.'

'It's free. *And* you get the print, and if you decide to...'

'Free? Oh, in that case...Rhi!'

So *there* she is. She is scrabbling amongst character pyjamas with her back to us. She knows I am here. She knows Caryl is talking to me. She is trying to *avoid* me.

Knowing this has an electrifying effect. I can feel all my adrenalin re-routing to my muscles. I can feel every empowering word I've read in every book I've got out of the library (central and local) resonating in my head. I can feel my waistline, stomach, thighs, boobs and face re-adjusting themselves into more desirable configurations. I can feel every one of the twenty-odd inches of altitude that separate my lofty causeway and her Sleeps and Smalls purchasing zone. I am woman. I am strong. I have right on my side and steel in my breast. I have, in short, the upper hand.

She turns around, slowly. Her face looks like a sucked sweet: boiled and red. She says, 'Oh. Erm...look...I...er...Caryl, I...er...think I...'

Caryl, who is busy slapping Oscar's cheeks in an effort to perk him up for the picture, says, 'Rhi, I thought I'd enter Oscar for this baby photo competition. It won't take long. You know Julia, don't you? Yes, of course you do! So what should I do, Julia? Do I just sit him on this fun fur podium here? Of course, he can't actually sit too well yet, can you, snuggles? But if I sort of crouch at the back, I can prop him up and...ooh! Look, Oscar, it's Izzles! Or is it Doodles?... Ahh. You like him, don't you? He just *so* loves the Tweenies. Oh come and look at his face, Rhi!'

But Caryl is fading into a soft focus wedding montage as she speaks. This is High Noon at the retail outlet corral.

I say, 'Of course I know Rhiannon. She's been to bed with my husband'. Which drops like a breeze block into the white noise, and instantly disperses it.

Caryl: 'What?'

Rhiannon: 'Julia, I...'

Me: 'Don't you "Julia, I..." me.'

Caryl: 'Pardon?'

Me (warming up): 'Didn't you know? Didn't she tell you, Caryl? Well, no, I guess it wouldn't be something I'd shout about either...'

25

Rhiannon: 'It's nothing to do with her. It's nothing to do with anyone except us and Richard. It's...'

Me (go for it, girl): 'And Emma and Max, maybe? Or was breaking up families just an unfortunate sideline? Have you got a *Seedlings* handbook about it I could buy?'

Rhiannon (redder still): 'I don't think this is the appropriate time to be...'

Me (textbook stuff): 'Oh, you don't, do you? Well I don't think it was very *appropriate* for you to have sex with my husband, either. So tough!'

Caryl: 'What?'

Rhiannon: 'Caryl, I'm going...'

Caryl (lashing Oscar back to his buggy): 'Rhiannon, wait!'

At this point Rani strolls back over the ramp, pausing only to ruffle Oscar's pink head as she passes Caryl – who is speeding to catch up with Rhiannon and all the scandal.

'Hey! Ugly, or what? Not a chance, that one,' says Rani. 'Sorry I've been so long. How's business?'

'None as yet,' I say. 'Look, I've just got to dash to the ladies. I won't be long. Set things up if we have any entrants, can you?' I have my hands balled into fists because I can't stop them shaking.

I leave Rani before she can sense the vibration on the stripped-pine effect flooring, and run past Chews, News and Blues and into Loos, where I lock myself in the furthest cubicle.

It says (somewhere, some book or other) that deep breathing coupled with mouthing a suitably calming mantra is very good in times of stress and agitation. Except that I can't think of anything. My mind seems to have gone off on some sort of fugue. So I simply stare at the cubicle door while my heartbeat comes down to something less like a rolling boil.

'Scott's Sanitation Services (UK) , Scott's Sanitation Services (UK), Scott's Sanitation Services (UK)...'

Which is all really peculiar.

Once I had calmed down sufficiently to function commercially, I went back to our stand on the causeway and told Rani all about it. Rani is almost pathologically single, being seriously gorgeous, seriously feisty and at odds with her parents at all times over the Polaroids of spotty second cousins etc. that well meaning relatives keep sending her from Poona. Rani calls a spade a spade. Which won't help her marital prospects any.

I told her I was confused about why I felt so much fury at Rhiannon when I'm feeling so nonplussed at the idea of having Richard back and am, indeed, considering the prospect of having a boyfriend (or boyfriends?) with such relish.

Rani thinks the one has nothing much to do with the other. She thinks Rhiannon is a bitch and a tart and that she probably got off lightly.

'But ahh,' she said, pointing a manicured talon. 'How would you feel if you knew Richard was still seeing her?'

I would be mortified, of course.

Is that it, then? That I can cast Richard aside only on the understanding that he remains celibate at number 7 Malachite Street?

I think perhaps it is.

Or is it just that I cannot bear the thought of Rhiannon De Laney having him?

Maybe.

Or do I just hate her, period, because she slept with my husband – regardless of what the outcome of that act turned out to be i.e. not as bad as I thought, bordering on being rather good in places, as it happens?

Perhaps.

Or am I just kidding myself? Do I really, *deep down*, still love Richard and want him back and am I just operating on a knee-jerk reaction level to the loss of pride engendered by becoming a victim, which is manifesting itself in a desire to have a sexual relationship with someone else? In short, an affair on the rebound?

Could be. I try to remember what it felt like all those years ago on the day when we both said 'I do'. I wish I could capture it; pull it out and inspect it; try it on again and see if it still fits. I remember a tall young man standing beside me. A long roman nose, just a hint of some stubble. A grey suit – too big for him – a slightly skewed button-hole, a faint sheen of sweat at the edge of his brow. I even remember his touch in the vestry, his whispered 'we did it!', his incredulous tone. I think I remember, too, how much I loved him. But that was then, wasn't it? And all this is now.

How *do* you untangle all the stuff in the middle and find your way back to the basic emotion? And, more to the point, should you even try? Aren't the feelings you have when you're older indivisible from the sum of the bits in between?

27

God, I don't know. I am so, *so* confused.

What I probably need right now is a bottle of wine and a take away curry.

By the time *Dial-A-Dhal* has my naan slapped against the side of the tandoor, I have begun to feel my equilibrium returning. I have forty two entrants, sixteen new family sittings booked, a pair of half-price *Pingu* slipper socks (plus discount) from the *Planet Kid* 'Don't Bin It!' bin, and there is an *EastEnders* hour long special on the telly.

And I have faced Rhiannon at last. The only way is up.

Chapter 6

THINK I'VE FINALLY ABSORBED some robust Celtic grit. Not quite to the extent of humming Men of Harlech in the bath or anything, but I can see some point to doing the lottery again. 'Up' is my new mission statement. Together with hackneyed but bracing couplets such as 'onwards and upwards' and 'fight the good fight' and 'seize the day' even. All well and good and to be thankful for.

Trouble is, I seem to find that even the simplest of social exchanges involve me in being branded the sad, hapless victim, which doesn't sit well with my thrusting new mind-set.

I was standing in the antechamber of Sainsbury's today – that part where you wipe the soft Welsh rain off your trolley, visit the ladies, or succumb to a tasting of whatever is currently being pushed (or more recently, and intriguingly, being urged to telephone Sainsbury's Bank [buy!buy!buy!] before launching into the weekly shop) when I found myself face to face with the terrifying Moira Bugle, who, as we all know locally, is *the* style guru of the professional woman in resting phase. I suspect Moira Bugle has been 'resting' since before tank tops came out first time around, but that's possibly why she's so darn good at it. She is to the noughties what the hostess trolley and pyjama suit were to the seventies and her *raison d'être* is the charity lunch. In short, she personifies the Lady of North Cardiff to whom we should all – in her opinion – aspire. But now that my status has so radically shifted, Moira Bugle doesn't frighten me any more. So I'm liberated at least, if still misunderstood.

'Julia, how *are* you, my lovely? It must be a couple of months since we saw you two in the Dog and Trouserleg.' She forms her glossy mouth into puckered enquiry. It's been three, in fact.

'That's because I've left Richard,' I told her.

Inhalation. 'Left him?'

'Well, thrown him out, really.'

'Thrown him *out?*'

'Well, he left, and I…'

'*Left* you, my lovely? How could he?' Hand on bosom. 'But why?'

'Because I told him to. Well, sort of. He…I…he slept with someone, and…well, we've split up, and…'

'With who? No, don't tell me. No, *do* tell me. Who?'

'Rhiannon De Laney.'

'Rhiannon De Laney? Rhiannon *De Laney*!'

Then, 'RHIANNON DE LANEY!' For the benefit of the lady plugging the leek potage, presumably.

'Yes, her.'

Moira's frosted pink fingers rattle the trolley. 'Great saints alive! So you've split up? I should say so. SHR!'

'SHR?'

'Serves Him Right, my darling. You poor *child* (Moira is forty-seven). How could he? And you so...so... Oh!' She embraces me, heartily.

Of course, what I really wanted to get across was that the leaving, though Richard's in a physical sense, was very much mine in a philosophical one. But I can't keep going around saying I've left Richard because people keep getting confused. My GP actually reached for my notes last week and began scribbling across my address. On the other hand, I don't want to say Richard's left me, because then people think that he really *has* left me – which winds me up, obviously, because there is a whole world of difference between your husband having a quick one (*two*) and you kicking him out, and him leaving you for another woman. Which means I have to start putting them straight which confuses them further and...pah! Why is life so complicated?

TTD Monday. Find succinct grouping of words to accurately describe potential (actual?) breakdown of marriage, with clear reference to housing arrangements, without sounding like a pathetic, sad person on *Jerry Springer.*

Trouble is, every time I find myself explaining the circumstances of Richard's departure to anyone I have this compelling urge to burst into tears regardless of whether I'm feeling happy at the time or not, which is both crazy and inconvenient, and will make people think I am just hanging-on-by-a-thread. And I cannot remonstrate with them about it because everyone knows that you only bang on about how you're definitely holding it all together when you're about as together as a half finished jumper with the knitting needle whipped out. And as soon as my face takes on that characteristic wrestling with itself appearance, people always want to clutch me to them and put their arms around me, which everybody also knows just makes it a zillion times worse. I feel a bit like an ear with a gobbet of wax in it. The more someone tries to gently tease bits out, the more it begins to hurt. Perhaps I (and my babes, of course) *should* leave the house. At least that way I won't have to keep explaining things all the time. I blame pregnancy. Before I got pregnant I watched the whole of *Gone With The Wind* without so much as a sniff. Now I cry at Bernard Matthews' chicken commercials. How low can you sink?

On this occasion however, I was rescued from the sobering prospect of having my chin wobble in front of Moira Bugle – which would have involved me in being made to sit down on a bench, copious squeezing of my upper arm, and quite possibly some hapless sixth former part-time shelf-stacker being dispatched to the staff room to fetch hot sweet tea and a bourbon biscuit – by the timely arrival of Mr Bennett, the man who brings me door-to-door kitchen gadgets and the like, and who Richard always insists we make some sort of purchase from as he is trying, apparently, to eke out a living. Two things struck me on seeing him. One was the Jaguar key fob in his hand and the other was Richard's clearly quite selective attachment to moral responsibility. Another note – TTD: mention my possible need to become a full-time home-based principal carer with special reference to burdens on state type stuff. That should put a cold Atlantic current under his stiffy.

Anyway, the arrival of Mr Bennett at least ensured that I was able to steer the conversation away from my marriage and on to the safer ground of my new plastic canapé maker.

'Well! ' said Moira, at last. 'That sounds like exactly the sort of thing I could use, wouldn't you say?' Moira is famous for her imaginative nibbles, but even Mr Bennett had shuffled away. Sales at any price? I think not.

'Probably more use than I'm likely to be making of it for the foreseeable future,' I said.

'Speaking of which,' Moira rattled on seamlessly, patting at the chestnut-coloured sculpture that was her hair. 'It's actually rather fortunate me bumping into you today. I was going to phone you...' Oh, yeah? 'To invite you over for dinner next weekend. Well, fair play, you *and* Richard, originally, but of course it would be just lovely if you could come along on your own. We don't hold with any of that *couples* nonsense, round our way, do we? *Do* say you're free.'

I toyed with the idea of invoking the old 'I don't think I'd be very good company' excuse but decided that as well as being untrue (of course I would – I am an item-of-interest) it would also sound pathetic. The least one can do in the face of such a blatant sympathy invitation, is to accept it graciously. Because, when all is said and done, what does it matter that Moira knows that I know that she had no more intention of inviting Richard and I over than swinging naked from her waxed pine Victorian airer? It's surely the thought that counts. And whatever criticisms one can (and should) level at her, her choice of pretending to have intended to is borne entirely out of a rigorously held belief that it would be embarrassing for me to be considered someone in need of sympathy and solace. Which is rather fine, when you think about it. So I said,

'Yes, of course I am.' And, 'Shall I bring some canapés, perhaps?'

Well. In moments of (wine-enhanced) good cheer I have developed a new image for myself: of someone scarred by experience but ultimately optimistic. And one of the things I am most optimistic about is the opportunity I now have to put myself about a bit, in a more wild and happening social scene than that centred around quiz nights and barn dances and dreary cocktail parties. And what do I have? I have an invitation to go to dinner with Moira and Derek Bugle, quite possibly the most staunchly conservative couple in Cardiff. To Moira, 'wild' equals a tit on the bird table. Mmmm. Can't wait. Really *cannot* wait.

I say this to Emma when I get home and she finds it amusing enough to tear herself away from her *High School Musical* DVD. And it is good to see her laughing again. She is totally Bugle aware, of course; not just from the various forays our association with the PTA have led us to make into their circle over the years, but also because Damon Bugle (why Damon? How Damon? So strange. So unaccountably *cool*), Moira's youngest, is two years above Emma at High School. He is something of a minor celebrity in the Chess Club, apparently, and has brought honour to the school in the recent South Wales championships. He is, all agree, going to go a long way in chess. Hastings, at least, where I think the nationals are held. He is also, Emma tells me, a complete geek, which I am trendy enough to appreciate is not a vote of confidence.

'What a hoot,' she says. 'Won't do much for your street cred, will it? Don't worry Mum, I'll keep it quiet for you.'

Emma, having emerged, scathed but essentially positive since her father's departure, has now restyled herself as a thoughtful and complex Bronte-esque character (themed accessories financed mainly by the blood money she's been wheedling out of him). She is anxious to turn me into as much of a sex goddess as can reasonably be achieved with someone so aged in order that I stay cool, and make Dad realise what a babe I really am. It seems not to matter to her that it was *I* that kicked *him* out, and that there is little doubt he'd be back like a shot given half a chance; it's clearly the infidelity itself that counts.

We have moved to a tangibly different place in our relationship. I have been scrupulously honest with her about why I asked her father to leave, and I think she respects me for being so. Also, I have allowed her to join me in using the word bitch (in the privacy of our own home, naturally) and I think she finds it as therapeutic as me. Having said *that,* I've recently been reading an interesting book called *Bonds that bind us* (us, as in women, apparently) which I thought would make appropriate light reading for the cuckoldess about town (why?). It has instructed me in the dire consequences for womankind if we feeble girlies insist on displacing our fury at our husbands and partners (men) at the people (other women) with whom they've transgressed. Given (it prattles on) that those people (the other women) have no personal duty of fidelity to us, doing so can only be harmful to us (women generally) as a group, and hinder our progress toward sisterhood and a free and equal status in society. Far better (it thinks, huh!) to accept that we do not have an inalienable right to expect a respect for fidelity from those people (other women) who do not have any contractual responsibility (marriage or similar commitment) toward us, and instead, ensure that our feelings of anger and betrayal are directed exclusively at the husband or partner who has failed in his responsibility toward us.

In other words, I should try not to instil in Emma any sense that it is Rhiannon who is at fault here. Simply that her father is a man and that men are pathetic souls with their forebrain just behind their foreskin and that it's a fact of life that men put it about a bit. For the good of womankind – and eventual world domination, and men kept in stud farms and subject to selective breeding and so on, of course. I think I'll throw *Bonds* away, actually.

The children love Richard. And Richard loves them. On the other hand, Rhiannon's a bitch.

What to wear, what to wear?

<u>What to wear:</u>
Long black (tight/plunging/backless etc) dress
Short black (tight but high neck) dress
Black Bootleg trousers plus Carvela boots plus what top?
(eating!!!)
Black jeans?
New outfit (what kind?) Think IMAGE

The trouble with going somewhere like Moira Bugle's is that you have to take a firm line with yourself about clothing. Either you go in regulation middle-class stuff – gold shoes, cotton/linen mix jumpers (appliquéd, of course) from *Coast* or M and S, velvet skirt/devore shirt combos etc. and resign yourself to blending seamlessly into the blur of middle-aged womanhood around you, or you don't. In which case you must decide in advance not to mind having yourself and your attire described as interesting, arresting, the sort of thing one would really *love* to wear if only one had the courage, and definitely hearing the word 'slapper' uttered in a stage whisper when you go to the loo. No contest, really.

Emma inspects my wardrobe (basically, as above, with knobs on) and decides that this is the time to make a definitive style statement. She eschews the ranks of standard civil engineering dinner dance frocks with a look that could frazzle a whole side of pig, and dismisses all my trendy bootleg and blouse combos as exactly what middle-class married women *would* think are cutting edge. They think, ergo they're not, it seems.

'There's a PDSA bag downstairs,' she says menacingly.

'I cannot consign my entire wardrobe to the bin,' I tell her loftily. 'I'm not made of money, you know.'

Grudgingly, she allows that I'll still need my usual black staples to go to work in, though as a photographer, apparently, I should consider it my duty to dress in as bohemian a fashion as possible. And it would be, I accept, more accommodating of baby sick.

'And I'll lend you,' she tells me, 'a few thongs and bits.'

'Thongs?'

'Leather thongs.'

'Leather thongs?'

'For your neck, Mum. God!'

But we agree, in the end, that an overall re-style is called for. Something younger, and snappier, more *Vogue* than *Family Circle*. But mainly, I suspect, something she could wear too.

Chapter 7

I AM GOING TO reinvent myself. Not the essential core of my being, of course; it's taken a bit of a pummelling of late, but I feel the essence of my inner self is basically sound and intact. Which is good to know, because someone at the school gate told me the other day that when her husband went off with an audio typist she felt like a used teabag for months. (Less encouraging is the fact that people I hardly know feel impelled to come up and discuss relationship crises with me at all. But I am sure I'll find a reassuring chapter about it in one of my books.)

No, it's more of a packaging thing, really. My packaging has become the grooming equivalent of a tin of Sainsbury's low sugar baked beans. And I was at school this afternoon and it struck me that almost everybody of my acquaintance has highlights in their hair. Eeeek! *I* have highlights! All my friends have highlights! The headmistress has highlights! Even the caretaker has highlights, and he's a man. I bet if I were to compile a list of all the people I know who have highlights it would run to several A4 sheets. But (and it's a significant but), Rhiannon *doesn't* have highlights. Rhiannon has a slippery, tumbling, tumultuous cascade of coppery auburn curls. The bitch.

Unsuitable (*no longer* suitable) Accessories:

Highlights
Fake Tan (Note: Moira is *orange*)
Jumpers with nautical motifs (unless on boat)
Whatever Christmas evening wear they are selling in M and S this autumn
Gold shoes

I have also made an appointment at Snip Sutton's Style Shack and added *Hair Monthly* to my Sainsbury's list. In actual fact Snip is really a bloke called Nigel Sutton who used to have the local OAP shampoo and set market covered. Until he came out. *He* doesn't have highlights. That must mean something.

Chapter 8

IT'S HAIR DAY TODAY. Hair today and gone tomorrow, as Eustace, my hair designer, chattily informs me. I get the impression he says that to pretty much every customer, every day. Which is fine for us, of course, but may well account for some of the more scathing glances he seems to attract from the cluster of spotty teenagers that are scattered around the salon manning brooms and towel bales and who are the hair designers of the future. I know they are this, incidentally, because while I was waiting I heard the receptionist telling a caller that if she would like to book an appointment with one of the Style Shack's hair designers of the future, she would not only get her hair done for free (bar conditioner) but also get her photograph taken, to be inserted in the loose leaf file of attractive styles that even hair designers of the future can manage.

I must confess to a moment of negativity here. Rhiannon has exactly the kind of skinflint cum extreme vanity personality combo to have indulged in a spot of coiffing styled by hair designers of the future. She has also always striven to be considered hip and hip types never plump for anything so crassly middle-class as having your hair done by a capable suburban hairdresser with a Nissan. Even if he *is* gay. I have flicked, therefore, through the mug shots. She is, alas, not there.

'What's it to be, then?' quips Eustace merrily. His hands are having sex with my hair as we speak, his long chocolate fingers darting playfully around and pummelling bits of my cranium.

I answer, pathetically (how many years since women's suffrage?), 'I don't really know' and 'what do you think might suit me?'

'Well, I think we need to lose this bob, my lovely. And chop into the nape.' He ducks to inspect it. 'And, hmm, we need height. We need height, we need volume. And colour. We need colour. We need...'

'We need something not too expensive,' I squeak. And, 'Oh, and I don't want highlights anymore.'

Once we've established that there is no such thing as highlights any more anyway, simply woven colour fusions tailored to the client's individual tonal profile (well, they still come out looking like highlights to me) Eustace tells me, in the manner of a hair designer very much of the present, that I'm to leave it to him and he'll simply wow me. Then I'm shuffled off by a pubescent called Cerys and subjected to ten minutes of vigorous shampooing at the sort of sink I have seen featured on *Watchdog*. The woman concerned suffered nerve compression (or something) of the neck, which resulted in her having some sort of stroke and then total, permanent paralysis from the neck down. No wonder I'm sweating.

By the time Eustace fetches up again however, I have suffered nothing more life threatening than total migration of the mascara to the ears. I look like a cartoon of someone who has been riding on the back of a motorbike at one hundred miles per hour. I ask you – who needs life-threatening? Isn't life unfair enough?

Yes, yes, yes and YES! I LOVE my hair! I can't walk in a straight line for trying to see myself in shop windows. I want to hug it, comb it, brush it, rub my hands on it, run my hands through it, wash it, dry it, then look at it some more. And you know what? It makes me like my face more too. And my neck, and my boobs and my stomach and my legs – oh, well, maybe not my legs – but pretty much everything else about myself. I feel totally, utterly rejuvenated. The second thing I do when I get home (post the half hour in the mirror, deciding that 34B is actually just great and that my legs are not so much short and fat as average length and muscular and that my eyes are not sludge but khaki and that having shoulders like a squaddie is really sexy and that it doesn't matter if there's a kink in my nose because when I smile – and am I smiling! – it miraculously disappears) is go to the phone in my bedroom (which is *by* the mirror) and telephone my mum to tell her about my hair. My mum is particularly good at being prattled at. No one else I know would tolerate it.

'Guess what?'

'What, dear?'

'I've had all my hair cut off and it looks absolutely brilliant. I can't imagine why I didn't do this years ago (I can't help but imagine that perhaps Richard wouldn't have had sex with Rhiannon De Laney if I'd done this years ago – but that's *so* silly). And I've had it coloured, a sort of coppery goldy colour with sort of blondy tips, and sort of spiked up at the top and it's all fluffy and tendrilly on my neck – but like, bristly, you know? And it looks so…so, well…I know! Sort of like Meg Ryan's but a bit more, sort of…well, funky.'

'Meg Ryan. Wasn't she that drunk woman? Or was she a doctor? What *was* it I've seen her in?'

'Oh, both, I think. But she'd better watch out if she comes to Cardiff. Julia Potter is on the scene now. Oh, I just can't tell you how pleased I am with it. Isn't it funny how your hair can change the whole shape of your face?'

'It is, dear. And I'm very pleased. It's nice to hear you sounding so jolly. Does Richard like it?'

'Mum! We're separated! I don't *care* what Richard thinks about it.' Of course I do. Or do I? Of course I do.

'Of course you do. Anyway, *you* like it and that's the main thing, isn't it?'

It isn't the main thing at all, of course.

The main thing, as everyone will tell you, is that everyone else likes it. And that Richard, particularly, likes it very, very much.

What a sad, sad woman I am. I know Richard doesn't even *care* about hair. So it wouldn't matter to him how I did my hair even if we were still together. And I know that, given that it was *I* who dumped him, there is no necessity for him to even have an opinion. But, God, I hope he likes it.

I'm not brave enough to let him see it when he comes to pick up Max and Emma (they are off to his flat for tea) so I say my goodbyes from the downstairs loo. Since then, though, I am becoming steadily more excited at the prospect of presenting myself, siren-like, on the doorstep; an item of almost unbearable sexual magnetism which he can no longer have.

But he catches me out by coming in through the back door when he brings them home again. I have my dressing gown on and my hand in the Pringles.

His eyebrows beetle alarmingly as he scans me. Then he finally speaks.

'Good God,' he says.

Max sniggers. Max, how could you?

'See?' he says, pointing (who'd have a son?). 'Ha, ha, ha. What did I tell you? She looks just like a pineapple, doesn't she?'

Three days later, a parcel arrives in the post.

My mother has sent me a small, misshapen *some*thing – the latest fruit, no doubt, of her creative muse. (My mother thinks she is the doyen of the Croydon Seniors Pottery Workshop, despite being, to my admittedly untutored eye, absolutely non-talented in three dimensional art. As a body, however, they are in receipt of a sizeable chunk of council funding and must therefore, I suppose, admit all-comers, or else. And I must be grateful – if ousted she may well turn her attention to dried floral arrangements. Which really doesn't bear thinking about.)

There is a note. It says:

Just a little something for your used tea bags. And don't worry about your hair. I'm sure Richard will come to love it. And remember – hair grows.

One of us is in denial here.

But it isn't me.

One of the most liberating things about not having a husband in residence is that it obviates the need to consult someone less artistic and enlightened than oneself concerning matters of taste. For the first time since blu-tacking every male under twenty to my room in a hall of residence, I am going to have free rein in colour scheming and soft furnishings. That I have no money is almost entirely irrelevant. Everyone knows that it's possible to completely transform your environment with little more than a couple of cans of inexpensive emulsion and some remnants of fabric (I have an old net curtain that I can dip-dye). Most important tool though is a skinny rib T-shirt in which to encourage builders' merchants to hack appropriately sized hunks from fashionable stone and hard landscaping-type items, which apparently never cost more than fifty pence.

The watchword with living space, as with one's person, is attention to detail, and careful accessorising.

Accessories (Lifestyle) I now need:

Gerbera daisies (real/silk – depending on season)
Test tubes (plus rack)
Terracotta Pots/Urns
A Smoothie maker
A Vauxhall Corsa*

*Query replace by eco-friendly Prius.

Of course, there's always a touch of insecurity about accessories, especially if you pick up most of your tips from the pile of magazines in the Time Of Your Life Photo Studio waiting area. At least two of them have pre-decimalisation cover prices. I really must make a committed effort to making my lifestyle a bit more *now*. Though I will not, naturally, start putting flan dishes of pebbles on my coffee table, or assorted novelty bottles filled with coloured water on my kitchen windowsill, like *she* does.

Richard hasn't the smallest idea about lifestyle as an expression of personal taste, which I presume is why he felt it necessary to pour scorn on my most recent accessorising when he came to pick up Max and take him swimming earlier. And once again, Max didn't help. Unlike Emma he has no sense of solidarity, and prefers to join with his father in what they clearly both consider to be completely harmless sniping.

'What's this?' Richard said, holding up my newest acquisition.

'It's curly willow,' I said. 'With integral fairy lights. In a burnished terracotta urn.'

'Yes, I can see *that*. I just wondered what its purpose was on the telephone table. Does it have a smell or something?'

'No.'

'Does it play a tune when the phone rings?'

'Of course not.'

'Then what's the point of it?'

'It's decorative.'

'It's looks like one of your mother's Dali flowerpot creations with some dead stalks stuck in it, to me. Har, har, har.'

Max: 'Har, har, har. If you think that's gross, you should see what Mum's put in the downstairs loo. Wait there!'

Oh, his sides were splitting, I can tell you.

'Ta ra!'

'What's *that*?'

'Dad, can't you *see*? It's a 'decorative wreath', of course. It has bits of orange, and shrivelled up chillies – see? – and, get this. *Twigs*. In little bunches. Oh and this is string, isn't it, Mum?'

'Ha, ha, very funny. You're both such wags, aren't you? For your information, smarty-pants that you both are, these were made by Emma, in her art class at school. I happen to think she shows a great deal of creativity. And I also happen to think it is very important to let our children know that we are both impressed by and proud of their artistic achievements, don't you, Richard?'

Hah! All utter rot, of course, but I know I can rely on Emma not to split on me.

40

(In actual fact, I have had to put my curly willow pot and wreath in the SCOPE bag that came this morning, because I read in *Homescene* yesterday that rustic is definitely out, and that galvanised metal and industrial flooring are both very much of the moment. Except in bedrooms, where turquoise and terracotta with flashes of copper are still acceptable – which is good because I just got the emulsion.)

But they are both treading a rocky road; Max, because I have absolute control over hours allotted to the new Playstation PSP his father has just bought him and Richard himself because if he persists in his current line of merry banter on these occasions (which, yes, I *do* understand are very healthy and psychologically enriching for all concerned) I will have no choice but to deposit the children at the front garden gate whilst scowling aggressively in an arms folded and legs slightly apart manner on the doorstep. Also I will start referring to him as 'your father' instead of Dad, and ring him frequently with requests for Nike AirMax trainers and Calvin Klein Puffa Body Warmers. We will soon see who's taking the piss then.

Chapter 9

DINNER PARTIES. WHO'D HAVE them?

It's currently trendy round our way to eschew the dinner party. Dinner parties appear to be no longer fashionable, and have been supplanted by:

Having a few close friends for supper (dinner party)

Having two close friends and their children over for Sunday Lunch (dinner party at lunchtime, plus chicken nuggets plus hangover during *Antiques Roadshow*)

Having a *How to Host a Murder* party (dinner party plus dressing up and farting around)

Entertaining business colleagues (dinner party where women do not know each other and always have to drive home)

Having a few close friends around after the pub shuts and phoning the Chinese take away for an Indian – or vice versa – and everyone falling asleep before it arrives (dinner party at our house)

Actually, I'm rather a good cook. When Richard and I were first married, we assembled forty-seven jars of herbs and spices, which I kept in almost fanatical alphabetical order along the back of the kitchen worktop. The saffron, in those days, was forty-four pence. I still have the whole jar of fenugreek.

And I used to love doing dinner parties. There is surely a time in everyone's life when a Saturday afternoon wouldn't be complete without a visit to a kitchen shop to buy gadgets and trivets and little paper chefs hats to put on racks of lamb. And I had the entire Robert Carrier collection *and* all the binders.

But that was then. I can't be fagged any more. Now I get stressed just thinking about them. Even thinking about going to *other* people's dinner parties. Especially if they've mentioned that they may flambé or something.

Which puts me on a completely different planet to Moira Bugle. Which I was anyway, of course, as I am thirty-eight trying to get away with thirty and she is about one hundred and two. And she is Moira Bugle. Which means she does as she damn well likes.

*   *   *

In the end I chose to attend Moira Bugle's soiree in one of those dresses that look a bit like underwear and have two layers; mine was sort of silvery underneath and sort of mauvy and lacy on top – very Madonna, very *now*. And I wore mauve strappy sandals (which Emma and I found in *the* most trendy shoe shop in Cardiff, which was uplifting) and one of those little beaded drawstring bags.

Emma said, 'You could go clubbing in that and no one would have a *clue* how old you are – if it wasn't for that big varicose vein up the back of your knee, you could be twenty-five, easily.'

Brilliant.

I had a great big fat repulsive throbbing *pulsating* vein up the back of my leg. Arrrrrgh! How could I ever go swimming again?

And I had completely forgotten about it. Really. I had *completely* forgotten its existence. I almost rang Richard then and there.

'That's it,' I would have said. 'That's the real reason I don't want you back. It's because you care so little for me that you didn't even see fit to mention the big throbbing vein on the back of my leg. Rat!' I mean, I could have had it injected, or lanced, or whatever they do to them, *years* ago. At least used concealer stick on it, or something. Which is what I eventually did. And popped it into my little mauve bag.

So off I went. I took a bottle of mid-priced eastern European white wine (trendy, or what?), a large bunch of freesias (all the same colour – class) and a box of *Ferrero Rocher* chocolates which I won in a prize draw (fortunately, Moira has no nose for clichés) and stood on her doorstep for a good half minute while she made the journey from kitchen to hall.

Moira and Derek are not only older, but also quite a bit richer than us. *Me.* They have a mock-Georgian house on the edge of the village that has a square footage that probably matches it. I was ushered vociferously into the lounge and presented by Moira (in shimmering *eau de nil* palazzo pants) to the already assembled throng. These were:

Moira's Derek – fifty-ish, something in local government, half-cut.

Caitlin and Stuart Goodrich – almost fifty-ish, both very nice. She makes embroidered cards. Stuart has some sort of business. Is Richard's big pal at the tennis club – *oof!*

Dawn and Boris Griffiths – Early forties (getting nearer) but big on beige. Her, local playgroup leader, sweet. Him, entirely unknown quantity but looks like sort who might grope bottoms.

And me. Which made seven in all. Seven? Moira? Surely not. Of course not. *Bing Bong!* went the door.

And then Howard Ringrose walked in. He of the biceps and hamstrings and suchlike. Toyboy and hunk and God Of Year Six. He? How? He? Moira? How on earth? *Why?*

Someone must have seen me ogling him in the playground. Or noticed a sheen of sweat on my upper lip while he ran through the fixture list for the summer term. Or must have noticed that the little artery that crosses my clavicle was pulsating ever so slightly as I said 'Hmm, that's what you call *not really muddy*, is it, Max?' in jocular fashion by the changing room door. Or, or, or...*and* told Moira. Eeek!

'Well,' said Moira chirpily, 'that seems to be all of us. Howard, I'm so glad you managed to join us. It seems Joan was quite adamant that you tear yourself away. Howard's mother,' she told us, 'has been rather poorly. But she didn't want Howard here missing the fun. What with SATs and all that. And I'll bet it's the only decent hot meal you'll be getting all weekend, is it not? Well! Drinkies, you two?'

I thought she was going to suffix the 'two' with 'youngsters', about which I would have had rather mixed feelings, but she went straight on to explain why she had invited a late twenty-something, cool person to a gathering of women on the very brink of hormonal dysfunction and men with hair hanging out of their noses. As you would. (I assumed my own presence had been explained earlier. And if not, why not? I was still fully fecund, even if the route to creation did have a 'road closed' sign across it.)

Joan, it turns out, is Howard's mother, and is also a friend of Moira's (Moira knows everyone old within a ten mile radius). Apparently, she now lives in Bristol – which is where Howard comes from, and it was Moira who told her about the vacancy at the primary school in the first place etc. etc. Who would have thought it?

'Anyway, nice to see you,' said Howard...

'Nice to see *you*.' Damn. So *obvious*.

'How are things going?'

Howard knew all about Richard, of course. I had to tell Emma and Max's teachers in case the standard of their school work suddenly plummeted and/or they burst into tears in the middle of PSE lessons or something. Which was wretched at the time, because I was in the bursting into tears stage myself, and the thought of my children bursting into tears in class made me want to burst into tears pretty much *all* the time, and what with Howard being my friend, and deeply sympathetic, I obviously did. Copiously. (Curiously, *thankfully*, Emma and Max had already moved on to the much more pragmatic 'Great! We can watch *Little Britain* without Dad moaning!' stage, of course.)

'Much better, now,' I said.

'I'm glad. I've been worried about you.'

Wow!

'By the way, I really like your hair like that.'

Yes!

So we had the dinner party. We had canapé things with what looked like burned bogies on them, then (at a table that looked just like those ones they set up in old-fashioned department store windows) some sort of cold soup, then goujons of something with home-made tartar sauce, then chicken breasts wrapped up in string with some sort of spicy stuffing inside them (and dauphin potatoes, broccoli, beans, artichoke hearts etc. etc.), then pavlova *or* fruit salad *or* chocolate crême brulées (*or* nothing, thanks, really. No, *really*) then about thirty-seven different varieties of cheese. Oh, and some grapes.

And of course I wasn't allowed to help with the washing up. While Moira and Caitlin and Dawn clattered purposefully to and fro, I was barred from the kitchen, and instructed to arrange myself in some part of their aircraft hanger lounge. This left me in the sort of conversational limbo that only a long-married woman at a suburban dinner party can find herself once the umbilical cord of the other females (and therefore chats about three-for-two offers and washing instructions) had been cut. If nothing else it shored up my flagging resolve that life, the universe and everything was probably happening elsewhere, and that I seriously needed to go out and find it.

Howard went off to phone and check on his mother. While my face subsided to its regular hue. Boris and Stuart (the latter's face had been set in a slight cringe all evening), had been clearly hoping to flick on the TV and catch up with the snooker or something. They both looked balefully across from their respective sofas as Moira announced my continuing presence with small snatches of what sounded like a press release, accompanied by the crackling of her static-charged trousers.

'Fair play. Julia's had a dreadful time of it lately. Can't have you beavering in the kitchen now, can we, my lovely?' and 'You stay by there, and just take care of the fellas for us, while we three get things straight.' And, bizarrely, 'So lovely to have such a pretty face amongst us!' as if they three were all hags. I felt totally discombobulated. It seemed to me that I had been diverted down an altogether different avenue from the one I had previously travelled. No longer (practically speaking) a wife, I was not deemed fit for bringing a pudding (I'd phoned and checked) or for kitchen responsibilities, and instead was assigned a purely decorative role. In short, the one Rhiannon usually had. Yet these were surely the very same women who would be shaking their heads in astonishment and horror if I shimmied into the downstairs loo for a quickie with one of their men. Was this some sort of test? Or did Moira feel it would be therapy for me to be in the company of a largish group of recumbent males for a while; that I could perhaps soak up sex, love, affection, attachment, androgens, shaving rash, sperm etc. by osmosis?

'So,' said Boris, finally. 'How's the painting going?'

'Painting?' said Derek, who was splayed on a vast sofa at the far end of the room. He was obviously glad to have been given a conversation to hang his small bag of pickled hosting skills on to. He pulled himself marginally more upright than flat. 'Didn't know you painted, Julia.'

'I think Boris has got the wrong end of the stick, Derek. I'm not a painter, I'm a...' But Derek, a good twenty feet away, was deaf as well as drunk.

'Painting! D'you hear that Moi? Julia paints!'

'No, I'm a...'

'D'you not paint then, Julia?' asked Boris. I shook my head.

'No. I'm a...'

'Painting? How lovely!'

Moira bustled in brightly. She clearly had Derek wired to a baby alarm. She carried her Bara Brith recipe tea towel ostentatiously, like a shield.

I said, 'Are you sure I can't help you out there?'

'Heavens no! The perc's perking. All shipshape and Bristol whatnot. I tell you what! Why don't we have coffee in the conservatory? Derek, lovely, open up, will you? Ah! Howard. How is your mother, dear? Could *you* have a bit of a wrestle with our patio doors?'

I wished I could go and phone *my* mother. I wished I could phone her up and say ' Mum, I am at a respectable dinner party and am fantasising about having really energetic sex with Max's teacher, who is under thirty, a fine physical specimen and who has that excruciatingly sexy combination of little boy/rugged army survival core documentary type person and who, I just *know*, knows I'm salivating over him. And if he doesn't, probably thinks I'm a complete dimble-wit anyway, who talks utter crap and is old and wrinkly, to boot. Oh, oh, oh. What am I to do?' sort of stuff.

But I couldn't. I'm a grown-up person and was therefore not under any physical or mental compulsion to follow him outside or hang around him or try and think up witty and alluring things to say to him. Especially as every time I got within a foot of him, I seemed to have lost the ability to formulate any interesting word strings.

But I was a mother. I was Max's mother. I should really put his case for the cricket team captaincy. So I joined Howard at the business end and held the curtains open for him.

'That's the way, you two,' said Moira. 'Coffee's almost up. Oop! What's this by here? Oh, Derek, how could you? I thought you told me you'd hoovered these chairs? Tsk. Bring a moppet in, will you, lovely? Ho hum, I don't know. People round and we've stains on our seats. What *is* this?' She rubbed. 'Looks like yoghurt or something. Tsk, tsk.'

I swivelled my knees and bowed out backwards. The conservatory, dark behind the swags, tails and general frippery of the soft furnishing arrangements, was cool and scented with jasmine. Real jasmine, unlike the horticultural assault that emanated from all the little bowls in the lounge. Real, heady, evocative of…I said, 'Is your mum okay?'

Howard's mother, he'd explained to me, had some sort of cancer. Not advanced, but serious enough that I had to arrange my face into something that didn't involve my tongue hanging out. But he was chirpy.

'She's just fine, as it happens. Sounded really upbeat. Her consultant's very pleased with her. Should we open the French doors as well, then? I don't think it's cold out. Shall I go and ask Moira?'

I had a vision of us in a *Fantasia* type cartoon. Going through one set of doors, then another, then another, until we eventually emerged in a forest carpeted with pretty cartoon flowers, wearing loin cloths and holding hands, while little birds fluttered about with ribbons in their beaks.

'I think she said to, didn't she? I guess we could sit outside, even. Even if they don't want to, I suppose we...yes, open them.'

Oh, God. Burble, burble, burble.

Howard did so, and the scent of jasmine was replaced by the unmistakable perfume of dew-dampened grass on a cool summer night. In the distance, the moon spread a soft milky glow over the hills of the graig, and the stars hung in fairy strings, twinkling and bright. It was just like in a period dramatisation of something by Dickens – apart from Moira's rustic wood donkey-shaped planter.

'Max,' I said, hoping to play my advantage. 'How's he doing right now? I've been so worried about him – more than Emma in fact. Him and Richard, well...well, he does seem more settled at home.' More settled than what? His father has given him state of the art iPod technology and pays him £10 to wash his car every week.

'Doing well,' Howard confirmed, striding across the patio with one hand in his chinos, then turning, arrestingly, his handsome profile tinged with gold from the halogen lamp. He smiled. 'Very well, considering.'

'And the cricket?'

'Which reminds me,' he said suddenly. 'I've been looking into getting the school registered in this new initiative the Sports Council are setting up. It involves the kids getting coaching from Welsh Internationals and so on. Tell you what. Let me take a note of your home number and I'll give you a ring with more details.' Then he whipped out a pen and a scrap of paper.

'242478' I said.

'242478. Great.'

The telephone rang at 00.21. So exotic, *so* daring. Written in the stars. (Plus reasonable alcohol intake.)

'Hello, Julia,' he breathed. 'Did I wake you?' As if.

'I'm in bed,' I answered. 'But I wasn't actually asleep.'

'I thought not.' Such breathtaking confidence, too. 'Well. Er...cricket.'

I loved that 'Er'.

'Are *you* in bed?'

'Yep.'

'Cricket?'

'I didn't really call you to talk about cricket.'

'No, I know.'

And then there was a pause. Just a tiny pause. But enough of one to make it quite clear that Howard was hovering meaningfully at the other end of the phone, and thinking of what to say next. Then he said 'Well.' Again.

'I'm sorry?'

'Well, I sort of thought you might feel you need a friend right now. How do you feel about dinner?'

Did he mean the dinner we'd just eaten or dinner as a concept? It couldn't be a repetition of an invitation. He hadn't actually asked me to dinner yet.

'Dinner?'

'Yes, dinner. Us.'

His voice was so deep that it resonated down the wire. Then I also remembered the contours of his bare chest at the lob-a-rock stall at last year's school fete. I began to feel a strange and wonderful heat in my stomach.

'I'm sorry,' I said again, feigning uninterested ignorance. 'Had you asked me to dinner?'

'No. But I am now.'

'Asking me to dinner?'

'Well, not to my place, exactly. I don't often cook anything worth inflicting on anyone. I meant food as in a restaurant.'

'What, Us? Go out to a restaurant together?'

'Yes.'

'On our own?'

'If you want to. I thought it might be nice to go out. You know. Chat and whatever.'

And that was that. Howard, me, dinner, *whatever*. Actually, I'm having difficulty imagining Howard, me, and dinner without a bolt-on scene in a rumpled bed. From the vantage point of my own bed (not, interestingly, the one I've in mind) I can see myself in the wardrobe mirror. I look, I think, rather nice against the terracotta tones of my new duvet cover – a bit of a catch, in fact, legs notwithstanding. That may, of course, have more than a little to do with the fact that I've taken my contact lenses out, but then, he might wear them himself, might he not? Seems like just about everyone does these days.

Dinner with Howard. *Dinner with Howard*. Well, well.

Chapter 10

I HAVE A DATE with the God Of Year Six. *I* have a date with the God Of Year Six. I have a date with the *God Of Year Six*. And let's not mince words, this is scary with a capital *Sc.* This is a date with the question of *whatever* hanging over it like...well, sex, of course. It will involve eating in a sexually-charged situation and, quite possibly, snogging (with sexually-driven chemical cocktail in nerve endings) as well. I have not snogged anybody other than Richard since I was twenty years old. Eeek!

Terrifying. What does one do on a date these days? And who can I find out from? Having spent the last week re-inventing myself as a post-feminist, postmodernist, post-the whole wifely package type person, I can hardly ring up anyone cool and hip and ask them for support and guidance.

So I telephone Lily. Lily and I have that special bond that only comes with shared wrestles with a breast pump. She has no truck, therefore, with any of my claptrap at the best of times. Also she thinks I'm so pathetic it can't hurt my reputation a jot.

'I'm going on a date.'

'Alors!! How eek-citing! Who with? What's 'e like? Is 'e gorgeous?'

Lily turns her French accent on and off like a central heating boiler during an unseasonable cold snap. I take it from all the spitting and gurgling that she is sitting with someone she wants to impress.

'You would hate him,' I reassure her. 'He's about as Gallic as a Bath bun and almost pathologically obsessed with rugby. Oh, and he drives a Ford.'

'Excellent. Your type, then.'

'So what do I wear? What do I talk about? And should I snog him so early on in our relationship?'

'Of course! Acch! Julia! Get your face from the sand! You sound as if you've become twelve again. If you want to snog him, you snog him. It's the new sex, you know.'

What a peculiar concept. And I'm not sure whether that makes it better or worse. All I know is that if I think about the idea of snogging someone I go all hot and cold. And it's not a lust-thing, honest. More a sitting O level Geography after two years faffing around at the back of the class painting my nails green with Christine Mumford type thing.

'Mum, I can't believe you're going to do that! It's *so* gross. And what am I supposed to say to everybody? Hmm?

This is Saturday and this is Max. Max is about as appalled as it is possible to be. Standing in the kitchen in his Bart Simpson boxer shorts, holding a pop tart and mug of tea (five sugars) he looks every inch his father. Crumpled, indignant and deeply disappointed in me. He puts down the tea and picks up his PSP. It bleeps and parps and pings for a bit. Max's PSP is a metaphoric stiff drink. I shake my head.

'You don't have to say anything to anybody, Max…'

'So it's a secret?' Ping.

'No, of course it's not a secret. It's just Mr Ringrose and I going out for a meal together. It's really no big deal.'

He digests this, eyeing me warily, as though I'm a carnivorous mammal.

'Is he your boyfriend?' Bleep.

'Of course not.'

'So why are you going out to a restaurant with him, then?'

'Just because he's a man doesn't mean he can't be my friend, does it?'

'You've never been out to a restaurant on your own with a man before, have you?'

'Not lately, but when I was…'

'Yeah, yeah, yeah. But I have a whole term left at primary. Can't you just wait till I'm gone, or something?'

Which, strangely, is exactly what went through my mind when Howard asked me out. So my son and I do have some sort of marriage of minds. But I can't do that, can I? The moment might pass. I might have grown hair on my chin by then, or lost some teeth.

'It's just a meal, Max. I'm not getting married to him or anything.'

'So he *is* your boyfriend! Mum, do you have any idea how embarrassing this is for me?' Bleep, parp, ping. Small explosion.

'She's your mother, Max. Embarrassment is part of the package.'

This is Emma, who slides in and manages to look superior, even though she is wearing a McFly T-shirt and a pair of novelty cheeseburger slippers. Max grunts his second 'gross' of the day, and slopes off to watch his normal Saturday morning diet of nubile presenters attached to short lengths of kettle flex and grouped on pink and purple sofas. Emma hooks her hair behind her ears and gives me a look.

'Does Dad know about this?'

'No. And it's none of…'

'…his business. O*kay*. I just *asked*. Don't throw a moody.'

God, why is conversation getting to be such hard work in this house? I can't help but feel we're on some slippery slope of family dysfunction which will culminate eventually in me having dockers round every night and screaming at the children to sod off and leave me alone while swigging Sainsbury's Gin straight from the bottle. It's a whole new ball game, this lone parenting lark.

Yet before I had Emma I was so certain I'd never say wait till your father gets home. We used to sit in little self-righteous NCT clusters and say: Dummies? Pish! bottle feeding? Tsk! Traditional female-oppression parenting roles where woman changes nappy and man goes to pub? Tut, tut, tut! How brave and true and strong and damn well *together* we were. We'd never *dream* of passing the burden of disciplinary responsibility to our partners. Perish the thought! That was for poor, sad, inadequate mothers who let their babies suck Smarties before they had finished every last wholesome mouthful of their home-made alfalfa sprout puree.

I still know some people like this. They exist in small pockets at the outer reaches of the high school PTA, campaigning for the Coke machines to be removed from the premises and inspecting the food science curriculum for E numbers. Sadly, I fell by the wayside early. It was all I could do to remember to make my children clean their teeth at night. And I said 'wait till your Father gets home' almost as soon as they were old enough to understand the full implications of currying disfavour with a man used to taking on entire town planning departments and reducing beefy site foremen to tears. Which is really pathetic, I know. And now it's too late. I can't say it any more. And my children, like tap-rooted perennial weeds, are sending out runners of disobedience as I speak.

Well what a turn-up.

Isn't it just amazing how you can really, really fancy someone one minute and then go right off them the next, over something that's nothing to do with hormones at all? I can't believe it.

Howard picked me up (to a chorus of much muffled whooping), and took me down to a trendy (much beaten metal) restaurant in the city centre, kindly inserting all sorts of information about the architectural and cultural niceties of Cardiff, and translating obscure Welsh street names along the way. Which I know was only because he was embarrassed, but was actually rather endearing. And informative too. I moved to Cardiff with one toddler in tow and heavily pregnant, so while Richard spent much corporate time hob-nobbing in the city, I spent much of mine dining in 'Mc' prefixed eateries, and getting to know all the toilets in Culverhouse Cross.

So. We've done the drinks, done the dinner, done the chit-chat about the state of Welsh Politics/Rugby, avoided having the chit-chat about Cardiff Bay (Howard being in the camp that believes the development of Cardiff Bay to be a terrible and mutilating act of social rape, and the end to talents such as Shirley Bassey being given to the world, and me being latterly in the camp that's pleased to see a bit of investment in the area, particularly as lump of said investment is going the way of Fielden, Jones and Potter, Consulting Engineers, and thus securing my children's hope of a university education). We've also done the argument over the bill, done the bill, done the dithering over whether to go on somewhere (going 'on' somewhere is a new concept for me; apart from the twenty-four hour Tesco store on the A48 at Gabalfa, I wouldn't know quite where to go on *to*). Then we've gone to his flat for a cup of coffee/foreplay/sex (eek!) or whatever, and there it is, all before me.

I don't know what I expected Howard's flat to be like. I wasn't even conscious that I'd formed much of an idea about it. But I obviously had, because I'm so disappointed. Actually, I *had* formed an idea. If I'm honest I expected it to be scruffy but welcoming, to smell of old leather and moss or something, and to have empty beer bottles on the mantelpiece and empty take away cartons as ashtrays. Except that Howard doesn't smoke, of course. But what we've got here is, well, prissy, quite frankly.

I know there's the odd person who takes the rise out of me because I like making lists of things, but this guy is so anally retentive you could tell every anal retentiveness pun you ever heard and you'd still be way short of the mark. He has everything in order. *Everything*. Not just the obvious things like CDs and paperbacks – the latter, I note, are carefully colour and height as well as author-

53

sorted. But things like magazines which he seems to have sorted by spine-widths. How sad can you get?

I waft around the living room, uttering explosive little oh! and oh, no! sounds at his records, his books, his choice of co-ordinating knick-knacks, knowing that at any moment he is going to return with a pair of bone china Clarice Cliff mugs and try, in no doubt equally logical fashion, to snog me. I pass the mantelpiece mirror and am arrested by the contrast between me (Meg Ryan meets pineapple and kohl pencil) and the room behind me (Homebase meets Upstairs Downstairs). Well, at least *I* look fine. Eye make up slightly smudgy, cheeks slightly flushed, hair tousled and looking surprisingly, well, tousled. Richard used to say that there is nothing so unsexy as a fastidiously groomed woman (which was always pretty handy) and that face powder and tights were the most wilt-inducing items a woman could tarnish herself with. And just when I've arrived at a point in my life when I can put the theory to the test with someone other than a thinning-on-top engineer I sense I am in the home of someone who may feel I'm simply a trollop. A slovenly slattern who's no better than she should be. I take another long look at my oozing-sexuality-without-trying-to image. I've done it so bloody well. What a terrible waste.

I cruise back across to the other side of the room, where the only encouraging note in this crashingly loud affirmation of niceness is the higgledy-piggledy pile of papers on the floor beside the sofa – work he is clearly in the middle of doing. I pick up the top one – a worksheet for his class, presumably – it's entitled 'Kool Kidneys' and is scattered with sweet little cartoon kidneys, with streetwise expressions and little stick legs. The text, hand-written in his familiar floppy hand, is accompanied by beautiful freehand drawings that explain filtration and describe how the glomerulus works. There is a packet of coloured pencils on the floor beside it with a label on them saying *Mr Ringrose's, Hands Off!* This is more like it.

It is all so poignantly touching that I find myself feeling guilty for thinking him prissy, and wanting to cry, or to hug him, or go for autumnal walks with him in Next overcoats, and sip hot chocolate huddled by the fire afterwards. Or even learn, heaven help me, to appreciate opera.

At which point he comes in, with mugs that are heavy, cheap and reassuringly non-matching, and blushes to find me inspecting his work. Okay, I like him again. Quite a lot. Oh, the relief, the relief.

'Never ends, I guess, the planning,' I say, replacing the sheet. And think *okay, I'm ready. You can kiss me now.*

He shrugs.

'I don't mind. I enjoy it. In some ways, it's the best and most challenging part of the job. You know, being able to teach them something in such a way that they don't feel taught. Do you know what I mean? They seem to absorb so much more when they're well motivated. It's great when it works.'

I realise that Howard is in the unfortunate (though entirely self-inflicted) situation of trying to chat up someone whose child he teaches. I suspect that in the staff room all sorts of completely outrageous things are said about the children and, I've no doubt, their parents. But he doesn't need to worry about me on that score.

'You don't need to worry about me on that score,' I say.

'What score?' he asks, looking shifty.

'The ultra-keen, ultra-critical parent score. I'm about as laissez-faire as they come. I have never, hand on heart, walked into school and queried a reading scheme decision. Honest. Though that's not to say I'm not a caring or committed parent, you understand. I worry about my kids just as much as the next mum. It's just that...'

He looks at me as if I've recently touched down in a space pod, then laughs in a really wholehearted way, big on decibels and everything.

'You don't have to worry about me on that score either.'

'I'm sorry?'

'I love the way you say "I'm sorry?" You say it such a lot, too. No, what I mean is, would you have said all that if I'd been a landscape gardener?'

Gosh, he's sharp.

'Yes. No. Oh, I don't know.' When can I say 'I'm sorry?' again?

'I don't doubt it. Shall I put a CD on?'

'Why not? What have you got?' This should be telling.

He puts down his coffee and moves in a sort of crouch that culminates in him kneeling in front of the pine-effect CD tower. I can see a chink of hairy leg between the top of his boot and the hem of his trousers. Oh! My stomach!

'How about some Puccini?' he says over his shoulder.

Go on. *Anything.* Just kiss me now.

*   *   *

I didn't get to kiss Howard, of course. Approximately ten minutes after we'd established a moratorium on our parent/teacher positions and had moved to the marginally more comfortable territory of both privately thinking about having a snog but pretending that we just wanted to chat about *Madama Butterfly*, my mobile chirruped. It was Emma, with the disconcerting news that there was a peculiar smell coming from Max's bedroom and could I come home as soon as possible in case the house burned down. Our delicate bubble of breathy abandon popped by a sharp prick of parental responsibility, I rattled straight home. Once there, I found that there was a small piece of bacon lodged on the little transformer thingy at the back of the TV. I cast it into Max's inflatable dustbin, threw out a couple of homilies about eating in the bedroom, then stomped off to deconstruct myself.

Then I got into bed, read a page of Lady Chatterley's Lover, and after thrashing about melodramatically for a while, eventually fell into a fitful sleep, my king size divan feeling as big as a field.

Chapter 11

LA LA LA LA la *la*
la la la la la *hum* hum *hum*
la la la hum hum *hum*
la la la hum hum *hum* hum *huuuuuummmmmmm*
dum dum *dum*
dum dum *dum*
dum dum *daaaaa* da *daaaaa*
la la *la* la la *la*
la *deeeeeee deee dy*.........

Yes, all right. I'm singing a lot. And there's nothing wrong with that. Well, except if you are listening to it, of course, but then that's your problem. I have to sing. I cannot help but sing. I sing because I am *in lurve*.

Okay. I know this is patently ridiculous. I am thirty-eight and have enough further education on board to know that this is what most (dreary, boring, *unimaginative*) people would consider to be a silly crush. But I just don't care. I feel like I have a big ball of custard or cotton wool or meringue or fairy lights inside me, and that I can barely contain it. I feel beautiful, *really* thin, and like I don't need lunch. I feel sexy (okay, horny) every time I think about him, and I think about him every five minutes or so. I feel, in short, *precisely* the way I felt the morning after the first night that Richard kissed me somewhere other than my mouth. To feel that way again is a wonderful, wonderful thing. Poor, poor Richard. Lucky, lucky me.

Rani is unimpressed.

'What the hell *is* that?'

'That snowman song. You *know*.'

'And I'm Mother bloody Theresa. Can't you at least learn the words and how to sing in tune, perhaps?'

I hug Doodles to my bosom.

'Hmmmm? Oh, yes…well, if it feels good do it, I say. Hum hum hum hum hum *huuuummmm*…'

She gives me one of those looks which are designed to make you feel stupid and self-conscious but which never do, of course, because your consciousness is wrapped up in a little bubble of happiness and won't allow anything that isn't fluffy or lovely in.

Which is why teenagers don't feel embarrassed about sending each other padded Valentine cards that are four feet high and have cartoon puppies on, I suppose.

'Anyway, your next family is here.'

'Hmmm?'

'And look comfortably off. Next, Gap, M and S *and* Will & Wanda's Baby Boutique bags…'

'Hmmm?'

'And the children, of which there are three, are all sitting on the sofa with their hands in their laps and *not* shouting, scowling or hitting each other.'

'Hmmmm?'

'And Howard Ringrose called. Would that be he? I said you were busy and would call him back later.'

'WHAT?'

God, I *really* hate Rani sometimes.

11.00 'I'm sorry, he's teaching at the moment.'

11.37 'Sorry, he's teaching. The bell goes at twelve. Shall I ask him to call you?' NO!

12.01 'I'm sorry, he's out on the field. Lunchtime Cricket Club. Try at a quarter to one. He'll be in for his lunch then.'

12.46 Clients. *Damn!*

12.59 Clients still. *Damn, damn!*

13.07 'I'm sorry, Mr Ringrose is in class. If it's urgent I could…' NO!

14.31 'Oh, dear. Playground duty, I'm afraid. Then he'll be in class till the end of the day, sorry. Is that Mrs Potter, by any chance?' *Damn!*

15.45 '*Helo! Mae Ysgol Gynradd Cefn Melin nawr ar gae. Oes I chi yn dewis gadel neges…*' Damn, sod, sod, damn.

17.12 Usher out clients, turn off lights, sling Milo, Izzles, Doodles et al. into toy box, chew nails. Go into ladies' powder room (yes, they do still call it that. This is *some* department store) in preference to hiking two kilometres to staff toilets, sit on loo and feel stressed. Must really get a grip. Must also re-familiarise self with primary school timetable, staff rotas etc. Emerge from loo to find Rani putting on chocolate-coloured lipstick, swathes of blusher and new tights (after-work date with unsuitable Caucasian *again*).

'Oh, you're here!' she says. 'That Howard just called again. I told him you'd gone home.'

Ow, ow, ow, ow, *ow*.

All in all, a bit of a night.

I got home, late, and in a complete strop, having realised, in a single gut-wrenching moment on the A48, that I did not have Howard's home number. What to do? What to do?

Once I got there I was greeted by:

a) Emma announcing that she was going out with her *friend* (plus prefix, three letters, first letter B) and would not therefore be available to have a Chinese take-away at her dad's flat (as per plan which was democratically arrived at and with her full and enthusiastic support) and could I let him know because he wasn't in his office when she tried to ring him and she couldn't get him on his mobile and she really couldn't wait any longer as the *friend* would be waiting on the corner by the bus shelter and thinking she had decided not to come.

(The natural conclusion to which would be that he would decide he didn't want to go out with her any more and would take up with someone else from their class and both would refuse to speak to Emma ever again etc. If he *was* a boyfriend, which, of course, he most definitely wasn't.)

And b) a really odd sounding message from Lily on the ansafone saying she needed to speak to me urgently and would come over tonight about nine-ish if she didn't hear from me otherwise. I was just playing it back for the second time (just in case there was also a message from Howard which had inadvertently got corrupted or something) when Richard arrived to pick up Max.

'Which reminds me,' he said confrontationally, stepping on to the *inside* doormat without so much as a by-your-leave or invitation from me to do so. 'The Outgoing Message. What have you done to it?'

'I've re-recorded it. So what?'

'Why?' Terse.

'Because it was your voice. You don't live here any more, do you? It confuses people.'

'Confuses who, exactly? Everyone we know knows who I am, don't they?'

He had a face on. That petulant look that he would often get on Friday nights. The look that said 'don't mess with me, I'm in a foul mood; I've had a bitch of a day'. The look that said 'will you please tell the kids to bugger off and leave me alone for a while' and shut itself in the lounge with a beer and the TV remote control while I tootled round obediently and cooked dinner. Well, tonight he had Max, *X-Men 2* on video and the Wing Wey Happy House set meal B. *And* he had to do his own washing up. Well, har bloody har. SHR!

'It's not the point,' I persisted, particularly irritated by his aggressive manner, given the compassionate thoughts I'd bestowed upon him earlier. 'No one's going to be leaving messages for you here in any case.'

'They might. Not everyone I work with is fully conversant with my personal life, you know. And it might be something important. The whole point of the OGM was that it gave people my mobile number so they could contact me urgently if they needed to.'

'So? I've got a larynx. I can give them your mobile number. Or you theirs. Or tell them to ring you at Malachite Street. Is it such a big deal?'

'Yes it is, frankly. It doesn't sound very good, does it?'

Neither, I thought, does 'I'm sorry but my husband doesn't live here any more on account of his disgraceful infidelity etc', which is what Richard was *really* worrying about. But I've moved on from petty point scoring, so, instead, I said, 'Then you'll just have to get another ansafone, won't you?'

'I should have that one.'

'Why?'

'Because you can't even work it properly.'

'Yes I can. I changed the OGM, didn't I?'

'No you can't. You're always cocking it up. It always goes wrong if you touch it.'

'Bloody cheek! No it doesn't.'

'Yes it does. And anyway, it's mine.'

'No it isn't.'

'Yes it is. I bought it.'

'For the family.'

'For me.'

'For the family. So that the children *in particular* could get in touch and leave a message if they needed to let us know they were going to be late or something and we were out. Actually.'

'But you're never out in the evenings.'

'I might be.'

'Pah! And stop bringing the bloody kids into things all the time, like you're some big paragon earth mother and I'm just some...'

'Unfaithful husband?'

60

'Oh, for God's sake! What *is* it with you?'

'Nothing. I just don't like you pushing me around.'

'Me? Push *you* around? That's rich! Here I am, kicked out of my own house and forced to live like a hermit in some grotty flat while you swan around lapping up the sympathy. I think you're actually enjoying this...God!'

'Hi Dad.' Max.

'Oh. Er, *hi* Max.' Dad.

'So,' I said, 'have a lovely evening, you two. Emma won't be coming, I'm afraid, as she is out with her friend. She did try to get hold of you but (master stroke!) your mobile was switched off. So sorry. Good night. Take care. See you later.'

*Note. Confront daughter re her recent tendency to be uncharacteristically shifty looking re male acquaintances. Hmmm. Older? Unsuitable? (if so, in what way?) Smoker? Bad lot? Swansea City fan? All of the above?

I stood in the hall for a few minutes after they left, making rude gestures with my fingers and sticking my tongue out. Well, he could sod off.

Then I felt really guilty about him living in a grotty flat when he had worked so hard for so many years to get us the (really quite nice) house we were all still living in. Then I felt cross with myself that I should feel guilty about that at all. Had it not been for Richard's career machinations, I would doubtless still be living in London; still pursuing the career that I'd never quite started. Being a mother, certainly, but someone for whom a man's largesse, or lack of, was not the controlling force in my life. And then I felt guilty about feeling like that about Richard because it was with my entire support and enthusiasm that he took the offered partnership in Cardiff in the first place. Had I ever once signalled a moment of indecision? Of wanting to be anything other than a wife and mother? Of wanting more than what he had so amply provided? And *had* I wanted more? Really? Hand on heart kind of stuff? And then I felt guilty about the flat once again.

Which was something I recognise I have avoided addressing as it questions the integrity of my whole stance as wronged wife with two kids who needs a house (or at least a reasonable amount of space) to live in, and brings into focus the female response to infidelity generally. In some ways (oh, really, Julia? Come *on*) it would be better if he was less sorry and remorseful and desperate to mend his marriage, and went off with Rhiannon De Laney, full stop. Then I wouldn't need to bother about the question of forgiveness and reconciliation at all. Which would suit me fine, because I'm in love with Howard now. Which was why, I suppose, I was feeling guilty in the first place.

Then, thinking that, I felt, as usual, as if I was just playing at being a proper grown-up, and that all my emotions were inappropriate ones. How could I be in love with someone else only three months since I thought I was still in love with Richard? How?

I ran a bath. What was love anyway? It was simply lust with cuddly bunnies attached. I resolved to stop casting myself as a character in a romantic film and instead as a matur(ing) thirty-something with her feet on the ground, who would keep matters of the heart in their proper perspective and take whatever life had to offer, as was my right as a woman. With this in mind, I did the whole *Cosmopolitan/She* bit and organised a 'bath as rejuvenating me-time' activity, incorporating:

> Glass of wine x 2
> Scented candle (air freshener) on soap shelf
> Church candles in egg cups around bath
> Bath oil
> Bath fizzer
> Essential oil burner on windowsill
> Sea sponge
> Half tube of *Pringles*
> *Lady Chatterley's Lover*

Because I had already finished the Pringles when the phone rang, the tube was on the bathroom floor. And the bathroom floor was wet.

And I was wet as well.

'Hi, Julia. Missed you again, ha ha. Er, Boro da! This is Howard......' Aarrrgh! Ouch! Oh, my bottom! Owwwww! No! Aarrgh! *'...I...er...suppose you must be out, so...er...well...er...perhaps you could give me a ring when...er...Well...'* Oh no, *please* don't hang up, grunt! Urrgh, please. *'...I...er...anyway. Give me a call. Bye.'*

Bugger.

Lily was on the doorstep half an hour later.

'So I had a brainwave!' I told her. 'I thought – I know! I can ring 1471, can't I? So I did, and he wasn't there of course, so I had to leave a message on *his* ansafone, which was so burbly and cringe-making it makes me shudder to even think about it, but then guess what? He called me back! He'd only gone out for a take-away and was really pleased I'd called him and I explained about you coming over and – here let me see to that wine box. You French have no idea about bulk packaging – and so I said I was sorry but I wasn't free tonight – well, what's left of it – but that I did have a fairly quiet weekend, as it happened, and he said would I like to go and see a film or something tomorrow evening, or whatever, and I said yes – of course! – and so we're going to the pictures tomorrow. Here – have a big glass – you're looking wan, and it is Friday night after all – and so there you have it. Brilliant, or what? Do you know what's on at the Odeon?'

'Pshhh! Julia. Listen to me. I have a big problem.' Gulp, slurp, swallow etc.

'Problem?'

'Big. And getting bigger and bigger. Julia, I am pregnant.'

'Pregnant? By who?'

'By Malcolm, of course. Who else would it be?'

Malcolm, as in tall stringy man in beige corduroy trousers and sweater. Malcolm as in woodwork teacher at adult education centre at college. Malcolm as in not-much-of-a-catch (apparently). Malcolm as in person who has surprisingly turned out to have had a sexual experience after all. And with *Lily*.

Cripes. This was a turn-up.

'Lily,' I said, effortlessly donning a maternal tone and ushering her into the kitchen. 'You shouldn't be drinking. Getting drunk is definitely on the no-no list now. Oh and congratulations, of course. Come here and let me hug you.'

'Pshhh!'

'No. I mean it. Con-grat-u-lations. One thing everyone knows is that no matter how you feel about this baby now, in time you will come to accept the idea. Indeed, become thrilled and full of wonder at the mystery of conception, and the miracle of life that will be the baby you give birth to.'

Note. By now I had consumed three glasses of wine and no dinner, due to *Lurve* etc. Privately rather taken with whole idea of making babies with Howard, even if I can't.

She sat down. 'But I don't want it.'

'Ah. You say that now…'

'But I don't. I don't want a baby. I am twenty-six, single, and the father is a dweeb.'

'A dweeb?'

'Definitely. It says so in the toilets at college.'

'Oh, that's just students for you.'

'The staff toilets.'

Hmmm. What to say next. That I was only twenty-four when I had Emma? Twenty-four. *Jesus*. And in love with her father. And happy. And expecting to remain so. Indefinitely. Maybe not. I am probably a very poor role model indeed. More wine, perhaps.

'Have a Pringle,' I offered. Then, sniffing a challenge, 'Okay, then why did you sleep with him?'

She stuffed about twelve in. Then shrugged. 'He made a lot of shelves for me. I was grateful.'

'Lily! How could you!'

'I don't *know*! Ask Richard. Hah! And I'm sorry, but I am drinking. I have to drink to forget.' So she did.

'Did you drive here?'

'I'll sleep over. Oh, Julia, why did I do this?'

'God knows. Why didn't you use contraception, you twot?'

'What's a twot?'

I considered.

'Like a dweeb, but more affectionately thought of.'

She ignored this. 'So. How do I get an abortion? And do you have any more Pringles?'

'Lily, don't panic. We have to think this through. Let me get some paper.'

Saturday breakfast.

Max. Three pop tarts (weekend splurge).

Emma. Grapefruit on muesli (why are teenage girls so predictable?).

Me. Nothing (bulk of winebox still sloshing about and taking up space).

Lily. Peanut butter on digestive biscuits plus tuna fish, plus glass of milk with mashed up banana in it. Lily has a face like a day old scone.

'So. What *is* this exactly?' says Emma, knowing very well.

'Give me that,' I snap (bulk of winebox still etc.etc.).

She doesn't. Instead she reads:

Options.

1. Keep, plus advise Malcolm, but ? future of relationship
2. Keep, plus advise Malcolm plus *end* relationship (firmness. ?
Paternal rights etc.)
3. Keep, but tell no one who Father is. (?work problems/
potential psycho. damage to child etc.)
4. Have abortion. Big step. Think! Think! Think!

'Mum, this is gross! And who's Malcolm? And what exactly is going
on around here...'

'Emma, it is not your mother. It is me.' (Lily.) 'Max! Go and
fetch me a piece of toilet paper, please. I need to blow my nose.'

'But...'

Me. '*Do* it.' He does. Lily slides her eyes after him and then
snaps them back to Emma.

'Pshhh! Okay, Emma. I am pregnant. I do not want a baby. I do
not know what to do. I am a fool. I am...'

'Oh, Lily! A baby! Oh, but that's brilliant! Oh, how could you
not want it? We'll help you, won't we? Mum? I'm old enough to
baby-sit now, and I could help look after it after school, couldn't I,
Mum? We're doing baby and childcare next term anyway, aren't we,
Mum? And it would be like, cool – you know. With you having
looked after us, and...oh, Lily, it's so brill!'

Oh God.

Oh *God*. Why can't I be more careful about leaving
incriminating scraps of paper around the house? Why didn't I learn
my lesson after last Christmas's game of dirty words scrabble?
(Consequence of which was that Max woke us on Christmas
morning not to ask if he could open his presents, but to ask us
instead what 'fellatio' meant and to query the 'd' in todger.)

But abortion. Oh *dear*! What a horrible thing to have to have an
opinion about. What a stressful thing to have to take a stance on.
What a crushing weight of responsibility to have dumped on me on a
day when all I wanted to do was moon around thinking about what to
wear for Date 2 with Howard tonight.

Okay. Have sent Lily back to bed to help pull her
face/body/psyche into shape. Now think.

Ummm.

Put yourself in similar position and consider best available option.

Ummm.

Imagine you're pregnant *now,* by Howard.

No, no, NO! Straight back to fluffy bunnies etc. plus opportunity to buy really nice buggy (had buggies and changing bags and cot duvets during that long, miserable 'pastels only' baby-merchandising decade.)

Imagine number of unwanted children in western world, coupled with spiralling family planning crisis in developing world. Consider ramifications of Mother Only as child-rearing option (football, satellite programming fluency, doing 'absolute last word on subject' type discipline etc.). This is more like it.

Termination – for and against (eat, for security purposes, after considering):

For

Doesn't want a baby
A woman's right to choose
Career/home/lifestyle difficulties
Will not have to marry (co-habit/share in upbringing with etc) unsuitable man.
Unwanted child bad thing to bring into world

Against

Wrong/act of murder etc. Foetus is living thing
Will scar conscience horribly etc.
Father's right to have child also
Will possibly regret
May damage reproductive system

Oh, this is *awful*. Especially given that I always had such a solid set of opinions in place about abortion. But it's like everything else, isn't it? For the majority, opinions are not informed by experience. I'm not qualified to advise Lily because I haven't been in that position myself. When I found myself (accidentally) pregnant with Emma, I couldn't have been more delighted a) because I was working at Arseface and Lecher (not their *real* names, obviously)

Portrait Studio and hating it passionately and b) because my then best friend had a baby and therefore didn't have to get up and go to work in the mornings, and could instead stay in wearing only a dressing gown and day-old mascara. Always (still is) my idea of heaven. Also, I loved my husband deeply, and was infused with all the usual sentimental feelings about having his genes intermingled with mine to produce a super-being.

Then I think of Malcolm Woodwork Teacher and can visualise a part of Lily's plight.

Lily woke up again at about midday, and we ate Pringles and taramasalata for lunch. Then, based on her estimate of being six weeks pregnant, we decided on a provisional plan of action. This would involve:

> Doing another pregnancy test
> Visiting doctor with view to counselling or similar
> Giving all options deep and reflective thought
> Making firm decision in next two weeks
> Telling another significant person in her life (think who) for balance of opinion
> Not panicking

She left at half-past two (having offered to come back and baby-sit M and E, in case of extreme lateness, i.e. sex with Howard) and said, 'I've made up my mind. I'm going to have an abortion. Can you help find me a clinic?'

Chapter 12

AFTER LILY LEFT, I looked in the Yellow Pages and was astonished to see that *Abortion Advice* was the second entry. Just like that, as bold as you like. It said to look under pregnancy, which I did, and there were about a zillion to choose from. Abortion, it seems, is now part of the social landscape, like the National Lottery and supermarket loyalty cards.

I rang the one with the small display ad, as per Richard's usually failsafe system (lineage: cheapskates, big display: sharks, and never call AAAA1111 plumbing/ taxi/ emergency gas repair Ltd – very big sharks with £150 call-out charges). I told the lady (who sounded *very* old – Marie Stopes maybe?) that I was enquiring for a friend.

'Yes, dear,' she said in that very predictable knowing way. I was about to add 'really, I actually am' but decided that would make her even more likely to think it was me with the unplanned pregnancy. So I asked her to send me a pamphlet instead.

'But don't you want to make an appointment?' she asked.

'But it's not…not yet, thank you.'

And then I felt really guilty for even being embarrassed to have someone who didn't even know me thinking that I was considering having an abortion, as if having an abortion was a nasty wicked thing to do (even if from some perspectives, and to some people, it patently is, but then they don't know the circumstances, do they?). And who was I, the lady at the abortion clinic, or anyone else to judge what a woman did in those circumstances? Given that it was they that were going to have to live with whatever decision they took. And so on.

And all I wanted to do was arrange my date with Howard, spend at least three and a half hours getting ready for it, and sing.

Chapter 13

WE'VE JUST BEEN TO see *The Devil Wears Prada*.

I was secretly quite astonished that Howard agreed to come and see something so blatantly girly (Richard would not have gone in a zillion years – not even if Sharon Stone was in it – though other, more perfect, husbands would, of course, to be kind to their wives). But Howard seemed really keen. I had expected him to suggest something involving car chases/male bonding/petty criminal activity etc., but he said, 'Great! I've been meaning to catch that for ages.'

It has been out for ages, of course, but our local cinema now has so many screens that they are probably still running *Born Free* in screen 87 at 4.35 am on the last Friday of every month with an R in it, or something. Such progress! I *love* the pictures.

I didn't take any Pringles (fledgling relationships are sensitive to overt displays of anti-social behaviour – which sneaking savoury snacks into cinemas clearly is), but instead said I'd like a small bag of salted popcorn. Which was a big mistake because it was only then that Howard said he wouldn't have anything, as he wasn't hungry. Typical! I then had to eat them as unobtrusively as possible (by sucking, mainly) so that he wouldn't have my piggery thrust in his face.

But it was a great film. One of those films where the audience all come out feeling like they love one another. Which would explain, I suppose, about orgies and so on when people went to shows like *Hair!* in the sixties.

So now we're in the car, in the queue to get out of the car park, and the sky is all big and spangly and velvety and full of the mysteries of the universe and the stars of all the dead souls who've gone to heaven, and though neither of us has acknowledged it yet, we have arrived at the pivotal moment. I say, 'Meryl Streep was brilliant, wasn't she?'

'Oh, she always is, isn't she?' says Howard, negotiating the exit bollard/young shrub landscaping arrangement and glancing across to check the road is clear. His eyes are so *shiny*. 'Did you see her in *The Hours*? So *compelling*.'

And so on and so forth till we approach the area in which Howard lives and which is on the way to where I live, and where it will be necessary for one of us to make reference to if and where we will have coffee and sex. But instead, Howard says, 'Do you fancy a kebab?'

I don't. I *love* kebabs, of course, and have been denied them as a marital food choice since Richard found a char grilled weevil in a shish, in '85. But I have sucked and chewed popcorn so carefully and for so long that my stomach thinks it has been fed a five-course meal (which proves what they say about sucking chocolate) and I want a kebab now like I want to undergo liposuction under local anaesthetic. Also, I am a garlic-free environment and wish to remain so for the duration. Ditto chilli, cabbage and that particularly pungent liquid fat that seeps out of the meat and soaks into the pitta bread. Which is dreadful, because everyone knows that men really can't stand women who don't enjoy their food. Especially ones that pick bits out of anything foreign with their faces wrinkled up in disgust.

'Mmm, yes. Why not? Do you know somewhere good?'

Of course Howard knows somewhere good. He is a single young buck with limited cooking ability and a big, man-size appetite to deal with. He knows exactly the sort of kebab house you'd expect him to know. Open half the night, manned by two chirpy Cypriots (father and son – son doubles as psychology lecturer at the University, by day, apparently), Awesome Kombat Death Zone arcade game blinking in the corner, row of metal bowls full of (surprisingly fresh-looking) salads, and starburst fluorescent stickers saying Chips £1.00! With Mayo £1.20! Curry Sauce's Available! etc. But no rum-babas. Kebab houses always had rum-babas in the seventies, I tell them, but they look at me as though I have recently beamed in from planet twit. Not in Wales they didn't, apparently.

'Shall we take them back to mine?' Howard suggests. 'Oh, yes. I'll have that, that, that and that, but not that. And I'll have a chilli, but no lemon. Oh and the garlic sauce too. And can you make sure it's on the meat but not the salad? Thanks.'

'Fine,' I say. 'And I'll just have cucumber. No. No onion thanks. And no sauce.'

'No sauce?' Howard exclaims. 'Are you *sure*?'

See?

Once we get back to his flat he has me open a bottle of wine (bought for the purpose?) while he bustles about and clears away the endearing combination of mess, papers and abandoned trainers that have added an attractive ambience to his flat. He then says 'I really need to take myself in hand,' without the smallest hint of irony in his voice.

'Where do we eat?' I ask.

Howard smiles fetchingly. 'Let's pig out on the sofa.'

But I can't help feeling that we've lost the plot, sex-wise. Call me old-fashioned. Call me a fuss-pot. Call me something derogatory out of a psychology textbook, if you will. But I can't see having a kebab as an arousing prelude to doing it. In fact, I can't see having a kebab as any sort pre-sex activity, unless it is a posh kebab, in a restaurant, with baclava for afters followed by a slow stroll through a sodium-enhanced urban landscape before laying on a sofa listening to an old Genesis album and smoking a joint while taking each others' clothes off as part of an elaborate sensual dance which evolves naturally into the mystical and spiritual conjoining of two beings. All of which may well be just nature's way of ensuring that parents recall their university days in such a way as to ensure they encourage their children to go but, hey, it was cool. It was sexy! Even Richard did it! Or did he? Or was it someone else? Or did I dream it, perhaps? Whatever. One thing's for sure. Sitting on Howard's sofa with the main light on is *not* sexy. A kebab, in this situation, should be something you fall upon ravenously *afterwards*, while sharing, by means of gaze, sigh and giggle, the rapturous high of the orgasms you just had. At the same time, of course.

But at least we're talking. Which has to be good. A couple of glasses of wine down the line and Howard has jollied me out of my grouchy mood (which he hadn't noticed anyway), and instead, we're into philosophy, big time. I've never known a man so able to have a conversation about feelings without walking away or trying to incorporate football into the conversation.

Me: 'Do you ever get the feeling that a person's motivation for doing something is sometimes the opposite of what you thought, and that, in response, your own reaction can sometimes be counter-productive to the effect you intended?'

Richard: 'It's funny you should say that. I was reading Danny Baker in the Times yesterday, and he was saying something very similar about the Hoddle/Gasgoigne situation. By the way, it's the UEFA cup second round tonight. What's for tea?'

*   *   *

71

Howard is different. Howard likes ideas. Howard is in touch with himself. Quite soon, I realise that our kebab plates (remnants of pitta welded to same by virtue of saturated fat solidifying etc) are gone and that he's pouring me more wine and that he's put something soft and twangy on the CD. And that we're close together on the sofa and that the light is unaccountably dimmer and that the cushions (in a range of accent colours to complement the knick-knacks) are making their presence felt more as an embodiment of squashiness rather than of naffness, and that I have *taken off my shoes.*

'It's good to be with someone who you can feel completely yourself with,' Howard is saying. He too is without footwear, having been finally persuaded that I am quite old enough to go home (eventually) by taxi so that he can have a glass of wine too. He has had four (absolute minimum), and has opened another bottle.

'Oh, you're *so* right,' I agree. 'Sometimes, you know, with Richard, I felt so much that I was channelling my focus so completely into my husband and family that I had lost – in a *deep* sense – what it was that I *am*. D'you know what I mean?'

'Mmm. Sometimes a person needs a jolt, a sudden loss of equilibrium, in order to find the inner space they need to understand who they are, don't they?'

'And it's hard when you're married, because marriage is, by it's very *nature*, an artificial state. You have to, like, compromise your identity: make life choices that are not necessarily those you would make for yourself. That must, by necessity, cause disruption to your psyche, and inner conflict. Yes. Inner conflict. D'you know what I mean?'

'I don't know about marriage. I don't do that stuff. But inner conflict is a big thing with me. Some days, it's like I'm, oh, I don't know, under the surface all the time? And like I can't break through it? I get glimpses of the person I could be and then – plunge! I'm back struggling for the light again. Whoever coined the phrase 'Existential Aloneness' must have had me in mind. That really *speaks* to me. And...more wine?'

'I'm sorry? Oh, no thanks. I'm drunk.'

'Drink your way through it. That's what I always do.'

'Oh, all *right*. Just a teeny, teeny splosh. To there! No! Okay. That's *all*. Okay?'

'Okay. *Sir*. You should be a teacher. You're really quite a strong person, aren't you? That's what I've always liked about you. You are so in control of your life. So focussed. Even when all this business with Richard and that Rhiannon happened, and you came to me, and you cried, and so on…you had such *dignity*, such self-possession, and I thought…'

'Wait! You called her *that* Rhiannon. Why did you do that? I mean, it's *great* that you did. I'm really pleased that you did because it says a lot for how you feel about me – in a way, sort of – but it's like it's been really interesting, because I've been reading all these books…'

'Which ones?'

'Oh, billions. All the ones in the health and lifestyle section in the Central Library, mainly. But it's like I've been working really hard on trying to maintain my dignity by not sinking into the usual trap of just hating Rhiannon and wanting to hit her or something, and trying to get in touch with my finer feelings and understand that she did what she did because she is flawed and had crises or problems earlier in her life that have made her the way she is…'

'What, a bitch, you mean?'

'Yes! But, like, someone who I can pity and not hate. Do you know what I mean? And the whole '*that* Rhiannon' bit is something I've been trying really hard not to think in terms of – for the children as much as anything…'

'Of course.'

'Of course. But it makes me feel so good that the result is that people I care about do it on my behalf instead. It's sort of enriching. It enriches me to hear *you* say it, whereas it damages me to do it myself. You know?'

'She'll always be *that* Rhiannon for me now. Oh… You're such a lovely person, Julia.'

'I'm sorry?'

'Let me cuddle you. You're so warm, I can almost feel the heat from you. Mmmmm. I'm so glad I've got to know you better. You've always been, well, there, I suppose. A small glow in the day – on the days that I've seen you – but I don't think it ever really registered with me before…'

'Me *neither*. It's been *exactly* the same for me! Why? It's like, karma, or something…'

'Karma, that fits. More wine?'

'Should I? Should you?'

'No, but isn't that just a phoney restriction society imposes on us? Why can't we just be? Why shouldn't we…'

'I mean mainly because I think we've had enough...I mean...I mean put your glass down, Howard. You're right. I *am* a very strong person and I *am* in control of my life and I have decided that what I would most like to do now is kiss you...'

'Would you? Then I should let you, shouldn't I?'

And so now we're kissing. Being, as we are, in a cuddling position already, I have simply tilted my head back a little, pulled Howard's head forward a little, and moved our faces together (slightly juxtaposed, naturally) so that our lips touch. As soon as they do, I am conscious of an almost unbearable surge of a familiar chemical reaction (I just can't help but analyse!) that starts deep in my stomach and moves outwards and downwards, so that within seconds my body, from navel to knee, is throbbing, pulsating, and quite possibly glowing – a sort of physical version of the bleepy red spot on those futuristic tracking maps the baddies use in James Bond films, to keep tabs on his Aston Martin.

I am also (and doesn't this just tell you everything about how crummy it is to be a self-conscious teenager) struggling mightily with a desire to put my hand in Howard's trousers. As if! Richard aside (our sexual history is an entirely different matter) if someone told me twenty years ago that I'd be anxious to grab a man's equipment while kissing him, I would have guffawed. Putting your hand on your boyfriend's trousers and feeling his willy was something girls did solely because if they didn't they might get chucked. Or was I missing something somewhere? In my case, by the time I had discovered that there were feelings you got in your stomach that caused you to behave in that way of your own volition, I was already at the clothes off and in bed stage, with Richard.

I tighten my hand around Howard's neck and open my mouth around his warm, moist lips. His lips part also, though sluggishly, it must be said, and his hands move in languid circles over my back, bumping into one another occasionally and snagging, here and there, on the fabric of my top. But they do not seem to be exhibiting any pressing need to grapple with my breasts or make a stab at broaching my waistband. So I stop kissing him.

'Are you all right?' I say. I sound *just* like my mother.

'Mmmm...um, actually, no. I feel sick.'

Grrreat.

Chapter 14

I AM IN CONTROL of my life. I am in touch with:

> Humanity (have taken charge of Lily's unexpected pregnancy crisis)
> Reality (have squared up to Richard re ansafone squabble and am mentally prepared for future ownership disputes)
> Sexuality (am *so* horny am rampant, and *cannot wait* for Howard to recover from his stomach bug/hangover combi)

And now I have an amazing career development too. Excitement, and big time.

In actual fact, I *am* a tad irritable with Howard. If he thinks I'm so great then why the hell was he sloshing Chianti down his face at such a lick last night? Where was his self control? (drink-wise). And where was his loss of control? (sex-wise). Perhaps it was just youth and inexperience (oh, come *on*, Julia). Or, or, OR – maybe he was nervous! Yes. That must be it. He is shy. Of course! Perhaps I need to offload Max and Emma for paternal overnight bonding session, and have Howard (*have* Howard) round here.

But I am buoyed enough by today's exciting development to recall that I am:

> Strong
> A warm person
> So lovely
> A small glow in Howard's day
> Focussed

Also, that I have:

> Dignity
> Self possession

It's a pretty scrumptious collection of things to be described as. Even if most of it (no, only a *bit* of it) is not true.

Anyway, being in possession of all these fine attributes (plus only half the hangover I expected – or is my liver showing signs of acclimatisation to its recently increased alcohol intake?) led me to spend a happy hour this morning compiling yet another list. A list of *Things I have never done* (two columns: a. wish I had, and will try to / b. don't intend to, if can help it).

And it was spooky that I got the career development phone call just then because whereas my b. list included such unappetising items such as *changed bulb in outside carriage lamp* and *cleaned out dustbins,* my a. list was in danger of turning into fiction/utter garbage; *become character actress/children's TV presenter or similar,* and *be rock star* (more of which later!). The only sensible items on it were *had own flat (room in hall of residence does not count)* and *be more considered/grown-up generally.* (Howard's comments notwithstanding – Howard is in *lurve* with me and thinks I am perfect.)

But now something really exciting has happened to me, I also find myself feeling passionately wistful (if that is strictly possible) about not having led a more driven and achieving life up to now. Not that I feel my life has been any more unexciting than most people's. Just that I feel there is a potential for greatness inside me which I have chosen to ignore. Or am I just arrogant?

Note – definition of being passionately wistful: standing at bedroom/Time Of Your Life Photo Studio window wringing hands/sighing heavily and saying oh, why didn't I stay in the New Malden Junior Theatre Club? Why? Why? I have so much to *give*.

At least I am achieving one item on my list. I am being considered, ordered and reflective in my thinking. Indeed, I am thinking at a rate previously unheard of in this house. But I must take care not to become over-analytical and introspective. No one will like me any more if I go around prattling on about being in touch with my real motivations unless I am drunk and with like-minded person i.e. Howard.

Anyhow, stuff profundity...SOMETHING REALLY EXCITING HAS HAPPENED TO ME. YYYYESSSSSSS!!!!!!!

And it's all thanks to Colin. I could kiss that man. Actually, I doubt that I could. But Colin's a darling, an absolute darling. If it hadn't been for getting married, having kids, wanting to spend a chunk of every day watching *Neighbours* and eating Hob Nobs I could have really been someone, photographically speaking. I could have been famous, rich, and also well stocked with classic quality separates from Harvey Nichols. Colin would have seen to it, because Colin was my mentor.

Richard's definition of Colin: a camp, slimy hack with nicotine-stained teeth.

My definition of Colin: all of the above, plus very nice bloke and good mate.

To say that Colin discovered me would be a tad melodramatic, but nevertheless, he did. He really did. He will definitely get a mention on the jacket when my first collection of photographs is published.

Colin was, and still is, editor of *Depth* magazine, a kind of middle-brow Sunday supplement. You know the type. Wouldn't tackle anything as stressful as genocide in obscure African states but, equally, wouldn't stoop to what minor celebrities like to eat for TV dinners. Think: unusual careers – pub sign painters or people who make handbags out of smoked salmon. And that's pretty much the mark. Lots of moody black-and-white photography, four to five features per week type thing.

Anyway, what Colin did was judge a photographic competition: a sort of bright new star type thing that they held every year. And I won it. I was nineteen and already at college and, kicking around a bit during the summer break (and feeling a bit full of myself), I entered. I did a whimsical kind of collage picture called 'the garden gate'. For it, I assembled:

My mum's cat, Tiddle
My old dog, Piper
A washing-up bowl full of water (splashed, dirty)
An empty milk bottle (on its side)
A squashed football
A Cindy Doll Punk Rocker that my mum had strangely kept as the main token of my childhood (food colouring plus bits of bin bag and safety pins)

I shot it in black and white at sunset (for the shadows; shadows are *good*) and fortuitously, Mrs Belvedere (my mum's next door neighbour) happened by with her shopping trolley and her hair in a head scarf that looked like a tea towel, just as I was about to go click. Then the cat spat and made a grab for her stockings.

Colin said '...shows an outstanding flair for composition coupled with impressive technical ability...' and a lot more encouraging stuff along those lines. And *Depth* were, I recall, particularly impressed by the 'juxtaposition of disparate images (squalor/old lady/fluffy pets/aggression etc.) that captured the very essence of modern urban life'.

Well, crap it may have been, New Malden it may have been, but it paid rather well: I got £500 plus a Pentax to die for and, best, a commission from *Depth* magazine to take photographs for a feature on what punks got up to down the King's Road on a Saturday afternoon.

(Which was, it turned out, mainly things like buying refill pads and half pounds of mince, pretty much like most students. But they didn't put that in the feature, of course.)

I've been doing stuff for Colin on and off ever since. Didn't land a job on *Depth* as soon as I came out of college (as if!), but, while I beavered happily at a small advertising photography studio (anything from tampon tests to trainers), Colin would give me the odd freelance commission, and made it clear that a little way down the line there'd be significantly more. But Richard and I were pretty much welded by then. By this time he was making his mark in the sludgy concrete of town planning, cutting a swathe through the bureaucratic mush. He was going places. And he was my hero. Does a *Good Housekeeping* gene get expressed in young women? That makes weddings and carpets and domesticity so desirable? Scary but, in my case, undeniably true. So I married, got pregnant, got a baby, got *sidetracked*. Somehow career plans seemed largely irrelevant; like pension provision, a next-year-perhaps kind of thing. By the time Max came along, of course, I'd all but given up freelancing; Richard had been offered his partnership in Cardiff, and having moved one hundred and forty miles westwards, I wasn't very handy for an impromptu shoot. Even if I'd been able. Richard worked long hours, and there was a clear if unspoken division of labour in our marriage; to have breached it would have involved not being a-proper-mother, and guilt, and Richard sulking and so on. But (thank God!) I did the odd thing for *Depth* still; kept the pilot light going, kept a smidgen of career aspiration alive.

And now this. *This!* This one's in a completely different league. On a completely different planet. In a parallel universe even, with aliens and lots of different-sized moons. I am *so* excited. Who shall I tell first?

In fact, I am going to tell no one. I have read that the need to tell other human beings about one's successes and excitements is a Victim Behaviour. It involves becoming reliant on other people for understanding/fulfilment/happiness etc. which in turn gives them power to make you unhappy, based on their response – or lack of. Apparently. If they should ask, fine. But it is of no consequence either way.

'Mum?'

'Julia?'

'Mum!'

'Hello dear. I'm glad you called. I telephoned last night and that French girl of yours was there. And you know I can't make head nor tail of anything she says. Is everything all right?'

'Yes, of course it is.'

'So where were you?'

'I went out.'

'Went out? You went out last week, didn't you?'

Great heavens above. What *is* it with people?

'Yes, and I went out again *this* week. To see a film.'

'But I thought your French girl said you were seeing Max's teacher.'

Hmmmm.

'I went to see a film *with* Max's teacher.'

'Oh. Is this a school thing, then?'

'Well, no. Not exactly. Except that Mr Ringrose and I thought we'd like to go and see a film together. *If* you've no objections.'

'All right. Don't get testy with me, dear. Anyway, you're all right. That's all I wanted to know…'

Hmmm.

'Okay.'

'So why did you telephone? And how's Richard?'

Hrrruummph.

'Julia?'

'Hello, Richard. What can I do for you?'

79

'I'm just calling about the outside of the house. I've had the quote from Evans's and I've told them to go ahead because it really needs doing as soon as possible. I noticed the other day that there was already a lot of peeling on the kitchen sill. I've said to use the walnut again. And I said next week would be okay, weather permitting. Is that going to be okay with you?'

'Yes, I suppose so. Except that I'm going to be in London on Wednesday...'

'Oh. Are you? Well. I suppose that doesn't matter. They don't actually need access. As long as you leave the gate open so they can get to the back...'

'I'll make sure I remember to unbolt it before I go. Er...to *London*.'

'Good. Well. Anyway. Everything all right?'

'Fine. *Particularly* fine...'

'Good. Kids okay?'

'Same as they were last time you saw them.'

'Good. So. Er. Back to work then. Er. Listen, Julia, are we going to talk soon, or something?'

Big sigh. *Big* sigh.

'Or something, Richard.'

'Sod you then. Bye.'

'That you, Ju?'

'Hi. I'm sorry to bother you on a Sunday, Rani, but I need to take a day's leave on Wednesday, and as you're not in tomorrow...well, I didn't want to leave it until the last minute.'

'Oh, no probs. I'm only vegging. Yeah, that should be okay. Greg can cover. There's nothing much doing far as I know. What are you up to on Wednesday then? Or shouldn't I ask?'

'Oh, no. I mean, yes. I've got to go to London. To meet with Colin. You know, my editor friend – from *Depth*. He's...'

'Sounds cool. What's the... No, Simon! Stop that! Sorry...'

'That's okay. He's asked me to...'

'Si-*mon*! Ha, ha! Stop! No! St...sorry, Ju. I'd better go. Friend round. You know. I'll see you Tuesday, okay?'

'Howard? I know you've got a hangover, and a bug, and I'm sorry to bother you, but I just had to ring you up because I've had some really exciting news today. I had a call earlier from the guy who I used to work freelance for, in London – did I tell you about him? –

80

and he's asked me if I'd like to shoot some of the pix for a series of features they're doing, *and* a hardback – coming out at Christmas, I think – which is – wait for it – a book about *Kite*! You know? As in the band? Me! Can you believe it? I'm so excited. They're playing Cardiff soon apparently – in fact, come to think of it, I think Emma was after tickets for that – and I'm to meet up with this music journalist and we're going to cover the gig itself, and do some shots before, in the dressing room etc., and then a bunch of aftershow stuff – that's what they have, you see, an aftershow party – very showbizzy, don't you think? And I get to snap all the stars! How about that? And, I mean, can you imagine how the book will *sell*? I mean, this band are just *mega*. Anyway, you must have run out of tape by now. Oops! Ring me as soon as you feel better, okay?'

When Emma got back from doing whatever it is fifteen-year-old girls do these days on Sunday afternoons with other fifteen-year-old girls, I pounced upon her with the kind of desperate enthusiasm I have not felt since finding out I got an A in my Art O Level and my mum was at the dentist having root canal work. Emma was gratifyingly impressed.

'Kite? *Really*? *Honestly*? But they're *mega*, Mum. (Who's picking up whose turn of phrase, here?) Wow.'

'I know.' (I really did, too.) 'And getting bigger all the time. Colin said their new album is tipped to go straight in at number one. It's coming out at the end of November. Hence the book. For Christmas.'

'And you'll be able to get their autographs, and maybe signed copies of the album and...and you could...Mum! You could get me tickets for the concert! And we could maybe meet them too! Oh, Mum, could I come and help? *Please*?'

All in all a very satisfying maternal moment. To *be* someone in my daughter's eyes.

Actually, there was a big part of me – bigger than it should have been, given the circumstances of the last four months or so – that said 'Richard'. Richard would really like to share this with me. Richard would understand just how exciting this thing is for me. How much of a big thing this is. Mum just doesn't understand these things. To Mum, a rock band is no different to a piece of Battenberg – just something she doesn't much care for but that is there, an entity on the earth. And she has no more concept of ambition than she does of quantum mechanics. And Rani – all she wants to do is go out with as many men as possible before she is forced into an unsuitable marriage to a man with a very long beard and a late night grocery shop. And Howard.

And Howard. God, I so much want to have sex with that man, and yet...and yet... And yet Howard knows me as mother, wife, person who is *so lovely*, but not as...

But not as the person who existed in this body fifteen, no, eighteen years ago, and who had such big, big dreams. Who was going to see the world, have her pictures splashed across acres of glossy newsprint, be interviewed in the quality press, be the subject of exhibitions even; be the person who was there when...well, when anything, *everything* big and important happened; the name up the side of the world's most compelling images... *the* name. Julia Potter. Julia Potter, Photographer. Only Richard knows these things. And I can't share this with him.

I am *so* cross with him. Still. Because whatever I want now; whatever I achieve at, fail at, get into, get out of, it makes no difference. A whole chunk of my life has been written off and discarded. A whole bunch of memories have to be shifted out and filed under 'bad bits'. I can't recall years twenty to thirty-eight without a tinge of regret, a trace of bitterness, maybe, or at the very least, an overlay of an unsatisfactory first chapter.

It's not fair. I so want to enjoy this.

Chapter 15

AH, LONDON, LONDON, LONDON. Home of everything that's happening and with it and dripping with wealth and the promise of stardom.

I am David Bailey. I am Terry O'Neill. I *am* Mitch Ikea.

'Ikeda.' Colin tells me. 'Mitch Ikeda, his name is.'

How does Colin know all this stuff? How can someone so sort of brownish and beige-ish and *old,* frankly, have his finger so firmly on the throbbing pulse of pop culture and the names of painfully trendy rock photographers? I suppose it must just suffuse into him while he stalks the corridors of his Dockside monolith in search of the woman with the snack trolley and the promise of a cheese bap.

Today, we couldn't be further from a cheese bap than a whelk is from a sturgeon's egg sac. After scooping me up from Paddington, Colin has brought me to *Builder*, a recently opened themed restaurant, which is proving to be trendy amongst those in the know. It has nooks full of trowels and old bricks and emulsion cans, and the menus are cut outs of comedy bottoms. Bizarre.

'So why didn't you ask that Mitch Ikeda to do it? Why did you ask me?'

It seems an obvious question. Whatever our personal history, *Depth* don't really need to trawl the murky bywaters of family portrait photography in order to get snaps of the biggest band in Britain. Do they?

Colin ignites a short cigarette and fixes me with one of his penetrating stares while a waitress in dungarees plops an ashtray in front of him.

'*You,*' he says, 'shouldn't knock yourself, sweetness. You are a talented, artistic and deeply creative photographer, and if you hadn't gone off and got hooked up with that fart you married,' (there is no love lost in either camp) 'you could have *been* Mitch Ikeda. Besides, there's not much chance of getting someone like that at this sort of notice, even if there was the tiniest chance he'd be keen to go somewhere like Cardiff for more than ten minutes at a stretch. And this was an in-house thing anyway. Besides, they've already been done once.'

'Been done?'

'Been done. Up at the MEN last month.'

'The MEN?'

'The MEN Arena, in *Man*chester. Sweetness, where *are* you? No, don't answer that. Now, babe.' He picks up his menu. 'What shall we have? I have to tell you, the guy who owns this place is a complete dickhead. Pops up all the time on that dreadful cooking show and swans about this place like a tit in a nursery. Don't touch the scallops, avoid anything Russian, and don't trust the specials – he's just clearing the fridge.'

I scan the contoured laminate and, beyond it, the coiffed and well-tailored clientele. 'So why do you come here?'

'Come here? I never do. I only brought you here because I thought you'd like to be able to go back and say you've been somewhere trendy.'

'Well, that's very sweet of you.'

Colin barks our drinks order to the waitress and asks, despite his warning, for borsch and then beef. I decide on a salad, and something involving a lamb chop, and then say, 'But if the pictures have already been done, why do you need some more?'

'Because, my darling, the first lot have been scuppered. Victims of the Feng Shui Seven, I'm afraid.'

'I'm sorry?'

'Donna got done by them last week.'

'But what…'

'You know Donna…'

I know *of* Donna. Donna Talbot is *Depth's* major contributing photographer. The person I could have been if I hadn't got hitched up with that fart etc. etc. She is very much of-her-ilk. She carries a bottle of designer mineral water rehydrating spray around in her handbag. Which has always told me everything I need to know. Except, perhaps, quite what it is one does with bottles of designer mineral water sprays. They would make your make-up drip, wouldn't they?

Colin blows a plume of smoke into the step ladder and scaffolding-strewn ceiling space. 'Well she had the negs round at her place – God knows why, when they should have been with me – and her place got stripped. And do I mean stripped. Right down to her colourwashed floorboards. Ha!'

I recall that Donna moved into one of those converted riverside warehouses on the Isle of Dogs, or somewhere. The sort that turn up in lifestyle magazines with the owner prattling about white space and minimalism and the integrity of willow as a representational artefact. And who can't hear the name Phillipe Starck without swooning.

I accept some wine and sip it. It tastes expensive. 'But who are the Feng Shui Seven?' I ask.

'Don't you know?' He stabs out his cigarette and the ashtray is immediately seized. 'Oh, it's such a hoot. It's this bunch of villains from New Cross – as yet still operating, as far as I know – who go into people's homes and offer to Feng Shui them – for vast tracts of cash, naturally. You know, all this bed moving and goldfish and thrusting yuccas and putting bits of flint on your window sill. All crap, but exactly the sort of thing that would appeal to Donna's philosophy of being stuck as far up her own bottom as it is possible to be.'

'But how did they get in?'

'Oh, as easily as you like. They told her, apparently, that it was important that certain manoeuvres be carried out at a particular point in some sort of celestial – or was it oriental? – cycle, which just happened to coincide with a shoot she was doing in Caithness. So she gave them the key.'

'Gave them the key – is she mad?'

'Quite mad. But, as she says, they were all in Ozwald Boateng suits, and one of them *was* Chinese. And Donna's from Torquay, remember. So. There you have it. No pix. No feature.'

He sits and beams while my starter is deposited in front of me. There are flowers in it. Garnish or food? Oh, the shame.

'So you rang me,' I say.

'So I rang you. I thought: Kite are playing Cardiff in three weeks time. Donna Talbot would no more visit Cardiff than Kamchatka. And who the hell else do I know that will schlepp down to Cardiff? Thank you, dear –' he takes charge of a large bowl with a hod carrier motif. 'But, ah! I thought. Julia Potter lives in Cardiff. And Julia Potter's husband has recently poked some trollop and been ousted. So Julia Potter could do with a fat cheque and some kudos right now. And besides,' Colin plucks my free hand from the table cloth, 'I have been in love with Julia Potter for nineteen years, and now she's available, and looking, if it's possible, even more gorgeous than ever she did.'

I pick up my fork. 'Don't start.'

'Why ever not?'

'Because you're married. Because you're not in love with me at all. You'd just like to have sex with me.'

'Oh, very strident. But it is true about the sex, yes. But sex in a strictly serial sense. Until my dick packs up, certainly – possibly longer, now that Viagra is a viable alternative to a stout rubber band. And Julia, I *am* in love with you. Just because I rub along with Mrs Colin does not mean I don't have the most intense feelings for you.'

'Oh shut up. If I said okay, leave your wife, come away with me and I'll shag you senseless till your teeth drop out, you would run a mile.'

'Ah, but come away where? I couldn't possibly go to Cardiff. I can't even read the bloody road signs, for one thing. Let's do Clapham. Clapham works for me. We could get a flat in one of those houses on the common and you could waft around in petticoats while I gaze dolefully out of the window agonising over whether my stanzas scan. Lets do it.'

I shunt the flowers to the plate rim. (They are not nasturtiums.) 'Can't. I'm moving into a new phase of my life in which I am going to eschew traditional male/female couplings and live as a free and sensual being, taking sexual gratification from whatever attractive males hove into view.' (Howard.)

He plunges his spoon into the mauve well in front of him. 'Well consider me hoved,' he says brightly. And loudly. 'We must do it on the table, *now!* But listen, Julia Potter, I detect a certain cutting edge in your usual array of soft and winsome charms. Life's cruel blows?'

'Not at all,' I tell him, as heads drop again around us. 'All healed. Consider it more a delightful and unexpected bonus. I must have buried it way back in a 'non-marriageable attributes' nook.'

'Well, if it's as robust a state of mind as you say, that is excellent news. You should never have married that dreary man in the first place. And it's fortunate also. Donna tells me that *Kite* have a fearful reputation, and a collective libido that could service Wyoming.'

It is *so* nice to see Colin.

The great thing about Colin is that apart from my family he is the only person I currently know that knew me before I knew Richard. Which gives him a special importance in my life. Not because he doesn't like him much (though it helps), but because it means he sees me differently from the way most people do. He sees me as Julia the talented and would-be famous photographer as opposed to Julia, as in wife of Richard, as in mother to Emma and Max, as in person for whom the domestic star shines most brightly in the firmament of life. Which matters. Of course it does. How many women are there in the world who have evolved into people who look after families and whose work has become just the thing that they do to fill in the time before the children get home? Too many.

And then there's the lust. Colin is not embarrassed about lusting after me because he didn't meet me at a dinner party *as someone's wife*. Every woman should have a Colin around.

A lovely, lovely, lovely, lovely, *lovely* day.

Almost.

When I left to go to London I had:

Locked house
Left back gate open (access for painters, as per instructions)
Put coloured wash on timer to coincide with return
Hauled large plastic vat of bolognaise sauce from snowy depths of freezer for convenient (yet nutritious) supper for self and children
Made arrangements for Max (at friend's house – to return following confirmatory phone call from self)
Made arrangements for Emma (Do not have anyone in while I am out – especially boys. Do not use phone except in extremis. Do not microwave tights)

When I returned, I had:

A police car outside my house
A broken window
Richard in my garden.

All rather worrisome.

Of course, drinking at lunchtime is the very best way to ensure that by seven p.m. you are anxious, nauseated, irritable and tired and that the front of your head will feel just like the bit in the roasting tin where the chicken has stuck. The bit you attack rigorously with a knife.

It was with some sluggishness therefore that I closed the taxi door behind me, and walked back into the maelstrom that was, these days, my life.

Richard had obviously heard the taxi because his head bobbed about above the garden gate like a skittish glove puppet.

'Hmmph,' he said, emerging. 'There you are at last.'

'Yes, here I am at last,' I agreed, with an entirely unforced edge of exasperation in my voice. 'And here are you. Where is Emma?'

'How should I know?' he snapped. 'You make all those arrangements these days.'

'But Emma should be home…'

'Yes, indeed she should. Which is another thing. But in the meantime, would you please go in and deal with the alarm.'

'The alarm?'

'Yes, the alarm, if you wouldn't mind, before it goes off again.'

At which point, it did.

I followed Richard into the house and switched it off.

'But why is the alarm going off, and what exactly are you doing here?'

'Because…' He rubbed his face with the palms of his hands. He looked very tense. 'Because Mr Evans accidentally broke a window and then set the alarm off.'

'But breaking a window wouldn't set the alarm off. It only…'

'Yes I *know* that. God, you are becoming aggressive these days. He broke the window when he was moving his ladder, and when he ducked to avoid being speared by a shard of flying glass he then jolted the ladder and the top of it hit the alarm box, causing it to go off. O*kay*?'

He turned and walked back into the kitchen, snubbing me. I let it go, in the interests of my chicken bit, and followed him, and then instantly regretted the slide into low-life that meant none of the breakfast had yet been cleared away. I could *feel* Richard noting it. Bastard.

'But why…'

'The police arrived following a telephone call from one of our, *your* community-spirited neighbours, who obviously thought the house was being broken into, being uninformed, *naturally*, of the fact that the outside of the windows were being painted. So they came and wanted to know what Mr Evans and Mr Evans's Youth Opportunities trainee were doing with a ladder up the side of our house, and so Mr Evans had no choice but to telephone me at work – seeing as you were gallivanting about in London –'

'I was not *gallivanting*…'

'Well, doing whatever it was that you were doing then. All I know is that I was in an important project meeting and that I have had to leave a small, frightened young engineer – who is already some thousands over budget, incidentally – in the hands of a property developer from Manchester, who will probably have eaten him between two slices of bread by the time I get back.'

'So?' I said. 'That's hardly my fault, is it?'

Richard gave me a look that said that absolutely *everything* was my fault since I ejected him from the premises. But he could not, of course, say this. So instead, he said, 'I am just going to see off the constable, Mr Evans and any lingering sightseers. And then I want a word with you.'

Richard wanting a word with me increased the scrapy chickeny scrubby bit to more of a cordless drill on hammer and caused the bilious small intestine full of banana flavoured blancmange (i.e. Chardonnay) to kick in and quiver as well.

What word? What sort of word? What sort of kind of word? I can recall pretty much every occasion in my life when someone (usually a grown-up, prior to this) has visited that particular brand of cruelty upon me. And here was another to add to my list. I stood, then sat, then stood again, while Richard dispensed apologies, platitudes and chummy waves in equal measure. Then I sat again, quaking. Though I knew not why. I had done nothing wrong.

He stomped back in, pulled out a chair (yes, *that* one), and sat down on it heavily.

'Right,' he said, combing his hair with his fingers. 'I don't want any nonsense about this. I want to know exactly what is going on, Julia. No flannel.'

'Flannel?'

'Yes, flannel. You may consider me to be some sort of low life, but just remember one thing…'

At which point he waggled a finger and threw me a look that said 'skinny rib, tsk! Baggy jeans, Yeuch! Trainers, *trainers*? Dear, dear me.'

'…remember that I have a role in this family, and that I take my responsibilities every bit as seriously as you. More so, to be honest, on recent evidence.'

As expected. 'Huh? I wouldn't…'

'Don't start. Just give it me straight.'

'Give you what?'

'*All* the facts.' He whipped out some paper. My pregnancy pamphlet. 'About this.'

Then he pointed, then looked at me pointedly, so I pointed back. 'Just where d'you find that?'

'Bah! You see? Flannel. For God's sake, just tell me. How many weeks?'

Ah! I see!

'Richard, it's not…'

'She's fifteen!'

'Twenty-six.'

'But…'

'It's Lily. And if you tell a soul, a *soul*, I will personally kill you. And just what did you think you were doing snooping around my house?'

'*Our* house. I still own it too, remember? And I wasn't snooping. I was trying to find the instructions for the alarm. Only it seems any semblance of order left this place when I did. So what's she going to do?'

'She hasn't decided yet. Well, she has, but I'm trying to decide her into being a bit less decided for a bit.'

He frowned. 'So she wants to get rid of it.'

I nodded. 'Which is all fine and…and, well, if it's what she wants. But I'm not sure…you know.'

'I know.' He paused to let his expression catch up with events. 'Look, I'm sorry about…jumping to conclusions and that. I…well, it couldn't have been you, could it? So I…'

'I know. Don't worry. It's been a long day, one way and another…'

'Mmmm. So. Successful? Your trip?'

'Yes. it was. I…'

'So. I'd better get back.'

So he did.

There were two messages on the ansafone. One from Emma, to say she'd be back about eight – having detoured to her friend's for homework and supper. And one from Howard.

'Hi, Julia. It's me. Great news! It all sounds very exciting. Listen. How about you, me…I don't know – pasta or something. At my place? Friday night? Or would you like to go out somewhere? Call me a.s.a.p.'

*   *   *

That 'pasta or something' is a bit of a bother. Despite everything I know about healthy eating – and the carnal athleticism of Italian men, for that matter – I find the idea of males in relation to pasta a bit off-putting. In novels, the hero never cooks pasta. He always knocks up a steak or an omelette, serves it with green salad, and makes *great* coffee.

But life is not art and art is not life. Food choices in fiction are not a realistic representation of things as they really are. Take picnics. Why do fictional picnics never include a pork pie? When I was young we always took pork pies on picnics. I wonder where Howard stands on pork pies.

I called him back.

'Do you want to go out then?' he asked.

'No. I'm happy to come to you. I just thought you told me you couldn't cook, so I...'

'Oh, I can't. But anyone can do pasta, can't they.'

Eeeek!

'I can't. Well, that's not true. I can. I do great spaghetti bolognaise. And I don't call it spag bol, or spag bog, or anything cringy like that. Ha, ha. And I have been known to make lasagne if pressed. But, no. If you're sure...'

'But the food's not important, is it? We can just have penne or cappelletti with some pesto. How does that sound?'

Oh *God.*

'Great. Eightish?'

The world has gone mad, that's what it is. Nobody does sex for its own sake any more. Just when I want to catch up with all the fun my un-hitched friends were having in their twenties, I am entirely out of step with the nation's sexual conscience. And women now write whole magazine features about how liberating and life-enhancing periods of celibacy are. But they generally have spots or hate men or are going through a fulfilment through creative handicrafts life-phase. They have a lot to answer for. Specifically, they have hunks like Howard thinking that it would be inappropriate to ask me for sex without first observing some sort of culinary ritual. And there was me thinking that grown-ups just did it.

I have not had sex for almost fifteen weeks. Which is over three months. Which is almost a third of a year. Which is a very long time, considering that for almost the whole of the past two decades I have been having sex once, twice, sometimes three times, and occasionally (generally after feeling inadequate reading those surveys that say *everyone* has sex at least three times a week) four times a week.

In fact, the only times I can recall having little or no sex are my two post-partum embroidered periods and when Richard went on a business trip to Brussels and got caught up in a lorry driver's dispute at the docks for four days. And after that – well. We certainly made up for it.

Which makes me sound like I'm sex mad. Which I'm not. Not when I'm getting some, anyway. Which is interesting in itself, because, though I blithely say I'm not *that* interested in sex, it is entirely from the perspective of someone who has not (up to now) known what it's like not to have any. I've been doing it since I first allowed Richard to make inroads into my flimsy barricade of girlish defences.

How do I know I'm not a nymphomaniac? I could be, easily. I've never been tested. Or rather, I am being tested now, and I seem to think about little else.

I am even thinking about it as I list the ingredients I'll need for the pavlova I have rashly offered to take round to Howard's. I am thinking: *Rude Food*. I am thinking whipped cream, strawberries, oral gratification etc. I am visualising us sitting on Howard's sofa, putting fingerfuls of pavlova into each other's mouths.

And the perfect end to a perfect day? Emma arriving home, one hour after her message said she would, and looking *flushed*.

I know *flushed*, of course. There are two kinds of flushed: the kind I've been feeling of late (frustrated, angsty, up one minute and down the next, wanting to have sex with Howard and so on). And the other kind. The kind that is generally associated with snogging and boyfriends and tussles with fastenings. Oh dear. I just don't feel ready for this.

Chapter 16

WHAT POSSESSED ME TO make a pavlova?

What possessed *me* to make a pavlova? I just don't *do* that stuff. I really don't know what has got into me. Just because Howard wants to spend half the evening cooking and the other half washing up doesn't mean I have to follow suit, does it? Surely all I need to do is *look* good enough to eat. In fact, what I should be doing right now is some serious grooming, and making a decision, underwear-wise. In keeping with my new role of photographer to the stars, I have invested in a couple of sets of Calvin Klein effect crop tops and knickers but can't decide if Howard would prefer black or grey marl.

But, instead, I'm making a pavlova, because I simply cannot resist the opportunity to show Howard that not only do I look good, but I cook good as well. It's so hard to escape the shackles of middle-class suburban housewifery.

If not parenting. Max is in a complete strop because he has been starving since he got home from school, but I can't cook his pizza until my meringue comes out, which won't be till seven, at least. And as his father is due to be picking him and Emma up at half past, he will have to shove the whole thing down his throat in about eight minutes. Or take it in a bag. Or eat crispbreads, like Emma, which is useful, at times.

'And why do you keep going out all the time?' he says. Other people's mums don't go out all the time like you do. And who is that cake for, anyway?'

Max does not know that I am going to Howard's tonight. I have decided not to tell him, in the interests of his mental health. Also because I hope I will be coming home rather late, and in a state of sweaty satiation, and do not wish to be interrogated about my movements. Hence the overnight stay.

'For a party,' I say.

'What party?'

'*A* party.'

'*What* party?'

'Yes, *what* party?'

Surprise, surprise. Emma is here.

'I'm going round to a friend's house for a party,' I say, again. 'A girl from work…'

'Rani?'

'No. Someone else. You don't know her. She's new. Listen, you two. Why don't you make sure you've got everything you need and bring your bags down ready. I don't want a last minute panic when Dad gets here.'

As they shuffle out, I catch bits of their conversation.

Emma says, 'You are such a derr-brain, Max. Mum's going round to Mr Ringrose's, no question.'

'Oh, ye-*uck*,' groans Max. That is *so* sick.'

In the end I decide not to take the pavlova. If I leave it in the oven until a week next Wednesday, it will probably firm up sufficiently to form the basis of something I can send Max in to school with for his end of term party. Instead, I take a bottle of wine and the punnet of strawberries. I can't take the cream as it's half-fat cream substitute and I wouldn't want Howard to think I was naff.

'You look good,' he remarks as I hand him my offering. 'And I'm glad you didn't go to a lot of fuss with dessert.' To which I want to reply '*I* am the dessert, ta ra!' But I don't, because he immediately turns and starts re-arranging the contents of his fridge to accommodate my punnet, and I have missed the moment.

He has laid the kitchen table with a cloth and some flowers and has various pots on the go on the stove.

'How's your mum?' I say.

'Oh, up and down. Bearing up. She has chemo next week, which sounds grisly, but, you know. It's better than…she'll be fine. Want some wine?'

So we plunge into dinner. Howard is all about tonight. The genial host, the perfect gent, the man about colour supplement ad, the glittering prize. He is wearing a roll-neck sweater, and looks just like James Bond and his pasta is perfect – how *could* I have held it against him! And we talk again. Lots. About all sorts of things. Boy can we talk! Hope we can make love with such verve and intensity, and with the same sort of effervescent ping-pong enthusiasm.

And I'm glad I abandoned the pavlova in the end. The strawberries turn out to be just right. Say what you like, but you just can't eat a puffed up, meringue-based dessert and look sexy. But you can *suck* strawberries. You can dip them in sugar (and the drop of fromage frais Howard had in his bountiful fridge) and kind of slide them between your lips… This dinner is no place for a pie slice and crumb showers.

We take our coffee into the lounge and Howard does his usual bit with the CD player. It seems like only moments, rather than almost a week, since we were here before, on the very same sofa, our minds (my mind, anyway) on the very same thing. Except this time we haven't drunk nearly as much. He's had three, I've had two. (I've been keeping an eye). I am ready for action. I have got the grey marl on. I have not eaten garlic. I have paused to re-tousle and re-sculpt my blond spikes. I have touched up my lip gloss and checked my teeth for pesto. This is it. This is it. This *has* to be it.

'So,' Howard says, and though he looks just like he has a licence to kill, he sounds just like Richard (licence to stand about looking pensive and reflective). 'The weekend at last.' He flips down the lid of the empty CD case.

'What are you up to?' he asks.

'I'm at your place,' I tell him. 'Sitting on your sofa, enjoying...'

'No, I mean...'

'Oh, I don't know yet. We'll see. What about you?'

He shrugs. 'Marking, marking...oh, and a bit of marking...ha, ha.' He then points. 'Is that coffee okay? It's a new Columbian blend. I wasn't sure how much to put in.'

Howard looks like he wants to get things together tonight but doesn't quite know what angle to take. How did someone so handsome get to be so shy? He must have had women pawing him since he was twelve. But it isn't just looks, of course, it's self-esteem, confidence, ego. Maybe he just needs some encouragement. I put my coffee down, kick my shoes off and swing my legs up underneath me.

'Mmmm,' I say, sliding them out along the sofa (almost black stockings under a mid-thigh Little Black Dress – my mother always said: if in doubt, go for a classic look. I think she was thinking more knitted separates than sex kitten, but the principle is sound). The light catches the gloss on the stockings just right. My legs don't look half bad. 'Mmmmm...' I say again. 'This is really nice...'

'Mmm...' Howard agrees. 'I'll have to remember the brand.'

Okay, Julia. You're just out of practice. I lean slightly to one side and pat the sofa.

'Come along,' I say, 'come and sit down with me.'

He does. Success! Now I need to consolidate. So I pull back the arm that did the patting and drape it across the back of the sofa, the hand only inches from the back of Howard's neck. I am just about to offer it up for the lightest of speculatory strokes when he turns towards me, looks me straight in the eye and says, 'I think we've got our wires crossed.'

Just like that.

I whip my legs round and back on to the floor. Which is where Howard is now looking.

'I mean...I don't mean *our* wires, as such. I mean...'

'You mean you don't find me attractive.' Which sounds really tight-assed, but you don't have a script to hand in these situations, do you? God! *All* that talking, and I managed to overlook his pheromones. Or absence thereof. How did that happen?

'Oh, no. God, no. It's not that...it's just that...'

'Howard, are you already going out with someone?'

'No! Well, yes, I am, I suppose. Yes. Yes, I am. Just.'

'Just?'

'Only just. Started going out, I mean. Look, the thing is, I really, really like you, and I...'

Oh, please. Not that old bedsock of an excuse.

'But you've started seeing someone else.'

Howard stands up and moves a few feet away. Is he expecting me to deck him? Should I?

'Julia, I don't know quite how to tell you this. The thing is, when you broke up with Richard and we started, well...'

'And *you* asked me out.'

'Not asked you out so much as asked if you fancied *going* out, which is...'

'Not different at all! Look, why are you splitting hairs? I don't understand what you're getting at. If there's some girl you've already...'

'There's no *girl*, Julia. His name is Nick.'

'I'm sorry?'

'Nick. I've known him a long time, of course, but...'

And then I fainted.

Okay, I didn't actually faint because you don't really faint in those situations, do you? But I could have done. I felt like I wanted to. I was certainly dizzy (I stood up too quickly). Swaying slightly, I said, 'What? You mean you're *Gay*?' in incredulous tones, which is exactly what you would say in response to a man telling you he has a boyfriend, but which was stupid, plainly. Of course he meant he was gay. And then I sat down again and said 'oh', and Howard came and sat down beside me and put his arm around me (not a *sniff* of hesitation now), and gave me some coffee and he said how sorry he was if – no, *that* – I got the idea that there was anything romantic between us, and that he hadn't meant that to happen, and that he was a bit embarrassed about last week and how we'd both had too much to drink and how he'd hoped (assumed) that I'd just shrug it off as us being drunk and...and...and...

And so that's that. Nick is the local co-ordinator for Earth Patrol, one of those thrusting ecological-warrior type charities, and he and Howard met through a school initiative some years back. And they play rugby for the same club. But neither of them acknowledged how they felt about each other because neither of them, up to a month or so ago, had 'come out'. Nick had even been involved in a couple of long-term heterosexual relationships, but they had both, ultimately, come to an end, because he felt unable to make the necessary commitment.

And now he and Howard are an item. And funnily enough (oh, I'm laughing fit to bust, me) I was a bit of a catalyst. Howard had, he tells me, always thought a lot of me; always felt we 'connected', apparently. Feels for me in every way that it is possible to feel for someone apart from sexually. That if I were a bloke...oh, *God*. And he was very upset about what happened with Richard. He had wanted us to become friends because he thought we would be good for one another – that we could support one another. And there was George Michael, of course. Howard rather likes George Michael. It was a *big thing*, he tells me, when George Michael came out. Like a portent, about him and Nick. Personally, I think George Michael sucks.

I sat and listened for a good hour or so, while Howard told me all about it, then we washed up together and drank cocoa in the kitchen. Then I went home.

Once inside (deep breaths, deep breaths, mantra, deep breaths) I feel better. Home is security, reliability, all things predictable and safe, Pringles etc. I remember four things. I am:

Strong
Warm
So lovely
A small glow in Howard's day

And because to shout and scream and call Howard a bastard (*another* one) would mean that I am really none of these things, I find myself wanting very much to forgive him all the angst he has caused me. It will, I know, be a learning experience. It will, I appreciate, mean that we can stay friends. It will, I accept, take a while to take in, and it will be, I realise, painful. In the meantime, I must learn to look on the bright side. I have a friend who trusts me enough to open his heart to me. I have a friend who is gay. My life will be enriched. I am part of the real world.

But once again, I am in bed alone and crying. The real world sucks as well.

Saturday morning. Lots of sun, lots of birds singing, lots of good old-fashioned summertime ambience generally. All things considered the no-hangover bonus has the edge on the no-sex downer. I may feel sick, but at least I don't feel *sick*.

Then I look down and see, on the floor beside the bed, my dress, my stockings and my trendy grey undies, looking swizzled, misshapen, cast off and forlorn.

Who am I kidding? I feel like the pits. I should have plumped for the hangover. At least it would have concentrated my mind elsewhere.

And isn't it strange? Eighteen years of marriage end and I spend at least half of the time I should spend grieving in daydreaming about *lurve*, sex and exciting new horizons. Yet dumped after three dates by a bloke I only just realised I even fancied and I feel awful. I am much more vulnerable and insecure than I had led myself to believe. I am a poor, sad little person. I am doubly rejected. I am not desirable. And I have a big slug-like vein up the back of my leg.

I'm just re-considering the whole purpose of my existence when a bang and a crash heralds the return of my children. My children who love me, at least.

'Mum? You up?' Max.

'Good party?' Emma.

'No and yes,' I quip chattily. There is no point in not continuing with the charade. I am a mother. I must laugh at adversity and put on a brave face at all times.

'Did you have a lovely time at Dad's?' I burble on, as their feet fall like boulders up the stair treads. 'I was just wondering if we should do something today. Go out somewhere, maybe. The beach, perhaps. We could give Lily a call. I'm sure she would like a day out...'

Max comes in and sits on the bed.

'Do we *have* to?'

'Well, I just thought...'

'Mum, I've already promised my friend that I'll go to town with her this afternoon...'

'No matter,' I say brightly. 'It was just a thought. There's plenty of things I should be getting on with here. Let's have a nice cooked breakfast, shall we?'

'Dad took us to MacDonald's on the way home.'

'MacDonald's? Your father?'

'Yeah,' says Max. 'Unreal, or what?'

'I think he's beginning to realise what normal fathers do,' says Emma, sagely. 'Nowhere to run, nowhere to hide. Not when you're an absentee father and have to be nice to your kids. Mum, look...'

I am blinking.

'...I could call and cancel. It *would* be nice to go out somewhere together, wouldn't it, Max?'

I shake my head gently, lest tears fly out and soak them.

'No, no. You don't want to let your friend down, Emma. You guys stick with your plans. I'm busy busy busy.'

An hour later, however, Max realises that he has left his new Playstation game (*Death and Amputation Rally 6*) at his father's and reminds me that the world will come to an abrupt and bloody end if he does not have access to it for the duration of the weekend. And just as Richard has learned to appreciate the importance of skills such as underwear husbandry and food shopping, so I have learned to show more sensitivity in matters relating to that part of the male fore-brain that controls mindless recreational pastimes. So I volunteer to drive him round to retrieve it.

Richard's flat is in one of those streets full of houses that are still wired up for servants, but that have evolved into crumbling piles that house sixteen well-proportioned flat-ettes. Filled mainly, presumably, by the offspring of the sort of people who may well have once had bells themselves.

I pull up outside number seven. Because it is on the wrong side of the street, I am kerbside. Max gets out and jogs up the path to a front door that opens on to what is, I assume, like a second home to him, but that is none of my business, not part of my life. The feeling is strange, and slightly unsettling. I almost want to drive around the block while I wait for him. But Richard comes out. He smells freshly showered. He has aftershave on. He says, 'Off you go then, Max, hurry along. I'm sure your mother has better things to do than hang around here.' Then he dips to speak to me.

'Good do?' he enquires, clearly assuming my puff-pastry features are the result of a wild night. He isn't, I note, affecting a martyred tone today. Hmmm.

'So so,' I say. 'I've been to better. Anyway…thanks for having the kids…you know…'

'You don't have to thank me,' he says, quick as you like. 'They are my children too.'

'I know, but…'

'No buts.' He waggles a finger. Then squints up the street into the sunshine. And says: 'So!'

What's with this 'so' all the time? I glance in the mirror and see a car pulling into the kerb behind me. Richard straightens.

'So. Here we are then. Got your game, Max? Yes? Jolly good. Well then. See you soon…'

As I start the engine, the driver of the car behind me starts to get out. You couldn't miss her of course; her hair stands a good three inches higher than her head. Big hair – so *eighties*. She gawps and bobs back down. And that's the picture I carry back home – of Rhiannon, in simian crouch by her hatchback, while Richard stands horrified, holding his head. I wind down my window, to lean out and wave, and mouth 'bastard' quietly, so Max can't hear.

'Phoning to apologise?'

It's Sunday. And almost eleven at night. He's called late, I guess, so the kids won't be up.

'No, I'm not, actually. Julia, I don't have to justify myself to you.'

'So why did you phone?'

I am feeling *very* snappy.

'Because I felt we needed to discuss things. For Christ's sake, can't we have a simple conversation without you bristling all the time?'

'I am not bristling. I just don't understand why you've rung me up to apologise about that woman, because it's absolutely none of my business, is it?'

'No, and I'm not apologising for anything, but I could see you were upset…'

'Well, wouldn't you be?'

'Of course I would. And I wanted you to know that the thing with Rhiannon…'

'I don't give a stuff what you and Rhiannon get up to, and furthermore…'

'How can you *say* that?'

'Because it's true! We are separated. You can do what you like.'

'You don't mean that…'

'Yes I do…'

'Because you're already hitched up with your toy boy, I suppose.'

'Since when?'

'I'm not stupid, Julia. I know all about you and Howard Ringrose.'

'Oh, do you, now? How?'

'How do you think?'

Max. And not really unexpected. Or unwanted, frankly. But now hopelessly out of kilter, of course.

'Well you know wrong, then, don't you?'

'So are you saying you're not seeing him?'

'Oh, I've been seeing him. But as a friend. Not in the way you think. As if you care anyway.'

'But I do. Of course I do. You have no idea…'

'I have every idea. I know just what it feels like, and I hope you've enjoyed it as much as I did. In fact, I hope the thought of me in bed with…'

'Julia, for God's sake! Why are you being like this?'

'Why do you think?'

'I don't know! I just want to try to…'

'Well you can't.'

'What?'

'So don't bother, okay?'

'Julia, for Christ's sake…'

'Okay? You've left me. It's not your business…'

'Julia, I didn't leave you. I *didn't* leave you. You left *me*. You *cannot* say…'

'Goodnight.'

101

* * *

God, I'm horrible. I listen to myself and I sound just *awful*. I sound like a screaming, ranting, whining, nasty, stroppy, belligerent, argumentative, bitter, sour-faced OLD COW. Is this what is going to become of me now? Am I going to turn into one of those women with grown-out perms and moustaches who go on daytime TV and rant about men?

Chapter 17

'JACINTA CAVE? WHAT KIND of stupid geeky name is that?'

'Must be her real one. No one would make up a name as silly as that, would they?'

'I don't know. Tom Cranshaw in my class tried to get everyone to start calling him Spawn of Godzilla last term.'

'Yeah, but he's mental, isn't he? The whole family is mental. Tom Craig's father is the one who was in the paper doing that sponsored maggot-eat.'

'Cool! If I could have a made-up name it would be Huntok Pincer.'

'Who's he?'

'The one with the special organ-dissolving powers in *Mutation Ninja Derby*.'

'Max, you're such a derr-brain. Mum, when *is* this woman coming? I have to meet Melanie at three by Superdrug. I'll never get there in time.'

Emma has been in a seriously bad mood since a) I noticed a love-bite on her neck and took appropriate grounding action re the boyfriend she insists she is not going out with, and b) her father (ironically, given a.) decreed her too young to attend the Kite (in fact *any*) concert, believing, as he does, that not only will she be fodder for every drug dealer/serial killer/rapist (circus press gang?) etc. in South Wales, but also that he needs to take a firm line now that her mother has become a hussy, tart and all-round-bad-influence, particularly in the areas of clothing/hair/lifestyle and lack of sensible *quiet* parenting. He has not, of course, said any of these things. He doesn't need to. Just as I don't need to tell him he isn't paying sufficient attention to his ear and nasal hair. A look generally suffices.

It's all a load of rubbish, of course. I have no life. While he has enjoyed not one but two (if not more, it now seems) jolly sessions of extra-marital sex, I have merely eaten a doner kebab and re-acquainted myself with the perils of crushes. But today is the first day of the rest of my existence, and I intend to give it a good kicking.

Since last Friday, Howard has called me at least five times. I am no longer Mata Hari but Mother Substitute (his real mother is not *au fait* with Howard's sexual orientation as she still calls homosexual men nancy boys/pansies/weirdos/not *nice*) and am being regaled with many detailed accounts of years of pent-up sexual and sociological tension. Furthermore, I must make appropriate politically correct noises vis-a-vis details of the *lurve* thing Howard and Nick have going on. Am scheduled also to meet Nick very soon, at dinner party-ette for three at Howard's (oh, cruel irony! But the pavlova base is now available, at least). Hope I will not get drunk and start asking personal questions about intricacies of their sex life, or stressing about the possibility of them snogging in front of me, as am fascinated and horrified in roughly equal measure.

Ditto situation with Lily. I am very embroiled in Lily's unplanned pregnancy. She has told no one, done nothing and is maintaining her relationship with Malcolm while he completes an MDF study nook cum storage facility for her. The girl has a breathtaking amount of nerve re adult relationships, but is so terrified of babies that she now crosses herself when she passes Mothercare. Much weeping, much wailing, but we have now procured an appointment at *a clinic*. I am to come also (as Mother Substitute, naturally).

And Richard has phoned to apologise for phoning-to-apologise for having Rhiannon round, and to say that I am absolutely right and that our private lives are now very much our own and that it would be ridiculous to spend any more time and mental energy getting tetchy with one another about them. Hmmmm.

By the time Colin phoned to firm up arrangements about the forthcoming shoot, I fully expected him to tell me that Mrs Colin had run off with Chippendale-type character and could he prevail upon me to become a Wife Substitute too. But instead he only commented that I always looked like a good shag but that now I looked like a great shag and that I looked, furthermore, like a woman who was begging for it. And that I have blossomed – finally. Which helped until I realised that I have no idea what Mrs Colin looks like and that she could quite possibly have a face like a bruised aubergine, or something, in which case I could extract little solace from Colin's slavering tone. I do not want to become the sad recipient of attentions from dirty old men who cannot do any better.

And I don't feel much like I've bloomed, quite frankly; more like I've slipped my leafy mooring in a high wind, been blown to the ground and then walked on by a retired Army Colonel in sturdy boots whilst walking his dog (who then piddles on me as well, perhaps?). But though I feel very much like Mrs Unwanted Wife from Abandonedville (*despite* my situation being entirely my choice) I do have the consolation of my Career Development and can at least look forward to hob-nobbing with famous people.

Incidentally:

I read in Emma's copy of *Teen Talk* that stomachs are here to stay for yet another summer, and so have decided to tart up my lower torso with either a lick of fake tan or one of those temporary tattoos of barbed wire. In a pair of fashionably loose-fitting combat trousers and in the sepulchral glow that Colin assures me still passes for light at pop concerts (as if he'd know), I may yet pass for someone nubile, taut, and entirely free from post-partum abdominal crenellations. Why, oh why, didn't I show more people my stomach when my belly button was still a deep and mysterious cleft in a landscape of firm and downy young flesh?

So now we're outside Cardiff Central Station, waiting for Jacinta Cave.

Who is, presumably, young, firm and in possession of a perfectly respectable abdominal area, as well as, if what Colin tells me is true, a good arse, so-so tits, and a nose ring.

I am trying to assemble this collection of erotica into something Max could use as an aid to identification, (Emma has by now opted to wait no longer and has removed herself stomp-fashion) when a sinewy young woman slides up to us and dumps an enormous Nike holdall on the ground. She seems to be wearing mainly black leather and sacking.

'You *have* to be Julia,' she announces, grinning through violently red lips.

Why do I *have* to be Julia? Post-marital hairdo, own teeth, cellulite?

'And you must be Jacinta,' I suggest, with appropriate gush. 'Good journey?'

'God-awful. No buffet, crap trolley service, and two blokes poking each other in the toilet most of the way here, *right* behind my seat…oh! Sorr-*ee*. Didn't see him. Oops!'

Max appears to have no concept of *poke* as a euphemism, thankfully, but I am distracted by unsavoury pictures of Howard and

Nick. I still have a great deal of deep-rooted prejudice-type baggage to deal with, obviously.

'Well,' I say, finally, 'you're here now. Let's get back and get sorted out.'

I pick up her bag, wondering if it might be full of French cigarettes, illegal substances and condoms, while Max helps her into the car and asks how much it costs to get your eyebrow pierced.

She has, in fact, sufficient metal furniture on her face and ears to hang a good sized net curtain from, and swathes of matt black hair, partly restrained by a clip. Her face is angular and pretty, if a little pale against the scarlet gash. She looks exactly as she should, given the nature of her work.

'Well, hello Cardiff,' she sings, lighting up. 'What's occurring?'

We have decided to go out.

Jacinta, who as well as writing for *Depth*, pens thrusting articles for the music press, would like to get the feel of Cardiff's *scene*, apparently, and so would like to hang out for a while tonight, soaking up Welsh Youth Culture and suchlike, and getting rat-arsed.

So when we got back, I spent some time considering what I believed to be the basics of the Cardiff scene and all I was able to come up with were:

St David's Hall

Atlantic Wharf Leisure Village

Arcades (v. trendy shops, but will be closed by time we get there)

Harry Ramsden's

College (whither *scene* (if any) on campus?)

A pretty poor show. Apart from a small kebab house on City Road, I realised I didn't know one single young/hip/happening place to hang out. Furthermore, I couldn't think of one young/hip/happening person to ask either. Besides Howard, who, on recent evidence, might well suggest somewhere a bit more hip and happening than was strictly necessary. So I telephoned Lily. Who is young enough at least to be able to point me in the right direction. And then Rani, for corroboration.

Then I telephoned Richard to advise him of my strictly work-related movements (good parenting brownie point – as if *I* should worry) and to tell him that the children had been told to telephone

106

him if they had any problems. I also paid Emma a small cash sum for baby-sitting responsibilities with a bolt-on promise of strict lock-out policy with regard to 'friends' wishing to assist.

In the end, we fetch up at the pub Rani suggested, a spit and sawdust rugby watering hole in St Mary Street, from where I hope such vibes as are to be found in the city will lead us to whatever *scene* is to be found nearby.

Jacinta loves it to bits. 'This is the stuff!' she coos. '*God*, like, history! Reality! Authenticity!' She clucks over old prints of Merthyr and Senghennyd. Should a dozen sooty miners swagger in singing *Myfanwy* in close part harmony, she would not, I suspect, bat so much as a lash.

'Jacinta – Lily, Lily – Jacinta, Jacinta – Rani, Rani – Jacinta. Lily, you and Rani have already met, haven't you?'

Lily nods. '*Seedlings* book party, February, wasn't it?'

Rani nudges me. 'At the home of the bitch.'

'Bitch?' This is Jacinta.

'Oh, no one,' I answer. Which is another thing. All those people I rustled up so that *she* could get the bumper family encyclopaedia atlas combo. Rani hasn't stopped going on about what a crock of shit her *Wax Lyrical!* batik book was ever since. She nods.

'Rhiannon's the bitch who shagged Jules's husband…'

'Yes, Julia, and speaking of Richard…' starts Lily.

'Richard? Ah, Richard!' Jacinta smiles. 'Colin said about him.'

I sip my wine. 'Did he?'

'Mmm. Said he was a dipstick. Is he?'

I'm not sure how to answer. 'Well…'

'Total. She can do much better, can't you?' says Rani. 'Hey, look at *him*.'

I look. 'He can't be more than fifteen, Rani!'

'Exactly. *Virile*. Go for it, Jules. He looks right up your street.'

But another *him* has clearly sidled up behind us. 'Julia?'

'I'm sorry?' *Damn*. Stuart Goodrich. Standing beside me, apparently part of some sort of after-work beano. Holding a pint, as he would, given that we are in a pub. Though not looking quite as happening as I had hoped for. At present it seems to be filled mainly with people in suits, holding mobiles, who are destined to be staggering home, smashed, before nine. Looking bemused, Stuart says, 'I didn't know you came in here.'

107

'I don't,' I say. 'I'm entertaining a visitor. Jacinta (I spread an introductory arm, but she's vanished) is working with me on a job. We're covering the *Kite* concert tomorrow night, for *Depth*.'

'Oh,' he says. 'Wow! Sounds very exciting…' He has obviously never had a conversation with Richard about the more high profile side of my early career. I suddenly, irrationally, find this intensely irritating. Like I've spent the last fifteen years submerged under a smelly duvet of quiet wifehood, making out like my husband's the only big I-am on the planet. (Richard? Oh he's rather well-known in town planning circles. Richard? Oh, I know, he's such a *whiz* with community architectural projects. Richard? Yes, it *was* him you saw in the Herald last Friday. Proud? I'm prostrate.) Why shouldn't *my* life be exciting? Why shouldn't *I* be someone? And mainly, why shouldn't I hang out in trendy pubs in town and look like I'm part of the action?

'More exciting than my life up to now, at any rate,' I tell him.

He looks like he doesn't know how to take this (which is unsurprising, as I've never voiced anything like this before) then says, 'Richard has always done right by you, Julia. I mean, apart from…well. Well, he's very unhappy. I mean…'

I am just about to formulate a resounding 'yeah, right' when Rani ambles back from the bar.

'Who's this?' she asks. Having met us here straight from work, she is already on her third. Richard would call her 'a loose cannon, that one.' (In which case, Rhiannon's a bazooka, with knobs on.)

'Stuart – Rani,' I say, noting that Lily has wandered off also, and noting, too, Stuart's badly concealed leer. Rani sees it as well.

'Hellooo,' she says, and is obviously about to launch into her exotic Indian bird bit, when a voice calls out, 'Goody, you animal! There's two pints lined up over here.'

Goody? Yuck! At the bar there is a huddle of Stuart clones, together with a couple of ageless women, with the sort of hair that can be tossed about a lot – in drinks, people's faces, taramasalata etc., and who are wearing power suits and astoundingly shiny, flesh coloured tights. It is one of these that is beckoning. Stuart looks shifty.

'How's Caitlin?' I ask.

'She's fine. Very…very busy em*broid*ering.'

'Hmmm,' I say.

'Hmmm,' says Rani.

'Well,' says Stuart. 'Nice to see you looking so well. Good…er…luck tomorrow then. Cheerio.'

Rani makes a totally overt appraisal as he returns to his commercial fold. 'Tosser,' she decides.

'Total.'

When I wake the next morning, I think I am dead and on a cloud, just like I half expected. But I'm not. The radio pings on and I realise that I am in fact in bed, and that I still have my contact lenses in.

After ten of the most excruciating minutes of my life (bar that first post-partum wee) I stumble downstairs to the kitchen. Lily, who exercised sufficient restraint last night for me to know that she really does not want to get rid of her baby, is sitting with a mug of marmite coloured coffee.

'Why have I got forty-seven beer mats in my handbag?' I ask her.

'Only forty-seven,' she says. 'It looked like more.'

'But why?'

'None of us could quite divine. But you were rattling on about how you wasted your time at college by going in *Habitat* a lot and pricing up Bauhaus chairs with Richard. I think you were anxious to make up for lost time.'

'By putting beer mats in my handbag?'

'To put on your wall.'

'What wall?'

'Who can say? You were keen to dismantle a bus shelter also, to get a poster for hair conditioner out of it.'

'A bus shelter?'

'You were the only person in your college who did not have a no-smoking sign from the London Underground or a traffic cone in their room. So you said. Apart from Richard, of course.'

'Of course! God, I must have been wasted.'

I make myself a less viscous shot of caffeine and sit down beside her.

'I went out with a bloke once who had a beer mat collection. He had three hundred odd of them, all different. All in rows on his bedroom ceiling. It's a thought. It could look quite groovy in the downstairs loo.'

Except that on closer inspection, I find that twenty-three of mine are identical, and say *Brains*.

There's a message in there somewhere.

Chapter 18

EVERYONE KNOWS THAT SHOWBIZ parties do not start until well after clapped-out, boring middle-aged provincial types have gone to bed, so I am working on the assumption that I will not be home until sometime after dawn casts its harsh light on my crow's feet, and have therefore asked Lily to stay one more night, to baby-sit the children for me. She is, of course, more than happy to do so, because poor, hapless Malcolm can't track her down.

While she is baby-sitting, and as a pre-cursor to abortion counselling, I have taken the liberty of getting hold of a copy of the classic video *Your Baby, Your Future* for her, as it is shot entirely in soft-focus and does not at any point allude to episiotomies or breast engorgement. Also, have primed Emma to:

Not drone incessantly about nappies or posset
Avoid *all* hostile contact with Max – priceless *Kite* autograph collection/lifting of now indefinite (Richard has spied the love-bite) grounding dependent

And Max to:

Stay mainly in his room and play on Playstation (big dose of grim-reality-of-parenting not good ploy at present)
Not attempt punch-up with Emma (financial recompense)
Not consume more than two pop tarts (unless not back before breakfast)

This is because we have had a full and frank discussion about the baby situation and have reached the conclusion that a woman who says she definitely wants an abortion and then bursts into violent tears crying 'oh, my baby!' is not a woman with a handle on her (metaphorical *or* actual) inner child. It is my duty, therefore, to present as positive an image of motherhood as it is possible for a woman with a varicose vein the size of a slug up the back of her knee can reasonably do.

But there *is* life after having babies. And I am certainly a role model for that. Tonight I have spiky hair, a leather necklace, glow in the dark club style earrings, khaki lipstick, a g-string, trainers with little silver reflector bits on them, and a robust looking piece of laminated card on a string, which says *Access All Areas*. Happening or what?

The look is somewhat spoiled by my camera looking like a big black willy protruding from just above my crotch but then I am *in the business*. Hey, it's cool.

Have borrowed Emma's Kite CD (*Flying High* – their second, and billion, squillion, zillion selling album) for research purposes. It contains the lyrics, the credits, some pretty ropey but presumably meaningful artwork, plus a montage of colour and black-and-white photos, depicting our heroes in a variety of locations, with wacky/morose/reflective/ebullient/lovelorn expressions on their faces. Plus obligatory beer, fags, hamburger boxes parked on all available horizontal surfaces.

Kite are:

Craig James – Lead guitar/vocals/keyboard (the good-looking, cocky, laddish one)
Tim 'Oiler' Linseed – Bass guitar/backing vocals/mandolin (the good-looking moody one)
Jonathan Sky – Rhythm guitar/sax (the not-so-good-looking but artistic, sensitive, ex-art college one)
And Davey Dean – Drums/percussion (the balding oaf)

Craig is credited with writing the music and a few of the lyrics, Jonathan Sky (understandably) with the bulk of the lyrics and Davey and Tim with 'arrangements and wanking'.

In the interests of capturing the essence of my subjects' personalities (and, therefore, attempting to shoot them with due attention to capturing the juxtaposition of disparate images and so on) I have studied this slim tome at some length. I have also made a respectable attempt at getting to know the songs and can now sing along to most of them. And, it has to be said (though not to Emma, as it will be distressing for her – it is bad enough that I don't wear a pinny), I really quite like the sound of them. Their songs somehow speak to me; not to my inner child exactly, but to my pubescent female full of angst yet ultimate optimism, coupled with adrenaline rush upon sight of any attractive male in vicinity, alongside crushing insecurity about shape of legs/nose/tits etc. and inability to hold intelligent conversation about Manchester United type area. Sort of.

In life, of course, they all look like sixth-formers.

Which isn't true of course, but my first impression, on meeting Kite, is spots, hair and pants. Not that any of them have excessively lengthy hair – just long, floppy fringes that hide half their faces, and (cause and effect?) a fair sprinkling of zits. And being young (and on drugs?) they're all lean and smooth-skinned, and to a man, they're all naked, except for their pants. Fortunately, these are of the baggy, boxer short variety, so I don't have to stare hard at the middle distance in an attempt to impose discipline on any wayward glances. They are all eating. Hamburger and chip boxes litter the floor, and there are milkshakes in place of bottles of beer. No one makes any reference to the clothing shortage, but then it is a hot night.

Kite's manager is called Nigel. He is a short man of about forty, with a shock of ginger hair and a livid scar across his forehead, which sits somewhat at odds with his cheerful persona. For he has the sunny and deeply obliging manner of a man on a fat percentage. He says, 'Boys, you know Jax...' mutter, mumble, chew, '...who's going to be covering the gig, and this is Julia Potter...' chew, grunt, nod, '...who'll be doing the pix. I think,' he turns to me, 'you'd like to get a few shots done beforehand, wouldn't you?'

Flushed and slightly breathless from the march along endless corridors, up and down endless flights of stairs and through endless unmarked fire doors that has brought us to their inner sanctum, I say, 'Yes. In fact, I'd really like to have you in your pants.'

Upon which, and in conjunction with a whole body, spontaneous combustion of a blush, I find myself the subject of jeers, titters, arm lock gestures and assorted invitations to extend my carnal repertoire.

But being blokey young blokes with six-packs, Kite seem quite happy to be posed and arranged semi naked, and made to squirt ketchup artistically and leer at the camera, while being quizzed on their set for tonight and their latest album. They may be boys, but they're pros. They are *stars,* I guess. Coo.

For a pop concert you need:

Big boots
A hard head

112

Very little clothing
Water
Ergo Waterproof make-up
Aggressive elbows but a very smiley face (*or* tattoos/shaven head combo)
To know that it's actually called a gig (for cool)
To know all the words (for interaction)
To be tall
Or to be able to jump up and down on the spot a lot (and if so, panty liners)
Or a ticket for a seat at the back, with the old folk

I am strenuously trying to recapture the essence and spirit of my pre-marital existence. Therefore, though I do not recall much of the concerts I went to back then, as I was usually drunk or blindly in love with whoever I went with and therefore suffering from sensory deficit in all but *Lurve* department, I elect to really *commune* with this musical feast.

At the end of the concert, therefore, I am wet, smelly, and have multiple cramps. I am crouched in the little space between the stage and the audience, which is fenced off and affords a good view of the band. It's been policed by six mean-looking but relentlessly cheerful roadies, whose job it has been (pretty much every ten minutes, all show) to manhandle the stage divers from the heads/shoulders/faces of the throng, and shimmy them back to the floor without cranial injury or limb damage. Then to steer them, none too gently, to the side, from where they would then generally make their tortuous way forward, climbed on some more heads and do it again.

I've been up on the stage itself, and down in the pit with the moshers at the front, but it is from here that I've taken a lot of my show shots. Despite a (literal) run-in or two with the guy from the record company who is making a video and has therefore been whizzing up and down adjacent to me on a little track, tutting, I've got what I think are some pretty impressive pictures – including a perfect moment when Craig James, having jumped a good four or five feet from the ground, flings his head back and launches the sweat from his fringe in a perfect arc behind him. Which is exactly the sort of thing any lead singer worth his substances would do. Isn't it? I'm well chuffed.

But the bright lights soon dispel the atmosphere. Where, only five minutes earlier, the place pulsated with the combined waving of several thousand teenage arms (and the smell of several thousand teenage armpits), it now has the ambience of a church hall following a particularly well attended jumble sale. All around me are hair slides, scrunchies, bobbles and cigarette packets, strewn among wet T-shirts, sweatshirts and vests. The floor is a sea of ripped plastic cups, which bob, like empty alien egg pods, on a thick muddy slush of fag ash and beer.

Jacinta finds me – she has made her report from the less hectic surroundings of the seating area at the back. She looks as fresh as it is possible to look if you're a goth and very taken with kohl and smoking.

'Yo, Julia!' she calls out. 'Lets hit the party!'

In fact, I end up hitting the party on my own. Once I've showered and changed, Jacinta has already vanished, so I make my way down to the function room alone. There seem to be two kinds of people at this party. People who either seem to be working hard at pretending they are really *in* with the band, or those affecting an air of total lack of interest. By skilfully combining the two I manage to get close in no time at all. To Craig James, who looks like he should be in bed. He is being talked at by just about everyone in earshot, and I join them to ask if he minds me taking a couple of shots.

'Must you?' he says.

'She must.' This is Nigel, Kite's manager, who seems never to take his eye off his ten percent.

'Oh, don't mind me, I'll just sort of shadow you all for a while…'

So that is what I spend the next hour doing. What we have is a deal whereby I can take any pictures I want as long as they get to see them all before any final choices are made.

And it's fun. After the initial half hour I spend trying not to gawp at the bounty of faces and names now assembled, I find that there are advantages to coming to this sort of thing later in life. While being interested, beguiled even, endures for some time, being awed is short-lived – these are just people at a party, after all. Rich and famous people, certainly, but still only people. Some of them even have M and S clothes. I am touched when a star from a leading soap asks me if I'd mind snapping him with the band. He's never, he says, made *Depth* up to now.

And I find that I am really enjoying a bit of spontaneous, seat of the pants, unstructured photography for a change.

I spend a fair while getting society page type pictures – the place is teeming with long-legged blonde women in very small skirts who all look related (did the record company ship them in as a bulk purchase?) and who seem to pop into the frame at every opportunity, clackety-clacking their ridiculous nails and parting glistening lips to show off their veneers. Jacinta weaves smoothly and confidently between them, scribbling things on her pad that they'll no doubt regret later. All very buzzy, very slick, very showbiz. And then I get punched on the nose.

I don't think I've ever been punched on the nose. I'd certainly no idea how much it hurts. But if you're going to be punched, who you're punched by does matter. I did, I concede, do rather well. I got punched on the nose by Heidi Harris, no less: heroine and pin-up and Queen of the Teens – the presenter of *Saturday! Happening! Live!* Max and Emma *would* be pleased.

Heidi Harris (as I find out much later), has a bit of a *lurve* thing with Jonathan Sky. Except that so has one Kayleigh Wilson, who is Jonathan's girlfriend (and childhood sweetheart, allegedly) and to whom he is due to become engaged. Last month, it seems, at some music award bash or other, Heidi Harris was spotted moving in for some serious mouth action, by a secretary (and spy) from *Gig* magazine, who passed on the good news to the incandescent Kayleigh, and then sat back to watch, as the two of them squared up to each other tonight.

Stop Press! Headline News! Potter's Best Snap!

Leading pop photographer, Julia Potter, narrowly escaped permanent disfigurement tonight, when she stepped in to separate two warring women at the glitzy aftershow that mega-group, Kite, put on, after their sell-out gig in Cardiff's CIA.

Fearless Potter (a young-looking 38) found herself slap-bang in the middle of a blazing row between Kayleigh Wilson, long-time girlfriend of the band's charismatic guitarist, Jonathan Sky, and the delectable teen pin-up, Heidi Harris, whose name has been linked with Sky's recently and who, it is rumoured, has romantic designs on the musician.

Wilson (21) said, 'The woman's a vampire. She should crawl straight back into the hole she came out of. If she thinks she can get her fangs into Jonathan, she's got another think coming.'

Potter recalls that the fists were certainly flying. 'I stepped in to try and separate them,' she told us, 'but they seemed intent on hurting one another. So I got myself between them, and just at that point Heidi lashed out. The punch knocked me senseless.'

Her only regret? That, actually being in the picture, she wasn't able to capture the moment herself. 'The last thing I remember was hearing a snap. And then I passed out,' she said, ruefully. It wasn't her nose, fortunately, only her camera – but this is one snap she wont forget for a while!

And what of Harris? Word is she's, ahem...gone to ground.

Okay, so it's a touch tarted up, but what's the point in having friends in high places if you can't make the most of your connections once in a while?

I didn't really pass out when she punched me, of course. Just fell in a heap while they carried on fighting. Jacinta, a roadie and Craig James broke them up.

'What the hell's going on?' Craig said, mainly to Heidi. Kayleigh, by now, was down on the floor with me, sobbing and clutching the side of her face. I suppose a left hook to rival Prince Naseem's is a mandatory requirement for Children's Television presenters these days.

'How the fuck should I know?' spat the unrepentant celebrity. Though in not quite the same chirpy tone that reverberates around our kitchen on a Saturday morning, it has to be said. 'This bloody mad cow just started on me...'

'And I'll bloody well start on you again if you so much as *expel air* in his direction, d'you hear me?' Kayleigh was back on her feet and about to launch another offensive when the him in question came jogging across.

'God, can't you just *chill*?' he said (rather unhelpfully, I thought, under the circumstances), then he bundled the scowling Kayleigh away. I was just staggering to my feet, in an effort to be noticed at all, when Craig James said, 'Christ, look at her! She's bleeding! God! You all right, Judith?'

'It's Julia...'

'Christ, give her some room, will you? Fucking bloody parties. Christ. Come on! Clear a space, for God's sake!'

'Uurgh…' I began, seeing blood on my camera, and all down my vest and in drips on the floor. 'Uurgh…' I went on. And then Jax took the picture.

'Uurgh,' agreed Craig.

And *then* I passed out.

Guess where I am now?

I came to a few moments later to find I'd been transferred to a sofa, where I lay in a light mist of dizzy exhaustion, while someone well-meaning tipped mineral water over my face. Then someone else trundled up with a wheelchair – they have just *everything* in these five star hotels, don't they? – and I was dispatched (the lead singer of Kite, no less, pushing) to a suite of rooms up on the hotel's top floor. Then a doctor appeared (do they keep him in the same cupboard, I wonder?) and pronounced the only fracture to be that of a camera lens cover. No trip to casualty. No ambulance home.

So they gave me an aspirin and left me to sleep. Which I did, for a while – being bashed up is *knackering* – and woke up an hour later to find Craig James in the room.

Now you can say what you like about money and privilege being unimportant, but there is simply nothing like waking up in a very big bed, with very crisp sheets, in a very grand room, with a very wide view, on the very top floor of a very posh hotel to make you rather covet some. But it a *tad* unsettling to then realise that it is the middle of the night, that you are barely dressed (Jacinta had taken off most of my clothing – I am in my own pants but an unfamiliar man's vest), and that you are alone in a room with a (male) virtual stranger. Who is probably at the apex of his virility curve and who is also, I notice, only in pants *again*. And, moreover, someone who is young enough not to have close acquaintance with stretch marks, cellulite, and stomachs that move like undercooked omelettes, and who would probably vomit if offered the chance.

I know this, incidentally, because just before I met Richard I had an aborted flingette with a lecturer from a neighbouring college. He was forty-two, but he may as well have been ninety once he removed his Aran sweater. Shockingly hairy, and his skin didn't fit. Does the same apply the other way around? Will Craig James – who can obviously get his leg over at the drop of a eyelid – try to take advantage of me? Will he part-ravish me then get a dekko at my lower abdomen, and go *Yeuch*? And be sick? And which would be

117

worse? The assault on my person, or the humiliation of proving too grotesque to be worth it?

I watch Craig James while I get my bearings. He is draped over an armchair, his long legs flopped over one arm, in front of the biggest TV screen I have seen outside of an American diner themed restaurant, on which there is some sort of ball game in progress. He is wearing headphones, and has a half-empty beer bottle plugged by a finger and dangling over the other side of the chair. He looks so young, yet completely at home in his palatial surroundings: like the child of a diplomat, perhaps. I recall that I read that Kite is comprised of four working-class lads born in working-class London. Yet the young guy here with me looks like he knows he belongs.

Wide awake now, I rustle the covers a little. He catches the movement, and turns around. Pop! goes the bottle, as he pulls out his finger. He yanks off the earphones and grunts an acknowledgement.

'Party over?' I say.

He picks up a small games console – like Max's but different – from the reproduction desk, and switches it on, absently, as he talks. (Good God, these things must be *breeding*.)

'Christ, no,' he says. 'It's only just started. They'll be at it till dawn.' He scratches his chest. It is now half past three.

'Oh. Don't you want to…'

'No, I fucking don't. I can't stand aftershows. Can't stand fucking parties at all.'

'Really?'

'Fucking hate them. It's all bloody liggers and sycophants. And arseholes who just happen to know your auntie's next door neighbour, and slappers who want to shove their tits in your face. Wanna beer?' He stands up and stretches muscular arms. Guitar player's arms, I suppose.

Rock stars want to have sex with anything going, don't they? Or maybe he's gay. Which would be a waste. If I was a young slapper I think I'd probably feel the same.

'Oh. Yes, please, and could I use your er…'

'Help yourself. It's just through there.' He reaches into a very maxi mini-bar.

'I've…er…got nothing on. Do you have something I could borrow, maybe?'

I feel like I'm asking for a napkin at a tea party. But he shrugs and says, 'So? I'm not looking,' and turns ostentatiously back towards the TV.

He does look, of course. I catch sight of him in the bathroom mirror as I pull the light cord. He waves as I shut the door. A 'how about it?' wave or an ironic wave? A wave that says 'so what', perhaps?

So what, for definite. I look the pits. And so *old*. I would be relieved if it wasn't so depressing. Even Colin wouldn't fancy me looking like this. Even an octogenarian with inoperable cataracts and a stick would make a run for it.

My hair is not so much spiky as just a wodge of felt, and my face looks just like it should do. Dirty, pasty, puffed-up and slightly bloody still around the nose, and with the beginnings of a monster black eye. I pinch one of the selection of toothbrushes on offer – for guests of the guests? – and give my mouth a good going over, then decide that I'm filthy and strip off my top for a wash. Under the downlighters, my boobs look like two peeled bananas. I put the vest back on and shuffle out again then I sit back down on the end of the bed. It doesn't cover my bottom, but the cellulite problem seems largely academic. He is, in any case, involved in some sort of complex on-screen manoeuvre. He hands me a beer, then sits back in his chair.

'Your face,' he says, snorting. 'Do you get stuck in like that a lot, then? I suppose you have to be a bit handy in your line of work.'

'Erm...yes,' I agree, thinking of the fist fights I frequently referee over Jake and Fizz.

'But she's a slag, that one.'

'I'm sorry?'

'A slag. That Harris bird. Jon's a prat.' He shakes his head then tips it back and takes a swig of his beer.

'It's true, then.'

'Course. He's always putting it about. Don't know why Kay sticks by him...' Which shows his age. And his innocence. Which is nice, I suppose. But the reality is that having a rich rock star fiancé probably isn't too tough an existence, particularly if you're feisty enough to repel all boarders. But perhaps she's met her match in the Valkyrie-like Heidi. I go along though.

'Perhaps she loves him.'

'Bollocks. It's dosh.'

Oh, all right then. Bollocks it is. I drink some beer, which tastes like nectar. I realise I haven't drunk anything in ages. Or eaten. The alcohol is giving me a buzz.

'I guess I should think about getting home.'

'Oh, aren't you staying?'

'Um, I don't think that would be…'

He snorts again. He's a laugh a minute, this one. 'In the ho*tel*.'

Cringe on cringe. 'Oh, I see. Yes, of course. No, I'm not. I'm local. I only live…oh! And I've got Jacinta Cave staying with me. I wonder what's happened to her? I should find her, shouldn't I? She'll be wondering…'

Craig James puts a hand up and shakes his head. Then he leans forward in his chair, legs apart, elbows on knees, hands on the bottle between his legs, expression suddenly engaging. He looks just like he does in one of the pictures on the album, and I wish my camera was handy so I could capture it myself, for Emma.

'Jax,' he says, 'will be wondering nothing. Except for perhaps where the KY is.'

'I'm sorry?'

'She'll be shagging old Nige about now.'

'Oh.' The manager.

'They're mates.'

'Mates?'

'Yeah. Like, good friends.'

'Oh.'

'And they usually meet up if we're touring.'

'Oh.'

'And his wife's not around, so it's good for him.'

'Oh.' *Oh*. I'll *bet*. For 'engaging', read leering. I stand up.

'Another beer? Or are you going? And are you taking that with you?'

He means the sheet, which I've inadvertently caught in my knickers. I pluck it out and thrust it back down on the bed.

'I think I'm going, actually. Except that I don't know where my trousers are.'

His eyes narrow. 'You having a moody?'

'No. I just think it's time I got back to my children.'

'Children?'

Hah! Thought that would floor him.

'Two.'

'No kidding.'

He looks vaguely animated and even impressed. Despite myself, I'm pleased.

'Eleven and fifteen.'

120

'No! Cool. You don't look it at *all*.' (Note: Young people are notoriously bad at guessing older people's ages. Note two: What constitutes 'at all'?) 'So, where are they?'

'At home, with my friend. Who is staying the night.'

'No dad?'

'Ex. I mean, not ex-dad. But ex-husband. I mean separated. I mean…anyway. Trousers?'

'I expect they've been sent down to be laundered by now. Why separated?'

'He slept with someone else. So I dumped him.' I've got that off pat now, I notice. Wordage, tone, style etc.

He says, 'Fucking bastard. I'm sorry,' and, incongruously, he seems to mean that as well. 'Look,' he says suddenly. 'Why don't you stay and have another beer? If your friend is staying over, then why don't you make the most of it? I would.'

'You sound like you know all about it.'

'I do. My old man wrote the guide book.'

I take the beer he hands me. We sit again, and I have the horrible feeling I'm about to take on the mantle of Mother Substitute. *Again.*

'Got any Pringles?' I say.

So I stayed a bit longer and we talked about how his old lady was completely 'fucked about' by his old man and about bastards generally. There weren't any Pringles but there was a breathtaking selection of savoury nibbly things, and lashings of beer. Then he lent me some jeans, and did an elaborate autograph for Emma on the hotel notepaper, which put me in mind of the experimental signatures we used to try out at high school. His involved a little dog, with floppy ears. He then let me take a couple more shots of him, gave me the Playstation portable-that-wasn't – just like that! – for Max, and called me a taxi. And then I went home.

'But what's he *like*?'

'He was nice. He was a very nice young man.'

'God, Mum, you sound just like Gran, do you know that?'

'But he was! That's *exactly* what he was.'

'But was he gorgeous?'

'I suppose so. Yes. If you're fifteen he's a nice-looking guy. They all are. Well, maybe not that Sky bloke, so much. But he obviously doesn't seem to have any shortage of admirers…'

'And his *jeans*. Can't I have them, Mum. *Please*?'

'Wow! A VS! *Yes*!' says Max, quite possibly computing rental charges as we speak.

'No, you can't,' I say. 'I shall be giving them back to him.'

'But look what Max got. It's not fair. And he's got yours.'

'The hotel has. And they know where to send them…'

'Oh, but *please*. He won't miss them. He's probably got millions.'

Which is true, and, in fact, as I left, he said keep them. But I won't. I will wash them, and send them back via Colin.

'So. How was last night?' I say. 'Everything okay?'

Max points at his sister. 'Except that *she* was on the phone for an *hour*. To her *boy*friend.'

'No, I wasn't!'

'Yes you were.'

'Yes, she was. One hour and ten minutes, in fact.' Lily shuffles into the kitchen and sits down. She is wearing my dressing gown. 'But it was him that phoned, so where is the problem, Max? Yeurrgh, I feel sick. Good God! Your eye!'

By the time Lily has inspected it another taxi pulls up, with Jacinta inside. I'd decided, given my knowledge of her probable activity and location, that she could find her own way home once she was ready. Which she has. And bar the black eye, she looks worse than me. Which was striven for, probably. And, if not, as Moira Bugle would doubtless say, SHR.

'You know what's worse than starting the day with a hangover?' she says, chattily. I consider quipping about guilty consciences, but can't be bothered. I shake my head instead. 'Starting the day still pissed-up, because you know it's all still to come. Jesus, that's some black eye you've got there. Ha, ha! Let's get some copy rung through to Colin, shall we?' She waggles her hand in her pocket. 'I've got the film here, and I'll be back in town by lunchtime. We could make Monday's Herald, with a bit of luck.'

'What? Mum in the paper?' clamours Emma. 'Cool!'

Max sighs.

'I just can't believe Heidi Harris would *do* something like that,' he says sadly.

*   *   *

122

Richard, naturally, arrived not too long after, and I had to let him come in because the kids weren't ready. We'd all been too busy helping Jax (who I provisionally/temporarily forgave) with her copy, and deciding which superlatives to shower upon me.

'What on earth have you been up to?' he asked, clutching a mug of coffee and looking like he was round to try and flog double-glazing.

'I got involved in a fight,' I said, grandly. I was beginning to rather enjoy my celebrity status.

'A fight? You?'

'Yes, me. I was trying to separate two women who were having a punch-up and I got this for my trouble.'

'Hmmm. And did you?'

'Did I what?'

'Separate them.'

'Not so you'd notice. I passed out, actually.'

'Good God.'

'But it isn't broken or anything. Though there was blood *everywhere*.'

'Good God.'

'Which is why I'm in these.' I shake a leg. Richard frowns. 'Mine are being laundered. I've had to borrow these from Craig James.'

'Good God. Craig Who?'

'The lead singer.'

'Lead singer?'

'Of Kite.'

'Kite?'

'The *band*.'

Richard shakes his head, slowly.

'Good God,' he says.

We are inhabiting separate worlds now, I think.

Chapter 19

BACK TO EARTH WITH a (literal) bump now. Real life must resume. But this week I at least have a packed programme of events:

Work   TOYL Face2Face finals (yawn)
School   Max's end of term party – make fairy cakes (yawn)
Social   Invites x 2:
Moira Bugle's charity buffet lunch for distressed hamsters (or whatever. Yawn plus eye contour concealer stick)
Dinner with Howard and Nick (High Point)
Pastoral   Take Lily to Clinic (Low Point)
Marital   Summit talk to discuss finalising of kids' holiday arrangements with Richard (Flash Point)

Despite an immediate future that involves little in the way of glitz and nothing in the way of sex (given all that up now – am obviously *past* it), I am at least enjoying a fair amount of local attention, since my picture was in The *Herald* on Monday. Though I eventually ended up as plain old *Photographer, Julia Potter* and the headline turned into *Heidi Harris in Party Punch-Up*, this was the *national* press, and I came out surprisingly well. Despite the blood situation, and the fact that most of me was folded up in an ungainly muddle of limbs on the floor, it captured, I feel, my derring-do.

The big news at work is that Angharad De Laney, the bitch's offspring, has made the local finals of the Face2Face competition, which means not only will I be expected to *be there* at the judging, but may also be expected to take the publicity shots as well. I am harbouring a serious and completely low-life desire to make her look as crappy as possible (which will be hard as she has a face-like-an-angel, though some bitch genes, obviously) and have to spend half an hour in the bath with my most strident empowering paperback, before I can cope with the prospect of her winning the final with anything less than a snarl. But I remind myself that I am now:

Famous
In the papers
Friend to the stars

and that I have not had an angsty thought – in fact, *any* thought – about the possible resumption of sex-thing between Richard and the bitch since the middle of last week, when I was still an unknown and feeling like shit.

Now why should that be?

Fairy cakes.

Making fairy cakes is absolutely *de rigueur* for the year six end of term party. It's up there with sewing in name tapes. As it should be. It has got to be the simplest culinary task on planet housewife. Four fat, four flour, four sugar, two eggs. Some icing, some smarties, some wax paper cases, a smile and a song and a pinny and done.

Except that I have none of those ingredients apart from some billion year old icing sugar, that has, in any case, turned itself into an attractive box shaped Damien Hurst type art installation, complete with petrified ants etc. This is by virtue of inter-carton communication between said sugar and a plastic pot of glacé cherries with an undiscovered hole.

All of which quite neatly defines my relationship with baking as an enjoyable pastime i.e. one Dundee cake every five years.

So I popped into Sainsbury's on my way home from work and almost collided with Moira Bugle, by the beans. She was travelling at some speed with a very full trolley and was clearly surprised when I leapt out and stopped her.

'Hello,' I said. 'Shopping for your charity lunch?'

'Hmm. Yes,' she said, pushing bits of stray hair from her forehead and blinking at, but not asking about, my black eye. 'Um, yes. How are you, lovely? All right, is it? Hmm. Oh dear, must dash…'

All very peculiar. One rarely escapes without at least fifteen minutes worth of posturing.

'Oh, and you really must come round to dinner with me sometime soon,' I said. Like you do.

'Oh, no! Goodness me, no! No, my lovely. I wouldn't want you to think…'

'No, you must,' I said brightly. 'We'll fix something up at the lunch.'

'No, please…'

Curiouser and curiouser. My cooking's not that bad. But perhaps, I thought suddenly, I am a social pariah. I decided not to push it. I didn't want the old buzzard round anyway.

'All right then. But canapés,' I quipped.

'Canapés?'

'For your lunch.' She'd say no, of course.

'Canapés. Yes, lovely. You make some canapés. Must dash now. Byeeee.'

Bugger.

But I'm glad I offered to make the canapés now, because I've quite enjoyed playing with my canapé cutter and have made a selection of quite exotic looking little fishy thingies, as a sort of dry run. And I have decided to bring these round to Howard's tonight, because I think homosexual men are probably far more appreciative of that kind of *detail* than straight ones. And I am right.

Howard, who has become even more handsome since love and happiness have visited his chiselled features, falls upon my tray with delight and enthusiasm and an altogether different timbre to his voice than his previous, non-gay one.

'These are *brill*iant, Julia! I didn't know you could do this sort of thing.'

'I try not to shout about it,' I say, casting about for signs of Nick as I shrug off my coat. 'Doesn't really suit my image. I wouldn't want it thought that I'm too domesticated. It's hardly sexy, is it?'

Howard laughs (ditto timbre) and squeezes my shoulder. I am so glad we have managed to develop such a wonderfully secure and honest relationship. I feel we are growing together. And there are so few people in my life that have so little expectation of me, except as a person they'd like to spend time with. What a shame we couldn't do this before. He says, 'I don't *know*. I suspect there's a man out there that would think so. Food can be *very* sexy. Can't it, love?'

And here's Nick.

I had thought it would be very easy to spot who was the man and who was the woman, and that with Howard being such a hunk, Nick would have to be the girl. But he is not at all what I expected. He looks rather like Howard, all biceps and eyebrows, and his hair, much like Howard's, is wavy and dark. He shakes my hand, then pulls me in for a cuddle.

'Well, hell*o*,' he says. 'So. Let's do this dinner thing, shall we?'

126

So we do. And though my canapés are completely outshone by Nick's berry soufflés with raspberry coulis, it's actually really enjoyable to sit back and watch them together. All the signs, the little looks, the little touches and glances – the signals that weren't there between Howard and me. They are all now in place. As they would be. These two are in love. And I find I don't mind in the least about the thing I had about Howard. Funny, but it doesn't seem real any more.

I drive home with a real sense of pleasure. Having Howard and Nick as my friends matters far more than I imagined it would. Like having two extra children, which is quite ridiculous, yet that's how I feel. I can see myself striding about on gay marches, protecting them from all the ills of the world, campaigning to raise money for Aids research, and feeling terribly modern and permissive and in touch with finer thoughts and feelings than most people. And I didn't *once* think about what they do in bed together, even when they had a quick kiss.

My canapés don't go down half so well at Moira Bugle's charity lunch. Suffering from total amnesia and clearly horrified that anyone has had the bare-faced cheek to bring a party food item across her threshold, she gives me a wild-eyed stare, before swiping them from me and marching out to the kitchen, bellowing a terse 'you shouldn't have' over her shoulder. I suspect they are in the bin before I have even removed my jacket, and been hustled into the fray.

I don't really know why I come to these things. All my books tell me I shouldn't do this stuff if I don't want to – there is probably even a chapter in one, headed 'How To Say No To Mrs Moira Bugle'. Yet I do. I suspect it fulfils some very deep-seated need that I have not, as yet, identified. Or perhaps I just fear that if I don't play a part, I will become ostracised by all the women I may end up having to share a rest home with one day. Though standing at the edge of the buffet table looking for someone who I both know and who isn't already engaged in intense debate about something entirely unimportant, I feel a bit ostracised already. Moira certainly doesn't want to talk to me any more.

I am rescued (if you like) by Caryl Phelps. She spots me as she moves in for a tuna vol au vent and makes a beeline. Caryl Phelps, now that she is conversant with the details regarding Richard and

Rhiannon, is anxious, it seems, to become my new friend. And to put her head on one side a lot and look compassionate and under*stand*ing. And to say 'but are you *really?*' when I say I'm all right. I short-change her a little, of course, by moving on to Oscar's recent lack of success in the Face2Face competition, but we both agree, ever so sweetly, that Rhiannon's Angharad has a very good chance, and wish *her* well, even if her mother has done a very sad and selfish (Caryl's words) thing.

'And what about Moira?' I say, steering the conversation away from how *hard* it must be, and how be*trayed* I must feel, by reaching for a brie and grape bridge roll and pointing. 'She seems a little distracted at the moment. Is she all right?'

'You don't know, then.'

I've obviously missed a lunch somewhere.

'No, I don't. Tell me. What?'

'Oh, she's in a complete state. It's *so* funny.' (Which is how friendship works, sometimes, in suburban circles.)

'What?'

'About Damon. The condoms.'

'I'm sorry?'

'The condoms that fell out of his wallet. Oh, it was so *funny*. Right in the middle of one of her big dinner parties. And apparently Richard…oh, I'm sorry…'

Oh. I get it.

'Don't be. Go on.'

'Well Richard was talking about taxis or something. He'd had some problem with some local firm always letting him down. I don't know, exactly. Anyway, Damon was just on his way out – it was still early. I think everyone had only just arrived. Anyway, Moira said that Damon had this friend in the chess club who had just started up some taxi company – can't imagine that, can you? Chess-playing taxi drivers. You sort of associate them with bicycles and woolly jumpers and so on – anyway, Moira apparently told Damon to give Richard one of their cards. So he got his wallet and pulled a card out for Richard, and a packet of three fell on the floor. Right in the middle of everyone. Can you imagine?'

I can.

'So what did he do?'

'Well, he went scarlet, apparently. As he would. And of course Moira bent down to pick them up, not knowing what they were –

though *everyone* else did apparently – and then she realised and just frog-marched Damon out of the room.'

'I can see it now. But isn't she over-reacting a little? I mean, he's sixteen, isn't he? With normal, healthy sixteen-year-old urges and suchlike.'

'Oh, I know. But I think it was just the shame of it. You know how prissy she is. She's just terminally embarrassed about it. And of course she's been telling everyone they belonged to his friend, which just makes it worse, really. And I think she just can't bear to think her little baby's having sex.'

'If he is. He might just be hoping. In which case he sounds like a responsible young man.'

'I agree, though the general consensus is the former. But who would have thought it? Damon Bugle. I mean, he's so...'

'Geeky,' I whisper. 'According to Emma.'

At which point we are stopped in our tittering by a cough and some clapping, and Moira addresses us with a clipboard and pen.

'Now ladies,' she says. 'The destruction of the Wetlands. I'm sure you'll agree that we need to do more...'

That night I had a dream about Damon's condoms. Except that it wasn't Damon, but Craig James who had them. We were in his hotel room, and he was blowing them up – multi-coloured ones, lots of them and tying them with guitar strings. I was dancing on the bed in my pants, I think. Then we climbed up onto the hotel roof and let them go, one by one, into the night sky. Craig said, 'Sex isn't safe any more, Mrs Potter.'

The alarm woke me before I could reply.

'So what we'll do is take you, Lily, inside for a chat, while your friend here has a coffee and a read. Okay?'

Lily nods.

'And did you bring your urine sample?'

Lily nods again.

'And after that, we'll see the Doctor. Okay?'

Lily nods a third time.

'And if Lily feels she'd like you to come in and join our discussions at all, later, then we'll call you. Okay?'

I nod as well.

The clinic is on the second floor of a rather neglected-looking office block in the centre of town. It has armchairs and lots of displays of silk flowers, and a lady who sits in a glassed-off reception (violent visitors?), who looks just like a picture-book grandma, and for all the world as if she should be knitting baby clothes.

What kind of elderly lady ends up doing voluntary work in an abortion clinic, I wonder? Does it require some sort of missionary zeal to prevent unwanted babies from having life foisted upon them, or do they just spot a small ad in *Pensioners' Weekly* or something and think 'ah, abortion – now that *would* make a change'. For this is very much an abortion clinic. Women come here because they do not want to be pregnant, and because they know they will not be made to feel any worse about things than they already do. But the air of sadness in the place is still almost palpable. And there are boxes of tissues on all three of the tables – more, no doubt, in the consulting rooms.

I scan the journals – obviously carefully selected. There is no place in here for family magazines: beaming children, whimsical scenes involving trikes and puppies. There is, though, a small box of toys in the corner. Clearly some of the people who come here are mums. I wonder how much more easy or difficult that would make it, then pick up the top one of a small pile of pamphlets. *Termination,* it reads. *What Happens Next.* Though it is carefully written in terms that are neutral, it makes for uncomfortable reading. And more uncomfortable still is the arrival some minutes later of what is clearly a mother and daughter combo: mother about my age, daughter about Emma's. Both are red-eyed – the young girl is still crying. I smile but they studiously avoid any eye contact. Anonymity, maybe? Or simply that this is just no place for smiles.

A half hour passes. I am just beginning to wonder about the depth of Lily's indecision, when there is a small banging sound and a very big cry. It's Lily's voice and for some seconds I hover half in and half out of my seat. Should I burst in, sheriff-style? Is she in the grip of a particularly physical form of therapy, or something? Has she hit the counsellor? Has the counsellor hit her? I decide, in the end, to do nothing, having read (where?) that both therapist and therapee can become quite agitated during counselling sessions and though I think I recall the book was more slanted towards reversion therapy for dysfunctional victims of domestic cruelty than aggressive pregnant French girls, I am anxious not to exacerbate an already distressing situation.

130

I wait on for several moments. The banging seems to have stopped. I prepare myself for a distraught and tearful scene. But then there is another almighty bang, followed by an only marginally less emphatic crash. And then a cheer goes up. A *cheer*. And then silence again. I glance up and catch the mother and daughter exchanging fearful looks. The receptionist comes in, clicking her biro.

'All right?' she enquires, casting anxious glances across at the firmly shut door. The others nod. I shrug. The receptionist goes away. More minutes pass, and then the door is swung open. I scan them, but don't see any signs of a struggle.

Though both Lily and the counsellor are smiling (though only *very* slightly, to do more would be inappropriate) neither exchanges a word of explanation with me as we prepare to leave.

'That's it, then,' she says, as we emerge on to the high street.

'That's it, *what*?' I demand.

'That's it, I'm keeping it. What else did you think?'

'Oh, Lily! I'm so glad. I knew you didn't really want to get rid of it.'

'Not it, Julia. *Her*. Yes, I looked at that lady and straight away I burst into tears. It was just as if I was going in there to be told that someone had died. Do you know? And I knew that I would keep feeling just like that for always. So she's staying. Pah! I am so stupid. You know, I even have a name! She is Aurélie.'

I don't dispute her logic, but instead hug her and then pat her stomach.

'Hello, Aurélie. Lily, you'll make the *best* mother. I know it was hard, but you really did make the right decision...'

Lily loops her arm through mine.

'So let's look at baby things. Mothercare, maybe?'

'A brilliant idea. But listen, what did she say to you? I mean, were you *really* that agitated? It sounded like there was a war going on in there...'

'That's because there was.'

'There was?'

'When the wasp flew in the window.' She shuddered. 'You know what I'm like about wasps.'

So now we're into a rather tedious Thursday, full of snivelling starlets and pushy mothers and no chance of respite until far into the evening.

Still, I'm mildly euphoric about the prospect of becoming a Godmother-to-be, and feel ready and willing to face (2Face) Rhiannon, and even to be sickly sweet to her child. Both in confections of cream and lace (Rhiannon's only marginally less OTT than Angharad's) they form a natural focal point – like an ornamental pond.

We have twelve children and babies on the shortlist, one of which will get a rosette (and complimentary sitting, naturally) then go forward to the national finals. The winner of this prestigious event then gets a brief (off-season) trip to Walt Disney World, and their face on the cover of *Family Choice*.

Angharad has to be odds-on favourite – many of the characters that looked so cheerful and cutesy mid-morning are now showing the strain of their post-bedtime outing, and, if not actually bawling, keep threatening to.

Our rotund Area Manager – an ageing clown-like figure who shows up once a month to 'gee us up' and grope bottoms, calls everyone to order, and assembles the children for a publicity shot – one in which he also appears, holding a randomly selected two-year-old, and also the cheesiest grin imaginable. Which is no joke if you are being repeatedly kicked in the crotch. SHR.

Then we mill, and re-group, then mill some more and then disperse, until it is time for the winning child to be announced. And wouldn't you know it? Angharad wins.

'Julia!' chortles the Area Manager. 'Why don't you do the honours for us!

We're terrifically proud of Julia,' he explains, reverentially, to the children, 'because she has recently been doing some very exciting photography, taking pictures of the very, very famous pop group, Bike, for a book. Isn't that exciting? Who's heard of Bike?'

Am I in some sort of trouble for freelancing, or is this torrent of gush loins-related? I wonder vaguely who I should berate for this misinformation but I'm cringing so much by now that I don't even bother to correct him. The children remain stony-faced and silent, until one pipes up with a chorus of *Round and Round the Mulberry Bush*. While I take the proffered rosette, I find myself humming a few bars of Kite's latest single, and wish myself, fervently, back in that other world. Then I advance on Angharad, shake hands with Rhiannon, and actually manage to walk back to my tripod *without* wiping my hand.

At the end, Rhiannon comes over to me.

'Look...' she begins to say, hands out, palms upwards. I look down at them, then at Angharad, who is standing right beside her. I shake my head.

'I'd rather not,' I reply.

We're being so terrifically grown-up and mature and all that stuff, that I've actually agreed to have Richard round for an hour or two, so that we can discuss the kids' and our holiday plans. Not that they much care. For Max, any enforced absence from his Playstation (and new Nintendo VS, of course) is torture and Emma has a permanent face on at the very idea of being separated from the boyfriend that she is continuing to maintain isn't one.

But *I* want to go on holiday, and Richard wants to go on holiday, and we obviously can't go together.

I've been having a few thoughts about Richard since seeing Rhiannon again, last night. I'm becoming frighteningly uninterested in him. In fact, I'm also confused about exactly why becoming uninterested should be something to be frightened about. We've split up, so surely that's a good thing, isn't it?

What I've mainly been doing, though is realising that me being so upset about the possibility of a Richard/Rhiannon thing resurfacing wasn't really about Richard at all. It was what Rani said. I don't want him but I still want him to want me. And I'm not even sure that I care about that now. Mad, eh? No man, no sex, no *nothing* in that department, so why do I feel so together?

'By the way,' I say, chattily, over some of that nice coffee Howard recommended, 'did you hear about Angharad winning the face2Face final?'

He gives me one of his looks.

'I'm not surprised. She's a pretty girl,' I add.

'Hmmm,' he says, getting his diary out.

Max is upstairs in his room and Emma is at a friend's house, so we can get on with the business of planning their school holidays without the fag of having to actually refer to them. Richard is keen to take them to the rainy corner of France for a week (no surprise there, then) and I am still undecided.

The main problem is that we both want to go away the week after next, having both, independently, booked the time off from work.

'So change it,' he says, smiling nicely. 'It's much easier for you.'

'No it isn't. It's harder. I'm not high up, like you.'

'But I've projects to see to and meetings already scheduled. For me to change involves inconveniencing lots of other people.'

I smile nicely too.

'And for me to change puts me in a difficult position with my boss. It's a very busy time. You know that.'

He continues to smile. 'But you are surely not so indispensable that you cannot change your holiday without the whole Time Of Your Life empire crumbling.'

I continue to smile also. 'Like your five-years-late millennium pod thing will, you mean?'

He politely ignores 'five-years-late millennium pod thing'. 'I mean that you are not going to lose your job just because you ask for a different week off.'

'But suppose Rani and Greg have already booked holidays? And I *might* lose my job. Now my extra-curricular activities are common knowledge, they might decide to kick me out and get a trainee in instead. And then where would we be?'

Less smile, more grimace. 'Don't be stupid.'

'Children cost money to bring up, Richard. With only one income...'

'Mummm!' this is Max. 'Colin someone on the phone!'

Richard sits and taps his pen on the table, tap, tap, tap, while I go out to the hall to answer the phone.

When I finally return he is looking less tense. He is drinking more coffee and smiling agreeably. He must have been doing deep breathing exercises or something. As per his own post-marital guidance literature, perhaps?

'I think...' he begins, but I hold up my hand.

'Don't worry,' I say. I *will* change my holiday. We're going to go away next week instead.'

'Oh!' he says. 'Where?'

'To Croydon.'

'Croydon?'

'To Croydon. To spend a week with my mum.'

Which, as it turns out, is probably going to be the best place for us.

Richard is just about to ask me what possible reason I could have for wanting to spend a week in a drab South London suburb eating entrails, when the rattle of the gate heralds Emma's return.

134

She comes in flushed, which is usual these days, and heaves her school bag from her shoulder.

'Good day?' I enquire.

'Good enough,' she replies. 'What are you doing here, Dad?'

'Organising our holiday.'

'Your father thought you'd enjoy spending a week in France, in a gite.' In the rain. While her father sits in a deckchair, in his (awful) sandals, scouring day-old newspapers and saying 'put the kettle on, Em'.

He starts to launch into how lucky he's been getting a place from a colleague on the council, especially given the short notice, what with everything that's happened and suchlike, but Emma has already perfected the Richard Potter special, and her withering expression completely dries his flow.

'And next week,' I add (is there no end to the horrors parents inflict on their children?) we're going to Croydon to spend a week with Gran.'

'Next *week*?'

'We leave Sunday.'

'*Sun*day?'

'As in the day after tomorrow. And we'll have to pack for both because Dad will drive to Gran's to collect you at the end of the week. You'll be going over by Eurotunnel. Won't that be exciting?'

'God!'

'Less of that tone with your mother, young lady.'

'And you'd better let me have your games kit and stuff out of that bag before you stomp off. I need to crack on with the washing.'

And *that* was when the photo fluttered out.

Looking back, I guess for Emma it must have been one of those dreadful, heart-stopping moments that you re-live all your life, in slow motion. Like when my mum pulled ten Player's No. 6 out of my school summer dress pocket. At the time, though, she moved like a splash of hot lava. Not fast enough though. Richard was nearer.

'Hello,' he said. 'Who's this?' Then his face dropped an inch.

After that, it began doing all sorts of strange things, involving colour, contour, eyeballs – the lot. And his voice went the usual half-octave lower. A sure sign that impending doom was due shortly. I leaned over to see.

'But that's him! It's him, Richard! Good grief!'

And then I thought: CONDOMS. Then: EMMA, then: SEX.

Richard said, 'So. Damon Bugle, no less.'

Emma sat down (I think her legs had decided they wanted to take no further part in things) and wrenched the picture from her father's hand.

'So?' she said, knowing full well that 'so' was the only appropriate response one could make to a confrontational parent with murder on his mind, but with a rather disturbingly vivid blush that totally belied her innocent air.

'So, Damon Bugle is your boyfriend, is he?' I said.

'Sort of.'

'What does 'sort of' mean, exactly?' Richard asked. We exchanged a look that wondered whether we should invoke the 'C' word at this juncture. I felt not. Emma shrugged.

'I thought you said Damon Bugle was a geek,' I went on. As opposed to the sex-crazed maniac that may have already deflowered our vastly under-aged daughter. Oh, God.

'Well he's not. He doesn't *just* play chess you know. He's also vice-captain of the sixth form debating society, for your infor*mation*. *And* he plays rugby for the Lions. And...'

She'd got it pretty bad.

'Okay,' said Richard. 'So he's not a geek. We get the picture. But what concerns me is that you've been very reluctant to discuss him with us, and you haven't brought him home either. You are entitled to your privacy, of *course*, but your mother and I have been very concerned about your behaviour lately. It's not like you to be furtive. And the love-bite...'

'Dad! It was only a *love* bite, for goodness sake. I'm fifteen, you know. Or hadn't you noticed?'

'And fifteen is too young to be getting up to the sort of thing that means you come home with a love-bite...'

At which point, Emma's face became redder still and tears began to plop out of her eyes. This is it, I thought. This is where she tells us she's pregnant. Then – hey, condoms, of *course*. My relief was immense. But then I thought: sex! My baby! She's only just got rid of her Barbies! I put my arm round her, prepared for the worst. She yanked it away.

'Oh, leave me alone, both of you!' she sobbed, rising from her seat. 'You just don't understand anything about anything. You don't care about me. You just don't understand *anything* about being in love. I *hate* you!' On which note, she fled from the kitchen.

136

'God, the little bastard,' said Richard. 'If I'd known...'

'Urghhhh,' I said, 'and there was me telling Caryl Phelps that Moira shouldn't have taken it so badly. Badly! And thinking what a responsible lad he must be! God! If only I'd known...'

'Do you think...'

'I dread to...'

'You don't think...'

'I hope not...'

'We'll have to...'

'I know. When she's calmed down...'

'Do you think I should...'

'No. Not now. Let's think about this for a while. We don't want to...'

'God, no. That's exactly what sends them straight into their arms, isn't it...'

'Exactly. God, I feel so *responsible*. I'm her Mother. I should have realised...'

'You're right. This *is* partly our fault. All this upheaval in her life, and...'

'And me being so wrapped up in myself, and...'

'I wouldn't say that...'

'Oh, but I have. What with work, and me being...'

'Well you have been...'

'And I've been worried about Lily, and spending a lot of time...'

'And you have been going out a fair bit...'

'And forgetting that she's really only a child still, and...'

'And it's hardly a good example, is it? All this gadding around...'

'Well I wouldn't exactly call it...'

'But you have been...'

'No, I *hav*en't. I was just saying...'

'And she *is* a girl, Julia. Look, I'm there for her, she knows that, but she's hardly going to come to me for advice about *that* sort of thing, is she? She needs a mother's guidance...'

'What do you mean '*gadding*'?'

'Simply that...'

'Oh. Oh! So you're Mr Squeaky Clean Stop At Home, are you?'

'Well I...'

'Well I nothing!'

137

'I certainly haven't been dressing up in strange clothes and pretending I was fifteen, quite frankly.'

'Oh, that's what I've been doing, is it? How dare you...'

'Look, I only meant...'

'You meant exactly what you said. *You* think Emma's going off the rails because of me. Because I'm a crap mother and that I'm more concerned with myself than with the good of my children. Well thanks a *lot*.'

'I said nothing of the kind. I just think *you* should think about the effect this is all having on the kids. Being carted back and forth all the time, and you going out with bloody hippies and whatnot. Children need stability. They need a secure family life. They need...'

'What you need is a kick in the balls. How *dare* you lecture me about family life! You were the one who poked that bitch round the corner. This is *your* fault, okay?'

I could almost see Richard's knees scrunch together as I said this. His superior tone made a bolt for it, too.

'Look, I know it was me who did *that*, but...'

I stood up. Same effect. He was visibly shrinking. 'Oh, and pardon me for taking offence!' I bellowed. 'I suppose I should have just said – oh, diddums, you must be feeling so *guilty*, poor thing. Please accept my apologies for feeling a teeny bit bloody upset about it. And what's with this '*that*'? You make it sound like you just put a shelf up wrong or something – that's if you ever bloody bothered to do that sort of thing in the first place – it was *infidelity*, Richard. You were unfaithful to me. Where's the book that says infidelity is no longer a bad thing? Huh?'

He stood up as well, arms across crotch, looking weary.

'I think I'd better go. This is getting us nowhere.'

'It's getting me bloody wild. Yes, you'd better.'

Bastard.

By the morning, the pace, tone and general ambience of the Potter household has subsided from seething hotbed of fury to a more manageable smouldering den of resentment. Emma and I are circumnavigating the house with care and lowered faces.

Despite being so angry with Richard that I want to hack off his willy and put it in a blender, my mood is lightened by two things.

The first of these is Max's admission that he took a small tube of writing icing with him to school yesterday, and surreptitiously autographed all my fairy cakes with the legend *JP (plus heart)*. That he went on to charge an illicit five pence for them is something I shall overlook. That it is a very sad woman who's day is lifted by something as inconsequential as a fan club of twenty-odd eleven-year -old boys I shall also overlook. I am clearly a star. They were sold out in minutes.

And then there is Moira and the canapé moment.

Moira Bugle, I realise, must have *known* about Emma. And must be living in fear *at this very instant*, that I, Julia Potter, celebrity brawler, may be on my way round to re-arrange her son's face. Hah! SHR!

But I'm still bloody mad. Thank heavens, for Richard's sake, for Croydon.

Now, I know that by the middle of next week I will be fantasising about stashing hamburgers, wine boxes and intelligent conversationalists under my bed, and attaching clothes pegs to my tongue to stop me from screaming at her, but sometimes my Mum is the *only* person who can make me feel better.

Within moments – no, micromoments – of me telephoning, she was enthusing about me, fit to bust. I almost decided she'd developed dementia and thought she was speaking to someone from Pottery Workshop *about* me. But no. The word 'you' was definitely in there.

'So I went down to Smith's and bought a dozen copies – I thought I'd pop a couple to your cousins in Penge. And, of course, everyone at Potty (Potty?) thinks it's all terribly exciting. In fact, Minnie Scrivens – you *know*, with the cellulitis – wondered if perhaps you might be able to get that television lady's autograph for her grandson. Anyway, I said I'd ask. I mean, she should really make some sort of amends, shouldn't she? Oh, and I've had a couple laminated – I thought I could use them as placemats, and I've written to Great Auntie Bet in Canada – she always likes to know what you're up to. Anyway, when you come you can see. I could get some done for you as well, if you like. Oh, and there's a thing! We're having a little bit of show on the Wednesday – nothing grand – just a small exhibition of the term's best efforts – my Mondrian ring tree's going in – did I tell you? And you could come along, and bring the children – oh, it would be lovely! Everyone's dying to meet you, now they've seen you in the paper.'

I fear this as only a woman who knows that she has been number one topic of conversation at a certain corner of Pottery Workshop for the past half-dozen years can. And now I have achieved cult status as well. I wonder if perhaps I should dye my hair green. It would be such a pity to disappoint.

'It all sounds wonderful,' I enthuse obediently. 'And the children are so looking forward to seeing you. And please don't worry about planning loads of meals and suchlike (some hope). I expect we'll be doing lots of day trips. We could even hit the coast a couple of times if it's nice.'

As always, I regret the word 'coast' immediately. For my mother, the word 'coast' evokes a Pavlovian response involving hard-boiled eggs, salad cream, two dozen brawn sandwiches, cold sausages, pork and egg pies, crisps, individual fruit tarts and (always) a Swiss roll. And topped with a treatise on burger bar catering. McDonald's, she'll say, serve such *un*healthy food.

'Anyway,' I go on, 'we can decide what to do when we get there, *can't* we.'

Which, short of extracting a promise in blood not to pillage Dewhursts, is the best I can do to promote culinary restraint. 'And now,' I say, 'I have a favour to ask you.'

So I distil Colin's message into manageable parts – in fact, mainly the part where she will be required to look after the children for the twenty-four hours between me speeding off to Brighton (where Kite are playing at the Rock Up Front festival next Friday) and the arrival of their father on the Saturday afternoon, ready to speed them across the channel for their annual fix of horizontal rain and garlic-infested roadside *frites* vans.

She homes, as I'd known she would, on to the part that involves access to said ex-husband without the complicating factor of truculent (sic) daughter.

'Oh, that'll be no problem at all,' she assures me. 'We'll have a lovely time. Perhaps Richard could come for lunch. He must be very proud of you, dear.'

Bah!

'Richard doesn't know.'

'Oh.'

'And I don't want you to tell him.'

'But…'

'Because it isn't his business.'

'But why *are* you going to Brighton, dear? I thought you'd already done the photographs for that newspaper.'

'I have, but they want a few more. This gig –'

'Gig?'

'Concert. It's part of some sort of charity roadshow. There will be lots of bands playing, and quite a few TV celebrities involved. And I think someone royal...Mum? Are you still there?'

'Royal? Actually *royal*? Which one? Not Princess Anne, I hope. I've never been keen on her. I've always preferred Princess Michael of Kent. I always like watching her on the tennis. Or is that the Duchess of Kent? Will you get to meet them? Goodness, how exciting...'

'I don't know. My brief is to shoot Kite. I really don't know much more until Colin firms up the details. I imagine there'll be some sort of aftershow, so I suppose...'

'Ooh, Julia, you sound so glamorous! Just wait till I tell Minnie! Now we'd better crack on. I'll put Max on the Z-bed and Emma in the spare room. Would you like the sofa or the li-lo?'

Chapter 20

Sunday
Sun, hot, lovely, lovely, lovely day etc.
I start the day feeling an unexpected seepage of positive mental attitude into loathsome depression/angst /fear of metamorphosis into second-rate single parent combi. (Why? Bizarre pre-menstrual turnaround?)

But it is short lived. Only fifteen minutes into the M4 corridor and am already experiencing in-car turbulence vis-a-vis selection of musical accompaniment. Decide to stamp authority on situation (and, therefore, hopefully, remainder of holiday) by declaring all knobs/stalks/buttons etc. as total exclusion zone and conducting said mission statement as 95 decibel tirade. Put Kite: *Flying High* on, volume twelve.

Fifteen minutes into Kite: *Flying High* suffer sudden and debilitating attack of parental guilt, as Max apoplectic about perceived favouritism towards sibling. Agree to drawing up of musical accompaniment rota, in tolerance-friendly fifteen minute cycles. Heated debate over inclusion of Radio Four's *Desert Island Discs*, as is forty-five minute programme but also family travelling tradition (unlike Early Learning Centre Favourite Nursery Rhyme Cassettes – a point of some pride *chez* Potter). By time have browbeaten offspring into sullen acceptance, programme is already at disc six, and guest's voice is tantalisingly familiar yet infuriatingly unidentifiable. Decide must be ageing theatrical (boring) luvvie and submit instead to fifteen minutes of *Throb* FM.

Five minutes in, experience pang of wistful regret that never quite mastered Richard style of mobile parenting, i.e. SHADDUPPPP!I'MDRIIIIVVVINGGGGG!!!!! followed by occasional ejection onto roadside for reinforcement purposes.

Later
Rest of population of South of England are clearly trying to go to my mother's house also. Sit in now stationary car, dispensing wine gums, and try to conjure mental picture of sitting in Mother's garden, developing tan, with large glass wine plus Pringles, buzz of

bees, scents of summer etc. Start and make stop again, this time at Happy Traveller, to partake of nutritious grease/chips/milkshake lunch, but coincide with coach party of Ghurkhas – none have assimilated concept of queuing, but they smile so engagingly as they shunt relentlessly forward that instead of grousing and bitching everyone nods and smiles and says ahhh.

Much later
Arrive at Mother's just as sun slides behind big cloud and nip forms in air. Sit in mother's kitchen drinking tea from leaky art-deco effect 'Potty' teapot, listening to buzz of moribund strip light, drinking in scent of giblets boiling etc.

Monday
Rain

God. Offal problem already underway. Mother has almost inexhaustible supply of animal organs with which to prepare meals (sic) for remainder of holiday, and produces frozen wodge of pigs liver from freezer as we breakfast. Emma (still very tense/taciturn etc) announces, 'I can see I'm going to spend the week vomiting, *Mother*' and flounces from room.

Mother entertains Max with mild (fifteen minutes or so) rant about powdered eggs, bread and dripping, digging for victory etc. Plus expresses concern about volatile nature of youth of today/additives in orange squash/rays that emanate from Sky satellite dishes causing leukaemia clusters.

See-sawing between mad, mad, mad at Richard and sensing seedling of self esteem in place concerning Brighton expedition/resurgence of proper career etc. But very damp at night. Wake in blue funk with bolt of terror about incontinence possibility, then recall properties of plastic lilos. Will camp on sofa from tomorrow.

Tuesday
Rain

Am good parent. Did museum combo today. Started with Natural History: dinosaurs (crap), sea life (crap) bugs (crap) followed by fossils (really crap). Had lunch in purpose built indoor picnic area (cheapskate sad family). Moved on to the newly re-vamped/restyled

143

(award-winning?) earth galleries (okay), and did earthquake simulation exhibit (crap plus, like, *really* bad taste, Mum).

Moved on once again, this time to more feverishly interactive exhibits of Science Museum. Paid extortionist on door, did engines (crap), miracle of reproduction (flicker of interest but 'Mum, *don't*!' if touched moving parts). Home to Croydon via Covent Garden and Piccadilly Circus, where did Goth Heaven type shops (wicked) and Trocadero (cool).

Derailment near New Cross afforded excellent opportunity to instil in offspring sadly lacking as yet sense of appreciation for heritage/history/culture, plus wealth of enriching experience visit to nation's finest museums brings.

'But it's boring.'

'No. it's...'

'Boring.'

'Tsk. You say that now, but you'll thank me for it later. Look at what you've learned today...'

'Mum, we do learning in school. This is the holidays.'

Wrong tack. 'Not learned then. Discovered, been amazed by...'

'You're right. I had no idea there were so many styles of Doc Marten. Why can't we live in London. Cardiff's so crap.'

'...the wonders of science and that amazing...'

'Boring, boring, boring, boring...'

'You wait till you're parents. You'll be bringing your own children to these places one day...'

'What for?'

'To look, to discover, to...'

'...be *bored*.'

Hah. Offspring will regret thinking museums-with-Mother outing worst that can happen to them. Will be taken next week to *Musées* instead, where will understand only one word in fifty-seven (Emma on German option at high school) and will be forced to listen to father recounting key points about Storming of the Bastille etc. Hah.

Eve.

Peak Experience Moment when Emma (screaming) found large blood vessel in nutritious brown stew offal-type dinner.

'That's an aorta, that is,' said Max.

Not a totally wasted day, then.

Wednesday
Low cloud, threatening rain

Shopping in Croydon. Not crap, as determined to make up for suspect parenting qualities by showering large chunk of promised pop photography fee on grateful (salivating) offspring. Return home from biggest, brightest shopping experience in South (apparently) with Tongue Twisting (or something) almost hang-out-looking-cool-by-themselves type *K-Swiss* trainers, and whole bag of seriously desirable *Bench* garb. Rashly quote cost. Mother speechless and dribbling.

And uncharacteristic and alarmingly frank telephone message from Richard, via Mother:
'He says can you ring him as soon as possible, and to tell you he's very sorry, and please can you talk. Julia, does this mean that Richard and you are *talking*... And are you and he *considering*...' etc. etc. ad nauseam.

Clever ruse on his part to commission Mother as running mate, as some half hour after putting her straight, am still subject of big sighs and wistful expressions. She will, any time now, get-photographs-out.

Eve.
Much hyped visit to local community centre to admire exhibits at Croydon Seniors Pottery Workshop Annual Show. Mother announces only seconds before arrival that I am to be guest of honour and that not only am I to present the prize in the 'freestyle' category, as befits my new status as deeply fashionable person, but also that I am expected to give small pottery-related speech (huh?) though strictly, of course, in my capacity as lay pottery fancier.

To this end, I spend some time taking my cup of disgusting tea for a turn around the trestles, and deep breathing to quell growing panic that I may too, some day, want to spend whole chunks of remaining time on planet gouging nooks and gullies from lumps of wet mud. Is there a sex thing at work here, I wonder? And will I get to do more of the real thing before it comes to this?

Freestyle winner turns out to be elderly man in checked shirt, knitted thing (jerkin?) and Hush Puppies the colour of baby poo. Unfortunately, his abstract piece, though painted mainly blue, looks so excruciatingly like a penis plus chicken skin testicles that am

145

forced to feign paroxysm of coughing to disguise involuntary guffaw. Finally settle on:

'Well, Mr Bledshawe, it's nice to see such imaginative and contemporary-looking work coming out of Croydon SPW. Is it ...er...splut...representational, at all? And...er...does it have a...ahem...name?'

He fixes me with a glassy grin.

'It's called *Cold Phallus*,' he says.

Am tense and tetchy with Mother to degree that cannot resist pointing at small flower type thing on way out, saying, 'And what's that one then – *My clitoris: a study*?'

Unfazed, she leans to read the card with the details.

'Barbara Pickles,' she reads. 'Hmmmm, it could well be.'

Later

Mood is deflected from unpalatable mental pictures of octogenarian sex games by copious anaesthesia-by-wine and by arrival, by courier (no less), of tickets/brief/itinerary/hotel accommodation details, from Colin. But still go to bed and dream of lonely pensioner vigorously (and fruitlessly) masturbating, by weak orange glow from one-bar electric fire. Arrive with soup, cheese sandwich and benevolent expression and find it is actually Richard.

Thursday

Very hot, very sunny, very little chance that maternal coast enthusiasm will be deflected

Mother up pre-dawn to hard boil eggs and make up flagons of squash.

Avoiding kitchen out of respect for integrity of stomach contents, spend gruelling half-hour with children saying things like 'you always love picnics once we get there' and 'but Eastbourne is so *cool* these days. They have joy riders now, you know' and even 'how about one hour's unlimited pier access plus five pounds each?'. Then spend more productive thirty seconds shouting 'GETUPGETWASHEDGETDRESSEDGET ONWITHIT**ORELSE**' while Mother out of earshot in toilet.

Coast idea soon seems ill-judged, as sit in crawl of maternal hatchbacks on A22 knowing full well that will sit in similar crawl of maternal hatchbacks again on M23/A23 on way to Brighton tomorrow. Arrive in Eastbourne and find parking space a mere 1.6 miles from sea front.

Children mutiny, then rally, as realise route seaward involves walking past *Skate Shack, Sport Locker, RamRomGameShop* and *MacDonald's*. But are thwarted in their quest for a Big MacBreakfast by approx. one million European language students clogging exterior and knocking old ladies' glasses off with neon backpacks.

Noon

Arrive on beach to find tide hurtling in at warp speed, and spend some moments in scientific appraisal of shingle wetness, in order to establish parameters of remaining beach availability. (As do not wish to sit within ten yards of any of other eight billion people on beach, in traditional sociable British style.) Finally make camp of twelve towels, two folding chairs, plastic sheet of dubious origin, cool box, carrier bag of crisps, Mother's Sun Lotions handbag, and £1.99 badminton set bought on prom. Spread picnic food in wide and daunting arc around us.

Noon plus ten minutes

Make new camp on higher up bit of beach.

After lunch (and departure of offspring to deposit £10 in pier management savings account) decide swim is called for, as blazing Eastbourne sun (hotter than Saharan sun, apparently) is melting the aspic in the pork pies and desiccating my contact lenses.

Begin process of strip to new sports-style bikini and audible gulp causes sudden realisation that there is something Mother does not know.

'Ooh!' she gasps, 'that looks painful. Did you get a boil, or something?'

Ah,' I reply. 'Not a boil, exactly…more a…more a…ring…'

'In your *tummy button*? Ugh! that's absolutely disgusting!'

'It's fashionable. *I* think it looks rather nice…'

She picks up a Kit Kat and snaps it asunder.

'Fashionable?' she splutters. 'The Third Reich was fashionable.'

Chapter 21

I FEEL KIND OF insulated this morning. I'm in a bit of a bubble. My personal escape pod (or, rather, Time-Of-Your-Life-Mondeo-Escape-Coupe) is speeding me on down shimmering tarmac, off to my new incarnation.

I had a call from Richard last night, halfway through dinner. I have avoided speaking to him all week, of course, because I fully expected to shout at him – which would have been inappropriate and ill-advised given the constant proximity of mother plus offspring. But I had to speak to him last night because he called to organise things with Emma and Max. I shut the kitchen door firmly and took it in the hall.

'Look,' he said, plunging straight into what he now obviously feels is his role as committed father, moral arbiter etc. 'I don't think it's very productive to keep this up, do you?'

I said, 'I'm sorry?' I still had a sprout in my mouth, so was caught off guard.

'I mean this aggressive stance you're taking all the time.'

Such breathtaking loftiness. I swallowed the sprout.

'I'm not sure productivity is the issue here, but if you mean aggressive in its common usage as the word to describe not returning a telephone call then, yes, I'm being *pretty* damned aggressive.'

'You see? That's *exactly* what I mean. I can't talk to you any more. I only wanted to apologise for Friday, but you seem intent on...on...'

'On not being apologised to, quite frankly. I didn't want to talk to you because I was very cross with you and...'

'And, as I am happy to admit, quite justifiably so. I was out of order, I know I was out of order...'

'And I wasn't particularly interested in hearing your apology. Been there, done that.'

'*God!* Julia, do you not have even the slightest sense that I might be suffering here too?'

I did. I do. Not sure (don't care) about the Rhiannon position, but my guess is he's not getting any more sex than I am. Tetchy, tetchy.

'No. But I'm glad you're taking the kids away for the week. It'll be your first ever bit of proper single parenthood. And in French.

148

And I hope it gives you an insight into what it's been like for me for the last few months, even though it doesn't involve work or Sainsbury's or packed lunches or anything. Oh, and don't let Max go anywhere muddy in his new trainers. Oh, and don't worry if Emma doesn't speak to you. Oh, and my mother is expecting you for lunch tomorrow. I reminded her that sautéed kidneys were your absolute favourite.'

When I stopped speaking there was complete silence. I thought he had hung up, but finally he spoke.

'Why are you being like this?'

To my credit, I thought for a moment before answering.

'Because,' I said at last, 'it makes me feel better.'

He laughed then. Not a big laugh or anything, just a small, ironic, unexpected, 'huh'-type laugh.

'Funny,' he said. 'But it makes me feel better too.'

Bastard. What did he mean by that?

There's some sort of sea change going on in my life all of a sudden, but I can't quite put my finger on what it is. One thing's for sure though, and that's that Richard doesn't like me any more. I don't mean doesn't love me, because I think he still does. Loves the wife he was unfaithful to, at any rate. I just don't think he can cope with the me I'm turning into. And I *am* changing. I feel like I'm becoming a more vibrant and successful version of my former self. That my potential – creatively, socially, emotionally – has been unlocked by the trauma of my relationship with Richard, and that all of a sudden I'm in control of my own future. Pretty scary stuff for your average bloke, I guess.

I find *I* like my new self very much. In fact I would say I'm almost *in love* with myself right now, which is bizarre. I'm finding a sensual pleasure in my own body. I like the ring in my belly button, like watching myself as I dress in the mornings, like to stroke my own shoulders, caress my own arms. Like to touch myself now, with no thoughts of loss or loneliness. *Really* like that I can make myself feel good on my own. Curiouser and curiouser. Mad old bag stuff.

I've been thumbing through the book I brought to Mum's with me, because I want to read somewhere that it's what people *do*.

*   *   *

Rock Up Front is one of those events that the music industry monolith stages every year just to prove that they have half an eye on humanity and not just on their obscene profit projections. A nine-hour concert, staged outdoors – the income from which will be directed this year at Earth Patrol – it will include sets by anyone currently big in the charts who they can 'persuade' to come for nothing (which seems to be everyone, pretty much), and will be shored up by gaggles of tittering DJs and kids TV types (Heidi Harris *for sure*), who will fill in the bits between bands. Much of it is to be televised, and all will be on video. In short, it is perhaps the most cost-effective bit of publicity anyone in the music industry could hope to enjoy this year. (I didn't actually know any of this stuff before, of course. Colin told me.)

Kite, as befits their megastar status, will be headlining. They will not, therefore, come on till well after nine tonight.

Rehearsals, however, will happen this morning, as will a whole range of publicity stuff. My job (Job!) is to get lots of pictures: Kite hanging out, Kite at the Earth Patrol stand, Kite cavorting about with celebrity folk. Also Kite on the beach (as if – Brighton? July?) and Kite – if it happens – doing impromptu jam sessions with other bands.

Biggest news of the moment, of course, is that Heidi Harris has gone public and announced that she and Jonathan Sky are now an item. So I am also, if possible, to get something appropriate re the Harris/Sky *lurve* thing. Hold the front page – I'll hold on to my nose.

There will be, Colin told me, lots of media interest: something I soon realise as I drive down the front.

Colin has organised a room for me in one of those big white hotels that line Brighton's prom. It's the hotel that Kite are staying at tonight – the better to get all those fly-on-the-wall pictures – and though there is also, apparently, a Kite trailer on site, they will be doing interviews for the music press here.

I cannot get within fifty yards of the place. The road is closed and the traffic is being sent up a side street and then herded, no doubt, into one of those labyrinthine diversion systems that bring you out facing the wrong way up the street you originally set off from. But as I draw closer, I spy a harassed-looking constable, and lower my window as I pull alongside.

'I want to get to that hotel,' I say politely. 'How am I supposed to do that?'

'Phwar,' he says, ambiguously. 'Not a chance, madam.'

'But I'm staying there.'

'Ah.' He peers in. 'Are you sure?'

I consider flashing my navel ring, as my badge of rock-chickdom, but the sun's beating down and the light is way too good.

'Of course. I'm with the press,' *God,* that sounds *brill*iant. 'I've got a pass here somewhere. Would you like to see it?'

My constable looks at me as though I'm Pamela Anderson and that I've offered to show him my tits. There is a perceptible change in his manner.

'Ah!' he says. 'Ahhhhh! That's the jobby I'm after!' He takes the pass, reverentially, and runs a finger across it.

'Just a tick, then,' he says.

He moves purposely forward and one by one removes a number of the row of traffic cones that block the road. Then, after a brief remonstration with a middle-aged couple in the Volvo just in front me, he stands and directs me through the resultant aperture, beaming as though I'd just climbed into his bed.

I don't know who is the saddest one here – him for seeming so absurdly pleased at being able to manoeuvre his cone forest for me, or me, for feeling like the Queen.

And the feeling does not diminish as I pull up outside the hotel entrance and have my car, my luggage and my (few remaining) pretensions to being a person of no consequence summarily removed by a man in a hat.

And Nigel – he of the absentee wife and percentage of billions – arrives in the foyer to greet me.

He isn't actually in the foyer *to* greet me, of course, but he happens to be there and makes a big show of being ever-so-pleased to see me. He doesn't even seem to need to consult the clipboard he is holding in order to remember my name.

'Julia, *hi*. You all right? Safe journey?'

'Fine, thank you,' I say, as you do.

'Listen,' he says, striding across to the check-in desk with me, 'be in your room for a while? I'll just deal with this lot and catch up with you in thirty or so. Let you have a game plan, okay?'

I nod, but he is already being swallowed up by a shoal of people who look unrelated and disparate yet have moved, I see, as one, in synchronicity with him. When, like the Pope, you're the main route to heaven, I guess a following of worshippers is to be expected.

I take my key and watch as they veer into a function room after him. God, I *love* all this stuff.

And it's a very nice room. Sort of Forte Post House with knobs on. I've got all sorts of things to hang outside my door, from cleaning requests to shoe shining chitties to breakfast order slips and Do Not Disturbs. I've unpacked, made some tea and inspected the bath foam, and am just flicking through to see if I can find something that says 'no entry, having wild sex play session with someone rich and important in the music biz', when there is a knock at the door.

It is Nigel, to let me know they are all going to the festival field – by chauffeured car, of course – in half an hour or so, where they will hang out in their trailer before a final sound check. In the meantime, he is ordering lunch for everyone: not the hotel buffet but the usual MacDonald's.

'You want me to get you a Big Mac?' he says.

Ah, the celebrity lifestyle.

The trailers are all parked in a large area that has been fenced in by eight-foot green netting, and which has rear access to the covered stage and a ramp that leads to a group of marquees, similarly fenced and enclosed. Like specimens, we are scrutinised minutely by a shifting assortment of young people, who stand at the fences, fingers laced through the wire.

'VIP area,' Jax explains. She has come over to join us. 'Hospitality tents, bar, portaloos with carpet in them and so on. That tent over there' – she points – 'I can't officially get into. But you can.' She nods at the card I have clipped to my T-Shirt. Like the one I had before, it says *Access all areas*; Jax's one, this time, is a gold plastic wrist band. It only says *VIP*.

'How come?' I say, intrigued by this curious hierarchy. I'm obviously a VVIP today.

'Because today I'm just covering the gig for the music press. You're actually working under contract to Kite, to some extent, with the book. You need to be able to go everywhere they go.'

'And that's the place to hang out, is it?' I say, my mind on the Harris/Sky debacle.

'Oh, def. All the cheesy arse-licking will be going on in that tent. Anyway, must dash. I'm supposed to be catching up with Nige about now.'

Hmmm. Still don't approve.

But the day is still young and there is, it turns out, plenty more scope for not approving of things. Kite are holed up in their trailer (twanging and humming in appropriate pop-star fashion) and some lesser band are making their bid for the stratosphere in the main arena, so I decide to take advantage of the relative lull, and do a circuit of the place. One of the first things to catch my eye, aside from the fact that what you can buy at the Rock Up Front Concert seems to consist only of chips, beer and Indian tie-dyed clothing, is the Earth Patrol stand.

I step inside and inhale a not unpleasant cocktail of grass and canvas. There are a number of display boards showing oil spills and de-forestation and suchlike, and photos of robust-looking men and women on boats (mostly in cagoules and all-terrain boots etc) splicing halyards and manning the topsail and tacking the tiller and so on, or, at any rate, things that I seem to recall being called that in the days when I read more a more eclectic selection of books.

All very worthy and active stuff, which is slightly incongruous against this country fayre setting, with the languid drone of insects and distant generator hum. As is what I find to the rear of the *EarthWatch* display.

My footfalls on the limp grass are silent, and I am in any case quickly arrested and motionless. My presence goes unheeded.

There are two other people in the tent. They are men – both Earth Patrollers, by the look of them; I check (for some reason) and see both are wearing big boots. The one with his back to me is half-sitting on the far edge of the souvenir trestle table, while the other one stands in front of him, very close. Their arms are entwined and they are kissing.

For a moment, I start, and can feel myself colour, then the new me kicks in and I mentally shrug. Politely, I turn, which is, of course, when they hear me. The one facing me looks up, our eyes meet and I move on.

It is only when the other one turns that I feel it. Though I can only see him out of the corner of my eye, I just know, in that instant, whose face I am about to see. And I am right. It is Nick. *Howard's* Nick.

I can't decide whether to simply leave or whether to stay and confront him. Ridiculously, I find myself looking at a poster about soil erosion instead. After all, I reason, I haven't seen or spoken to Howard in almost two weeks. How do these things work? Is the romance over, then? And it's really none of my business. Except that Nick moves towards me now looking smiley and welcoming in exactly the way that one would if one was guilty as hell but hoping for damage limitation.

'Julia! Fancy you being down here!'

'You too,' I say. 'I thought you did Wales.'

The words come out sounding curt but he ignores that and carries on.

'Yes and no. Wales is my main brief, but some of EP's activities are nationwide. Who gets involved is largely a matter of who's around, who's available.'

Unfortunate turn of phrase. We both watch the other guy rearrange pamphlets for a moment. God, he's not even good-looking. Has a face like a stoat.

'Why are you here, then?' he goes on, nodding towards my badge and cameras.

'Work. Is Howard with you, then?' I say. 'I would imagine he'd enjoy something like this.'

Nick lowers his gaze.

'Um, no. He was going to come along, but his mother isn't too well at the moment. She's…'

'Not well? How bad is she?'

'She's back in hospital. She's…'

I feel an intense wave of anger, the likes of which I haven't felt about anyone or anything, bar Richard, in a long time. Howard is my friend, and this guy is taking the piss. I want to hit him (Richard's right, of course. I am becoming *very* aggressive of late), but instead I glance across at pamphlet man and say, 'So you thought you'd find someone else to keep you occupied, did you?'

To which he really has no answer. Though he does supply one. It is (well, *well*), 'It's nothing to do with you.'

'It's everything to do with me. Howard is my friend. Is this what it's all about with you guys, then? Shag who you like, when you like? Is this just a quickie, to keep you going till you get back?'

I realise I'm beginning to rant. And somewhat melodramatically. They were only kissing, after all. Not exactly having sex on the fact sheets.

He folds his arms.

'So you're going to rush off and tell him now, are you? Like that will help anything? Turn something that is nothing into something that might...'

So he was/has/*is* going to shag him.

'Nothing?'

Pamphlet man has moved onto *Katrina – the aftermath,* and almost out of earshot. Nick lowers his voice and tries for logic and reason.

'It's just sex. It isn't important. I don't think you really understand these things, do you?'

Rubbish. This is Richard all over again.

I say, 'I understand deceit.'

And stomp off across the grass.

And such is my air of preoccupied scowling that a rustle starts up at the fence round the compound, and I realise the waves are intended for me.

But there is no pleasure to be had in being assumed a pop star. I let myself into the trailer feeling impotent and furious and relieved to find it now empty. I simply do not know what I should do.

If I call Howard and tell him, am I not, as Nick said, just going to make things worse? If his mother is very ill that's the last thing he needs. And yet how can I just stand back and let this guy betray him? I consider his words about it all meaning nothing. *Bastard.* How can it mean nothing? *Bastard.* And won't he just keep right on doing it? Yes, of course he will. *Bastard.* And then there is Aids. *God.* I feel a shudder go through me. Perhaps I should go right back out there and ask him if he'd like me to fetch him a condom. Here, Nick. Shag away. Just, you know, doing my bit for the planet.

I do nothing, of course. I open the fridge and take out a Coke, then sit down at the table amongst the baseball caps and guitar cases and little plastic baskets that Kite keep their wallets and keys and loose change in, and wonder why people have to hurt each other all the time.

I do not wonder for long. Within moments the trailer is full of voices and sweaty bodies and the snap of ring pulls, and the curiously reassuring company of these overgrown Max clones.

'Snap-snap time?' says Tim. 'Here –'

He puts a finger up each nostril and one each side of his mouth. I oblige by whipping my camera to my face and catching it before he can remove them.

'Off the record,' he says, on his way back out.

'For my private collection,' I reassure him.

'You want to watch her,' says Nigel, who passes him in the doorway. She'll have that lot in *Hello!* if you're not careful. So. What's next. Hmmm. Oh. Symbiosis. Christ. Get the windows shut, Craig. Then Heidi's doing the Young Patrollers comp. winners. Then, yes…Julia, do you want to come along to the signing with us?'

'Yes, I do. But Nigel, is there a phone somewhere I could use?'

He throws me his mobile then pulls a beer from the fridge.

'Right, you guys. See you in thirty,' he says.

Craig and Davey take their cans and bags of crisps to the other end of the trailer. I move over to the bench seat by the window to pick up a signal. This caravan, inside, is just like any other. Dralon and pink floral curtains and Formica.

Howard answers almost immediately and I feel suddenly unprepared for his cheerful tone.

'Julia! How are you? Are you at Rock Up Front?'

I say yes, and he tells me how he's been trying to get hold of me, to let me know how he and Nick were supposed to be going too, but how he couldn't because of his mum being so ill.

'And did you meet up with Nick yet? I told him to look out for you. Though I wasn't sure if you'd be slumming it with the proles.'

Which is about the size of it, in Nick's case, unbeknown to him.

'Yes, just a moment ago. That's why I called. He told me about your mum not being very well…'

'No. She's not too good, but bearing up. They've taken her back in.'

'I know. Is she okay. I mean…'

I flounder. What I want to say is 'is she dying?' but I realise I just don't have the vocabulary to hand to put it any other way. How did I get to be so old without learning how to deal with stuff like this? But he rescues me, of course.

'They're sorting out a hospice place for her. She's not in any pain.' He chuckles. 'Bit spaced out though. How's Nick? Working hard, I hope.'

I find a laugh from somewhere and send it along to meet his.

'Not at all,' I say. 'Looks like a pretty cushy number to me.'

'Are you going to get together with him later? I thought you two lost souls could…'

'Er…no. I have to stick with Kite pretty much right through now. And they're not doing their set till nine, and then there's going to be some sort of TV appeal going out. I have to get shots of all that stuff. You know…'

'Sure. He'll just have to keep himself out of trouble, won't he?'

'I wish you'd been able to come, Howard.'

'I know. Another time. Hey, and I'm getting next term's curriculum planning licked into shape, so it's not all bad. You're home tomorrow?'

'Sunday. Colin booked me into the hotel for two nights in case we decide to do a shoot tomorrow. Or sleep, more likely, after tonight's revels. Look, I hope your mum's okay…'

'She's doing all right. Look, give my love to Nick, yeah? And a kiss?'

Bastard.

I stab the power off. Something in the set of my shoulders must be giving me away, because I hear a sound behind me and a voice says,

'Something up, Mrs Potter?'

Craig has taken to calling me Mrs Potter since we met again this morning. I didn't like it at first – what with the Richard connection and all that – but now I find I rather like it.

'Oh, nothing.' I sigh and sit down.

He sits also.

'Yes there is.'

'Oh, it's just that I just heard that a friend of mine's mum isn't very well. She has cancer. I don't think she's got very long.'

'Oh, I'm sorry. What kind of cancer?'

It's a reasonable enough question, but I realise I don't even really know.

'I think she has secondaries in her bones, or something. I don't know. I don't actually know her that well. It's just that my friend…'

'She's cut up, I suppose. Who wouldn't be?'

'He – he's a he, my friend – Howard – he sounded so…so *okay.* You know? It's so…'

'Well, that's good, isn't it? That he's okay, coping…'

'I know, but…oh…'

I twist my lens cover round and round and round. Is this really something I should be talking about?

'Nothing,' I finish.

'What? Tell me.'

'Well, it's just that I just found out the guy he is with is seeing someone else. Here. *Now*. That's all. And I don't know if I should tell him, you know, with his Mum…'

'So he's gay, yes? So I wouldn't bother. It's probably no big deal. Or maybe…'

'Which is just what *he* said. That it was nothing. *Bastard.*'

'Then maybe it isn't. You know, maybe they are both okay about that sort of thing…'

'Okay? How can it be okay? Howard loves him, and he's screwing some other guy.'

'So what. Sex is just sex. If he says it means nothing then maybe he's telling the truth. I'd keep schtum, if I were you.'

'Sex is just sex? You sound just like my husband did. Let me tell you, it may be nothing to the person doing it, but is sure as hell is something to the one who gets betrayed.'

He spreads his palms.

'Which is just what I'm saying. What he doesn't know can't hurt him. But if he's going to be hurt it's going to happen anyway, isn't it?'

I stare at him, realisation dawning. I'm just not in step with the world any more. Sex is just some cheap commodity. And if nobody knows, then…

I stand up, and realise I'm shaking. Shouldn't have turned down the burger earlier.

'Like your manager's wife, I suppose. While he's having sex with Jacinta Cave? No problem, eh? Just a bit of fun?'

'What *are* you on about?'

'I guess if everybody's doing it, why not, eh? *Eh?*'

'What the hell do you know about it?'

'Everything I need to, by the look of things. I guess I'm just some sort of dinosaur…'

He stands as well, towering over me.

'Julia, Nigel's wife's two hundred miles away in hospital, for fuck's sake. Has been for almost three years now. She's quadriplegic. We don't even know if she's…look, I thought you knew about the accident…'

'Accident? What accident?'

'The car smash. Look, you didn't…'

But he doesn't get a chance to tell me what it is I didn't, because tears muscle in and rearrange my face for me, and I start (infuriatingly) weeping and wailing all over him.

158

He, of course, does the only thing to do in such circumstances, and puts an arm around me. We sit back down, and while I sniff and snuffle and sob and suchlike, he says, 'Bloody hell! What the fuck did I say?'

I shake my head and accept the sweet-wrapper sized swizzle of pink tissue he's found for me.

'Nothing!' I cry, 'Oh, God. I feel *awful*. I'm just so bloody – so *fucking* fed up.'

'Whoah! You swore!'

'I'm sorry.' I feel my face begin to redden.

He smiles. 'Hey, but it's not such a big deal, is it? Your friend will be fine. He's a grown-up. He'll sort it.'

'Oh, I know. I'm just so, oh, I don't know, disappointed, I guess…'

'Hardly something to cry about.'

'I know. I'm not crying about that, I suppose.'

'What then?'

I blow gingerly into my pink scrap.

'Life.'

He laughs. 'Ah. Only a little thing then.'

I laugh too, despite myself.

'*My* life, and how it doesn't seem to be shaping up quite how I imagined it. I suppose I've been deluding myself. I thought that once I got over what Richard did life would be different, somehow. All excitement and adventure and new possibilities and old lost opportunities coming around again, and, and…'

He glances up as a muffled cheer fills the caravan momentarily. Then turns back to me.

'And?'

'And it's all the same shit.'

'You swore again!'

'I didn't.'

'You did. You said shit.'

I manage another laugh. I'm beginning to feel better. 'For someone who swears every other word, you are really quite puritanical, aren't you? Don't you like me swearing?'

His shoulders move. 'It's not that. It's just…I don't know…unexpected.'

'That's only because you see me as different from you. As someone older. As a mother and so on.'

159

He knocks back some Coke, stands up, sits down again, looks petulant. 'I don't, you know.'

'Yeah, you do. It's not a conscious thing. You can't help it. Like I can't help being with all of you and being reminded of my children. Not because you're children – you're all twenty-odd, aren't you? But because your outlook is so much more like theirs. And I don't mean that in any way as an insult. I guess it's just that your worries are different to mine.'

'I'm twenty-four. And I don't.'

'Don't what?'

'I don't see you as a mother. Someone older, yeah. Course I do, but…'

'There you are, then.'

'No. Not at *all*. As someone I…'

And then (we are back to sitting side by side on the bench seat) he looks away, and then back, and then smiles and then shrugs. And seems to me more childlike and innocent than he can possibly imagine, yet when his arm snakes around me to finish what he is obviously finding difficult to put into words, the child is suddenly gone.

The trailer door started rattling only seconds later, and then Nigel crashed in, with Jonathan Sky not far behind.

'Right,' Nigel said. 'Fall in. Signing session in five. The tent between the main bar and the arena. We've got back access and Security's got some characters organised for us. You ready?'

To us. We nodded. Both stood.

'…just get my trainers,' said Craig, bouncing off down the trailer. A rhapsody of ripples and tendons and chiselled shoulder blades and hamstrings and his flop-flopping hair shiny and bouncing as he walked.

So. Here we go again. I felt:

> Strange
> Trembly (through low blood sugar, most probably)
> Confused
> A bit silly
> Like I needed a cold shower/stern word with myself about all of the above

160

But I didn't do either. The tent Kite had been given to sign copies of their new album in (for the zillion-strong queue that now snaked like a conga on The Day The Earth Stood Still across the grass) wasn't far from the Earth Patrol one, so once I'd taken some pix of Craig and Jonathan with the first few of the adoring zillion, I nipped out.

It was by now around five and the concert had developed a snoozy quality. The afternoon sets over, and the evening ones still to come, everyone over twelve seemed to be quietly milling, while the children hyperventilated over Heidi Harris in the arena.

And the Earth Patrol tent was clearly as convivial a place to hang out as any, and a welcome respite from the still-hot afternoon sun. There were several people in there, most wearing appropriately grave and earnest expressions, and emitting the occasional tut-tut or sigh.

I couldn't give a stuff. Pamphlet man was nowhere to be seen, but Nick was in place at his souvenir trestle, dispensing ball-points and rainbow erasers and badges, and urging anyone with facial hair or sandals to sign up as a member and help save the world. I strode up to him, my *Access All Areas* pass swinging, talisman-like, to and fro across my chest. I said,

'Howard sends you his love – oh, and a kiss and a hug as well – and says try to keep out of trouble, won't you? And I just thought I ought to let you know that if I hear you've been anywhere near that sad excuse for a holiday romance boyfriend of yours, not only will I tell Howard, but I will also, personally, kick your face in, delicious bloody raspberry bloody coulis or not.'

Nick blinked then started furiously arranging Polar Cap Snowstorms. He said nothing. I left. So did everyone else.

I think it was the heat.

Because I didn't want to hang around looking fretful and irresolute, I had a word with Nigel and got Kite's driver to take me back to the hotel for a while.

Jax was sitting on one of the squashy sofas big hotels seem to like scattering at random around their public areas, and scribbling in what I now came to see was characteristic fashion. She looked completely engrossed, but I felt a sudden compulsion to let her know that I understood about Nigel and her and his wife and so on, even though she new nothing of what I'd thought in the first place. She looked up at the sound of my approach. I took off my camera and lens and sat down beside her.

'You staying here as well?'

'Not really. Kind of. I've got my car. I might shove off later. See how it goes. What you up to?'

'I thought I'd sleep for a couple of hours, have a shower and go back over later. They're not on till last, and I've shot plenty of film.'

Jax put her pad down and stretched.

'Mmm. Sounds like a good idea. Hot, isn't it? I'd go for a dip in the sea but I can't even be bothered to walk across the road to the beach.'

'If you want to use my shower you're very welcome.'

She shook her head.

'Thanks. But no probs. I've got Nige's key.'

I nodded.

'Have you known him a long time? You seem very close.'

'Couple of years. We met at a St John's Ambulance first-aid course, of all places.'

'How come?' It seemed a rather unlikely venue.

'I was staff writing for *Gig* magazine at the time. Company policy. Someone had to be a trained first-aider in the office. I was the newest. I got lumbered. And Nige – well, you know about his wife, don't you?'

I nodded again.

'I know she was involved in some sort of car accident.'

'They both were. A bad smash. Head on. He had a bad time afterwards – you know, blaming himself – though it wasn't his fault at all. I think, with the course, he was kind of exorcising his demons – you know, he feels if he'd had some sort of training, then – well, you know. Anyway, we got talking – him and I both being in the music business, and then we met up again when I covered Kite's first tour. We always had this rapport, you know.' She laughed. 'Despite him being such a wrinkly!'

'It must be so hard for him...'

'Yeah. I think it is. He lives for the band now, pretty much. They're like his surrogate family. He and Vicky didn't have any kids. They were waiting – ironic, isn't it? – until his lifestyle was a bit less hectic. With Kite just taking off and everything, they didn't expect to be seeing too much of each other for a while. Funny how life works out. Makes you realise how much you've got to live for the moment. Still...'

She stood and picked up her pad. '...I never did have any problem doing that. You going to the party?'

'I guess so,' I said.

After Jax had gone I sat in the foyer for a while longer, letting the air-conditioning cool me, and thinking about Richard and the children speeding under the sea on their way to the uncharted territory of their first holiday alone. And me, who would normally be with them (checking my lists to confirm I packed tea towels and ant powder, most likely) sitting instead in a five star hotel, wearing jean shorts and trainers, having just been kissed by a pop star.

Funny, like Jax said.

Chapter 22

'SO WHY KITE, THEN?'

It is almost two in the morning. We're in the marquee where the people with the right accessories (i.e. the *Access All Areas* passes) get to come and chill out after the day's endeavours, before moving on to some trendy club or other, where the serious aftershow will really begin. With some eight bands and solo artists performing, plus an army of TV presenters, radio stars and music industry big-wigs, there are a fair few people in the tent. The place is seething and hot and is beginning to smell more like compost than meadow. And there is now a definite sponginess underfoot.

The voice is that of Donna Talbot. I don't know quite how she wheedled her way in here, seeing as she is only covering the gig freelance for *Sound* magazine, but she did and she has and we haven't up to now spoken. She is livid, I know, that Colin gave me this job. That I'm in with the in-crowd. That I'm here at all. She called me a provincial (provincial what?). It breaks my heart, therefore, that I do not have an answer for her.

'Because…' I begin, and here, fortunately, is Tim Linseed to help me.

'Because it's what we got paid for our first proper gig.'

'Oh, how *clever*,' she says, clearly not thinking so at all. 'I always think it's fascinating to find out how bands got their names.' She angles her back very slightly towards me before addressing him. 'Did you know that Symbiosis called themselves that after the bassist found he had contracted roundworm?'

'No, I didn't,' says Tim. 'By the way, Julia, Nige wanted me to ask if you still wanted to do this beach thing. He thinks if we aim for four-ish or five-ish, we'll have it to ourselves, and have some half-decent light. He wanted to run it by you. You're the expert. What d'you think? I don't mind, and I don't think Craig does. And Davey's rat-arsed already, so he'll do whatever we tell him. Don't know where the fuck Jon is, though.'

Yes! Donna's face has fallen in on itself. And she has something on a cocktail stick in freeze-frame on the way to her mouth. Hah! SHR!

But it's a short-lived delight, because I don't really want to do it. And the reason (pathetic) I don't want to do it is because:

a) I've been kissed. I've been kissed by Craig James. I've been *kissed* by *Craig James*. (Though he may well call it snogging.)

and:

b) Craig James is now avoiding me.

Bugger, bugger, bugger. What the hell do I do now? Given only a) I could just about manage. Given just b) I don't suppose I'd have noticed. But given them both is just about the worst thing that can happen to anyone, let alone someone who has turned not reading other people's (presumably screamingly obvious) signals into a Turner-prize-winning installation. I feel like a hot tap that's been left on. Fluid and steamy and relentlessly emptying, till the tank dries up and shrivels and eventually rusts. It's really no wonder that I want to go home.

But I can't. I'm at work. And I have a) plus b) to contend with. It's bad enough having this development happening in the first place. (Just when I've got used to celibacy and reading articles about post-menopausal women learning to hang glide.) Don't know how to feel about it. Don't know how to deal with it. Except that I am beginning to realise that my body/Id/hypothalamus or whatever, is clamouring for a return to my fall-back position of the last thirty-eight years (well, thirty-three-odd – Patrick Borrell in Reception class was the first.)

Fall-back position is patently bad. Fall-back position involves becoming completely focussed on the object in question plus suffering impaired sensory reception for all other stimuli. Fall-back position also involves endless analysis of every tiny thing the subject does, appears to do, looks as though he might consider doing, in relation to perceived interest/lack (eek!) of interest in self. Fall-back position involves total inability to concentrate on anything else *at all*. In short, fall-back position is to be avoided at all costs.

I am thirty-eight. Why does this still happen to me? I should have grown out of this by now.

Funny, isn't it? When I was seventeen, I thought it was simply a function of being seventeen. When I fell in love with Richard, I thought it was simply a function of being in love. When I lighted upon Howard as a sex-object, as opposed to just having him as a

165

friend while fall-back position still channelled, if sluggishly at times, towards Richard, I thought it was simply a function of being a (stressed and lacking any self-esteem type) cuckold and/or being short of sex.

Now, in a tent (sober) at ten past two in the morning, I realise a simple and elegant truth. It is simply a function of *being me.*

Undesirable me?
Halitosis me?
Wrinkled me?
Desperate/clingy looking me?
Ancient me?
Two-paper-bag me?

Richard-joke: Went to bed with a new bird last night. I wouldn't say she was ugly, but I had to wear a paper bag over my own head, just in case hers fell off.

Boom bloody boom. One of Stuart's, no doubt. Drawn from that deep, deep well of crap jokes that men tell, to put shagging and birds in their proper perspective. Ho, ho.

I keep telling myself that Colin fancies me, but it doesn't make me feel any better. In fact, it makes me feel marginally worse. Like I did when, at sixteen, I had a bubble-cut perm. I was asked to dance no less than five times that evening. But each man that tried sported some sort of hair loss. And here I am, whipping myself up into a frenzy of dithering vapours about a child-man of twenty-four!

Why, oh why can't it just happen the way it is supposed to? Why can't I meet someone, find myself fantastically attracted to him, find that he's fantastically attracted to me as well, have sex, have a *lurve* thing, and kind of take it from there? Why?

Well, it sure as hell ain't gonna be happening tonight, Ju. Whatever slant I try to put on things, Craig James does not want to be anywhere near me.

All the little details are in place. I'm here, towards the back of the tent, with a rag-taggle, loosely Kite-based ensemble. And Craig is up the front with goodness knows who. There seems an almost endless procession of people (TV, radio and generally *beautiful* people) who want to be inside the aura – an aura I hadn't really, up to this moment, acknowledged, but which, *boy!* am I suddenly noticing now. Who *are* these people? I make out Heidi Harris,

Jonathan Sky, a sometime presenter of the National Lottery, and a weather girl who looks as clued up about isobars as I am about the physics of nuclear fission.

And our eyes are failing to meet.

And failing at every reasonable opportunity they would normally have for meeting. Every scan of the room involves a blink just about *then*, every pass to and fro involves a careful detour, every reason to connect involves a third party. One such arrives now. It is Nigel.

'You going to come and hit this party?' He seems ebullient and happy. A concerted effort, and I slip out of my reverie long enough to wonder how much private agony he carries behind those pale, shiny eyes. And I wonder also, if he's just been to bed with Jacinta. She's gone home now, Tim told me, her job done. Done in all senses? I wish she was still here to divert my attention.

'I'm not sure,' I begin. 'I'm rather tired, actually. I got up so early to drive here, and...'

'Pah! Believe me, you'll get your best stuff tonight. They're all on free hooch, don't forget. And anyway, you can sleep till Thursday if you want to.'

I almost actually *say*, 'No I can't. Time Of Your Life are expecting me Monday. The Tweenies will fret it they're left in their box.' But I don't. My whole lifestyle seems suddenly hopeless. A sad excuse for a life, in fact. And then there are the beach shots.

'And hang on,' he goes on, saying it for me. 'What about...'

And reminds me that it was my bright idea to do a shoot on the beach in the first place.

Not mine at all, of course. Colin's or someone's. But I nod and recant.

And off we all go to the party.

Where I have decided to be pro-active. One can only be avoided if one is consciously striving to instigate contact. I am therefore intent on doing anything but. Which isn't, as it turns out, difficult. We come in two cars: him first, and me later, and by the time I arrive he is six deep in groupies. He couldn't see me if his life depended on it. Too much glare from the lip gloss and ironed hair, and the dazzle of super-sheer one denier tights.

I spend much of it pro-active in a far-flung corner. By the time Colin and I decide we should go greet the dawn on the shingle, I feel crumpled, dejected and one hundred and seven.

167

Brighton beach, like any beach, is never quite so beautiful as when it is empty and lit by an oversized sun. There is a cloudscape so pink and so luminous that if one were to paint it one's work would be considered childish. A pewter sea rolls carpets of foam on to the pebbles and the sharp caw of seagulls cuts through the cool salty air. It is beautiful. It makes all my senses tingle. And that I'm as far away from the drudgery of my normal working life that I could sit down and cry right now, this minute. I don't want to go back to it.

'Fuck me, it's parky. Got a sweatshirt in there, Nige?'

Tim is striding about the shingle flapping his arms across his chest. Gusts of breath cloud his face as he speaks. Nigel produces some sort of wind-cheater type garment. One of several he has brought in a canvas holdall, for the shoot. As ever, prepared. As ever, organised. I recall what Jax said about Kite being his family. Far away from their relatives for much of the year, they could, I decide, do a lot worse.

Craig, who up till now has exhibited an absorbing attachment to a close study of the crusting of fauna attached to the groynes (this after exhibiting an attachment to a close study of the paving stones of Brighton's front), wanders over to be given one also. We didn't bring Davey or Jon, in the end: the one was too pissed and the other too busy. Heidi Harris's charms proved too alluring.

'Right,' I say, conscious of the sun's upward progress and anxious to maintain the brisk (brusque, frankly) tone I've decided to adopt as another defence against falling back to fall-back position. 'Let's get this sorted. Off you both go, up the beach. Over there.'

Nigel, who is, thankfully, unaware of the pathetic tableaux being played out in front of him, says, 'Why don't they skim some stones or something. Look like they'd rather be skimming than shagging ha, ha.'

And suddenly, we can hear sirens.

We all turn to watch, as headlamps arc whitely against the now pink-washed buildings, and strobe as they flash past the promenade rails. There are four or five cars, all moving quickly along the empty road.

'What the hell's going on?' says Nigel, picking up his holdall and setting off up the beach. Craig and Tim jog across, and we too make our way back up to the steps. The sirens have stopped now, but the blue-red still flashes, just off the main road.

'Isn't that the club we were at?' asks Tim. 'What can this be all about?'

By the time we too have reached the promenade, Nigel is already on his way back across the road towards us.

'Drugs bust,' he mouths. 'It's seething in there.'

'So's Davey and Jon,' says Tim.

Nigel shakes his head.' I couldn't see either of them. With any luck Dave'll be comatose somewhere, and Jon'll be with Heidi.' He pushes his hand across his forehead. The scar looks the colour of coral in the dawn light. 'Look,' he says. I'll go and sort what I can. Best bet for you is to get back to the hotel. We don't want your faces in this, if we can help it.'

He turns and runs back across the road, and we start walking the few hundred yards to the hotel.

'God, what a long day,' I say, to them both.

'Fucking parties,' says Craig, to no one in particular, but least of all me.

Tim nods.

'Fucking right.'

And hell, I'm fed up. At the start of today I was:

Happy
Optimistic
In control
Excited

Now, despite having done what I *know* is some seriously good work, I am:

Miserable
Negative
Feeling dissatisfied with the life I have
Scared about the prospect of a new one

I'm also wide awake. I can't relax, can't sleep, can't face watching a film. What I need, I decide, is a deep, bubbly, five-star bath and to not stress myself about unsatisfactory encounters with boys. I can get that at home, thanks.

But wouldn't you just *know*. I am in the middle of giving myself a ylang-ylang-scented foam moustache and trying out *shaver socket only* (shaver socket *on*-ly, tra la la la *la*-la) as a new mantra, when I hear a soft knocking. It is almost six a.m., but I did not order

169

a paper. Neither did I order breakfast, an alarm call, my shoes to be polished, ironing, a pedicure, or a complimentary aromatherapy massage.

But the knocking persists. I rise, meringue-like, from the water, and put my dripping self into the white five-star/ robe. It is so heavy that I am stooping slightly as I answer the door.

And there he is.

T-Shirt, the ubiquitous boxers, and a carrier bag saying *Cardiff Royal Hotel; For Your Laundry*.

'I er,' he begins, as my fall-back position (military tattoo pulse/goldfish mouth/tendency to pant/lose grip) promptly re-asserts itself.

'I er,' he expands, '...thought, I er, I ought to give you back these. Wasn't sure what time you'd be off.'

As he stands before me, a rangy, sprung form against a sedate backdrop of flock and carved dado rail, all I can think of is this. How can someone who can get up and sing/jump about/play the guitar one-handed backwards whilst doing the splits in mid air/act natural/be composed/*swagger*, even, in front of thousands and thousands and thousands of people, have conversations with thirty-eight-year-old women of no consequence that start (and seem to continue) with the words I, er?

He proffers the bag. I take it.

Of course. It's easy. He is embarrassed. He had a quick snog in an unguarded (I've decided – compassionate) moment and then thought 'ooh er, now I'm going to have this old bird hanging around thinking I fancy her'. And he feels a bit guilty that he's avoided me ever since. And so why is he still hovering in the doorway? Come to think of it, why didn't he just have Nigel give me this? Whatever it is. What *is* it? I open the bag. Inside are my trousers. And something else. Two something else's. Tubular. I put my hand in.

'Pringles,' he says.

'So I see. Look, I, er...' (Oh dear. *I'm* at it now.)

'I wasn't sure which flavour you liked so I had Nige get two.'

'Oh. Well, thanks. I like both of these. I...(why not torture myself a bit more? hey, it's only a lust thing)...would you like to come in for a moment?'

'Yeah, I would.'

I head for the mini-bar while he closes the door. I think naked/robe/robe/naked, in roughly equal measure. Then I think stupid woman, shut up, don't be ridiculous. Then I give up on thinking because my brain is whirring and despite everything logic is telling me there is something primeval going on in my stomach again. Daft.

Then he says, 'Look. I just wanted to say I'm sorry.'

'You don't have to,' I quip (a lie). 'Do you want a beer or something?'

'Yeah, okay. Yes. But I am. I was completely out of order, you know. Today.'

'Don't apologise,' I say, crouched over the mini-bar and trying to hold the robe together while ferreting for lager. 'It was just one of those things. I was upset. You were very kind. I…'

'But I shouldn't have…you know…here, there's the bottle opener…tried it on, like.'

Pish! goes the bottle top. P-i-s-h-!

Tried it on, like.

Someone – must be me – says, 'I'm sorry?'

'So, like I said, I'm really sorry.'

'*Sorry*?'

'I was well out of order.'

I can almost feel wheels turning. Doing a flip-through of file cards to find just the right one. The one that will put into some sort of order the idea that my (still goldfish) mouth wants to convey. Flip, flip, flip. Eventually, I light upon:

'You weren't out of order at all.'

'Wasn't I?'

He sits down on the bed with his beer and looks up. I shake my head.

'No. Not at *all*.'

'You mean…'

Now I nod, but say nothing. A girl has her modesty.

But I don't need to speak. Craig James pulls the robe, plus me in it, and captures me in a warm, squidgey, lovely, crushing, breathless, scented, urgent, *wonderful* embrace. I am being held. Properly held, for the first time in months. How do people manage to live without this?

'Fuck me, Mrs Potter!' he remarks, without irony. 'Fuck me!'

Watch this space, CJ.

Wow.

'So you thought…'

'I know! And *you* thought…'

'Sure I did. I thought, God, you stupid fucker. She'll think you're a right derr-brain. I half expected you to slap me. When Nige came in…'

'When Nigel came in all I thought was: oh, no! I want more.'

'Did you? *Really*?'

'I really did. I thought *wow*. I hadn't actually realised up to that point that I fancied you. It just never occurred to me that you were an option.'

'I suppose I felt the same. I mean, you know. Kids and all that. Except that as soon as I saw you again yesterday morning, I realised why I hadn't got around to getting your jeans back to you.'

'God, isn't that strange? All along, I've been saying to myself, send Colin those jeans to get back to Craig James, but I always didn't quite get around to it. Weird.'

'Not weird. Karma. I realised straight away yesterday how attracted to you I had been.'

'Attracted? I love that word. Go on. How attracted?'

'Really attracted. This much attracted.'

'Mmmmm. How much attracted?'

'Incredibly attracted.'

'Fantastically so?'

'*Fantastically* attracted.'

'Wow. *Wow*. Pringle?'

'Sex.'

Chapter 23

SO WHAT NOW?

When I woke up it was quarter to four on a sunny Saturday afternoon. Strangely, Craig James was still in my bed, sprawled and in the sort of heavy, immobile sleep that eventually catches up with those who are physically sated. And boy, are we sated. But I couldn't sleep any more. I'm already in that post-childbirth phase of life that insists that every waking moment is utilised in some sort of productive endeavour. So, instead, I spent several glorious minutes productively looking. Admiring his curves and his bumps and his contours. Fixating on hairs and on freckles and moles, and on the way the fine hair at the nape of his neck formed small waves and whorls, like a field of ripe wheat in a stiff summer breeze.

Happiness is capricious. But I had caught some at last.

I showered, slipped on a pair of my CK effect pants, then padded around for a bit in the room, catching glimpses of someone I'd lost touch with some time back and hugging myself with joy that I'd found her again.

There is nothing like a long bout of sexual athletics to make you feel thin and toned and gorgeous. Except, perhaps, long distance running. But as that usually involves scraping your hair back, scrubbing your face, and not having any orgasms (as far as I know – though it *is* a popular sport), sex wins hands down, any time. Especially sex with someone with plenty of youthful enthusiasm. Sod experience – give me a good slug of libido. I can explain all the twiddly bits.

Listen to me, I thought. What am I *like?*

Craig slept on, and I sat for a while on the balcony. Apart from the now familiar gaggle of teenage girls in the car park (who were privy, presumably, to some insider information about Kite's movements – or lack of), there were few people moving along our pretty stretch of front, fewer still on the beach. All off retail-park shopping, no doubt, as people do on a Saturday: buying freezers and vacuum cleaners and new school shoes for next term. Doing, in short, all those deeply unsatisfying yet necessary chores which are the stuff of ordinary life. Not having sex with Young Pop Icons. Not making love. Not feeling suffused with desire and abandon. Not being in touch with their inner children. Not exploring their G-Spots. Not feeling like *this*.

And across the twinkling jade water, in a fusty Gallic gîte, my husband and children were no doubt already stoking an elderly barbecue, on which to cook strings of horrible French sausages with bits of twig in.

Knock knock.
    'Who's there?'
    'It's me.'
    'Me who?'
    'Me who have big white chief randy bastard to collect. Open the fuck up.'

Nigel looked fresh and rested and full of his usual verve. And showing not the slightest surprise at the whereabouts of his musical prodigy. He came in and kicked Craig while I called Room Service for coffee. I had added a large T-Shirt to the pants. It said 'Kite - Hard and Happening tour. Which was rather appropriate.

And get this:

Time to call time on 'Charity' Drug-ins?

Thirty seven-people were arrested last night at Brighton's fashionable Swank Bar, including Game Show supremo Ted Bunting, Pop goddess Minxie and children's TV presenter, Heidi Harris. The raid, organised at short notice following an anonymous tip-off, also netted drugs with an estimated street value of eight thousand pounds.

Derek Handel, of Brighton and Hove constabulary, said 'We were all very disappointed to find so many high-profile celebrities indulging in such anti-social practices. Some of these people are heroes to young children. They look up to them and they deserve better.'

The arrests, which were all on drugs-related charges, were made in the small hours of last night, during a party organised for the participants of the Rock Up Front concert, the music industry's annual fund-raising fest.

'It's disgraceful,' commented Councillor Geraint Ogilvy, the councillor who brought Rock Up Front to Brighton in the first place, despite concerns from some residents about noise levels and

hooliganism. 'We were thrilled to be able to host such a forward-thinking event, and, like everyone, full of admiration for the stars who gave freely of their time and their talent. That a few of them went on to disgrace themselves is something we deeply regret.'

Regret today too, perhaps, for the usually effervescent Ms Harris, who spent a night in the cells and has now been released on bail. Harris (25) was in the news recently, after a fight at a popular London nightspot, over her relationship with Kite bassist Jonathan Sky. On that occasion she scuffled with the musician's former fiancée, and broke the nose of the on-duty 'Depth' photographer (ironically also arrested last night). The question now is how much of a role Harris's alleged drug habit may have played in that incident, and what sort of media future she now has. TV bosses, however, were unavailable for comment.

Sky himself was arrested also, but released without charge shortly after.

'And get *this*,' Nigel said. 'Guess who phoned with the tip-off?'

We both shook our heads.

'It was Kayleigh, of course.'

'How do you know?'

'Because she's already been on the phone to Jon, this afternoon. She's cock-a-fucking-hoop. She's one of a kind, that one.'

Craig bounced out of bed, naked, and unconcerned to be so. He took the paper from Nigel.

'Christ, I wouldn't rate her chances if Heidi Harris finds out.'

'I don't think Jon has even the smallest intention of telling her about it. And you two keep schtum, won't you?'

'Hey, 'I said, re-reading the piece over Craig's downy shoulder. 'Hang on! What about this? It says I had my nose broken! And…and that I've been arrested as well! How did that happen? I wasn't even there!'

'Your name's not actually in it. I shouldn't worry. *Depth* have plenty of photographers, don't they? It's just bog-standard crap reporting. Quite normal.'

'But anyone could look at an old copy of the *Herald* and find out my name. And think I was on drugs or something. Like, people I *know*. And where on earth did they get the idea to put that in the first place?'

Nigel moved to the doorway to help the breathless waitress who had just arrived with the coffee tray, while Craig simply sat on the bed with a pillow over his groin. Cups rattled furiously, as Nigel went on, 'I shouldn't worry about it. I doubt it will hit Cardiff. It just made a good link with the punch-up last month. And who's going to be arsed to find out your name when they've got Heidi Harris and Ted Bunting in the frame?'

I poured out the coffee while Craig did his little dog cartoon on the Room Service slip. Such a thoughtful touch. God. *Lurve* alert, *and how*.

And Nigel, I decided, was probably right. Who *would* be arsed? No one.

Wrong again, J.

Chapter 24

SEASIDE
Sun
Sea
Sand
Sandcastles
Surf
Seashells
Starfish
Spray
Salt
Styrofoam Cups
Seagulls

'Sex.'
'No, no, NO! You can't say the S word!'
'All right. Um...... Swordfish.'
'No. Can't have it. You can't see any.'
'I can.'
'No, you can't.'
'Yes I can. In the Sealife Centre. So *there*.'
'No you can't. You can't actually *see* them. The rule is...'
'Okay, *okay*. Um...um...hell, *sex*.'

The things you do.

Kite were supposed to be doing a live radio interview and phone in for *Surf FM* early Saturday evening, but Nigel cancelled it because of the drug raid story. Which suited everyone fine.

'Didn't want to talk to some dickhead DJ with a playlist he got out of his own backside anyway,' Davey announced, with rare animation. And was speaking for the rest of the band also, it seemed. So there was half of Saturday night to kill.

When Nigel left, Craig showered and shaved (with my pink razor) then padded off to his own room in my high density towelling.

'Wouldn't it be nice,' I'd remarked, putting on mascara while he shampooed his hair, 'if we could go out for a walk on the beach, or something. You must really miss being able to do things like that.'

'Not often. I'm a bit of a lazy bugger. (Patently untrue. He was fit and energetic and driven.) I quite like being chauffeured everywhere and brought take-aways.'

'Who wouldn't? But surely you'll tire of it eventually.'

'I can't imagine it now. But I suppose after Kite my face won't be slapped all over the place the way it is now, so it won't be a problem any more.'

'I wouldn't bank on it. Look at people like Sting, or Phil Collins…'

'I'd rather not, thanks.'

'But you might end up like that, might you not?'

'Not. For definite. Once we've done all we can with Kite I'm going to open a little specialist music shop off Shaftesbury Avenue and spend my days selling Fenders and Gibsons and jamming with elderly session musicians.'

'Really?'

'Of course I'm fucking not! I'll be living it up! I'll have fucking millions! And perhaps I'll buy Wales, so I can have you as my own private serf…hah! What do you think, Mrs Sexygorgeous Potter?'

When he came back, even I didn't recognise him.

'Baggy clothes, sunglasses, hat. The job's done. Where are we walking?'

So we're down at the quiet end of the beach and though I have seen several teenagers staring and obviously wondering, not one has been sufficiently bold to confront him. Which is lovely. I have him all to myself.

'Sunhat! There!'

'Does it say Kiss Me Quick?'

'No…*Reebok*, it looks like. But there's another one.'

'And what does that say?'

'It says *CJ 4 JP*'

'Oh, come *on*…'

'Come on what? I'd make a very good magistrate. Have the likes of you fucking dope-head *Depth* photographers banged up, that's for sure.'

'Har, har. Very funny. Sandwiches.'

'Sex.'

'*Not* allowed…'

'Sex. *Really*. Over there. You see that boat?'

'What boat?'

'Over there. Way up the beach. Past the windsurfer. Orange sail. Yes?'

'Well look a little past that. There's some sort of hut. You see? Where some old geezer probably keeps his maggots and so on...'

'Yuck. Yes...'

'Well just beyond that, a little further down the shingle, is an old boat. Upside down. And propped up at one end by an oilcan. Being painted, I suppose. Or pitched, perhaps.'

'Yes...'

'Well that's it.'

'But it's deserted over there. I can't see anyone at all, let alone two people having sex...'

'Well of course you can't...'

'But you said...'

'What I said was *Sex. Really. Over there.*'

'But there isn't...'

'But there will be. Just as soon as we're under it.'

I said *you're joking*, and *but we can't* and even *but what if somebody sees us?* To which Craig quite reasonably replied *I'm not*, and *we can*, and *they won't*. All of which was true. Like any other oily, boaty, ropey out of the way bit of beach on a sultry summer Saturday evening, it had been passed over in favour of clean bits with deckchairs and proximity to tea stands and kiosks and toilets. And if some crusty old sea dog should happen along here, he'd probably, Craig reasoned, consider it a bonus.

And my body was clearly in agreement. The gentle heat that had been quietly simmering in my lower torso all afternoon was fired up, whoosh!, like a boiler, before the words 'under it' were out of his mouth.

We jogged the few yards past the windsurfer (surfer abandoned? Drowned?) and on to an area of knobbly, oil-darkened shingle, that was littered with old bits of rope and driftwood.

'We can't do it on this,' I said, privately expecting we'd manage.

'No probs,' he replied, veering off across the stones. 'We'll use this!' It was a large slice of ancient tyre tread, culled, no doubt from a junk yard, and to be used, I supposed, as a buffer for the front of a boat.

That it would provide instead buffering for my backside touched me as too ridiculous for words and I laughed.

Craig tutted and pulled me by the hand.

'Under that boat, Mrs Potter, and look lively about it, or I'll have you on fatigues for the rest of the voyage.'

Obediently, I crawled on in. It was a big, deep boat, and would seat six or so, comfortably. The seats themselves, three wide and greying wooden planks, formed the cross beams of our roof. With the prow propped, and facing seawards, our domed hidey hole put me instantly in mind of a mini Sydney Opera House, thrusting out towards a shimmering blue seascape. Craig, though, had more prosaic matters on his mind.

'You realise that if the Man from Atlantis emerges from the waves here, he's going to get a cracking view of your arse.'

'And yours.'

'I shall have to keep my shorts on. Can't afford to be recognised, remember? There's fuck-all space for an autograph session in here.'

I pulled him towards me. 'Come on, be serious. Now you've got me here I expect to be ravished. Indeed I *demand* to be ravished…'

'So stop talking and let me get on with it.'

He hooked his thumbs under the hem of my T-Shirt, and slid it up over my head. Cool air brushed my nipples and I thought I might implode.

'Then get on with it!'

He covered one with his lips.

'Thwex,' he said.

'Ahhh……… What? I'm sorry?'

His head lifted.

'I said *sex*.'

It moved over. Reconnected.

'Okay……oh, my *God*……oh, *yes*!… Ok*ay*, one point!'

When we got back to the hotel, the gaggle of girls had become more of a flock, so we fiddled our way round the dustbins and beer crates and entered via the fire exit just off the kitchens.

'Packing up, I guess,' Craig remarked. 'Wagons at dawn.'

Thoughts of tomorrow began to nibble at my consciousness. Tomorrow, the next day, the day after that. How many years had I been here already? It felt like forever.

'When do you actually leave?'

'Not sure, exactly. I have a date in Streatham at one o'clock sharp.'

'Date?'

'With my mum, and roast lamb and mint sauce. Wanna come?'

God, *yes*.

'I can't. I have to get back. Quite apart from anything else I have a deadline to meet. I have to get all my pictures uploaded and sorted. The printers will need them – the book's due out in December... and I have to meet with Colin to discuss the pictures and, oh...'

'And then?'

We had reached his room. He slid his keycard across the lock and turned the handle. The other hand, warm and strong, still held mine.

'And then...and then, who knows? I have a day job. I suppose I'll get on and do it. Click, click, smile, please. Like you do. Unless Colin comes up with any exciting new commissions...'

'And your husband? Your marriage?'

He let go of my hand and strode across the room. 'Coke, wine, beer, something?'

I shook my head.

'Ugh! I don't want to talk about that. Don't want to even *think* about that. That's someone else altogether. I'm a rock-chick-groupie-babe-good-time girl. Now gimme a beer.'

He flipped off the top and passed it to me. Like the blanket of dusk that was darkening the sky and the room, a terrible melancholy seemed to have settled on me.

And no strings of coloured lightbulbs to cheer it.

He kissed me and said, 'No way. You're not that.'

Then he seemed to change gear, and picked his guitar up. He smiled.

'Sit yourself down, Mrs Sexygorgeous Potter, and let me play you a bit of a tune.'

Which is exactly what he did. He told me he'd been 'fiddling around' with it for a few weeks, and that he was really excited by it, and that he thought it had the makings of a really good single. And that he hadn't run it by Jonathan yet, and that he was going to play it to his mum tomorrow. And that his mum (though not remotely musical) had a real ear for a tune and that when he was a teenager, and his mates were all out all the time on the pull, he'd spend hour upon hour in his bedroom, practising on his guitar and composing, and sometimes she'd put her head round the door and tell him, yes, or no, or to try changing a chord or two.

And how much he wished he could persuade her to let him buy her a flat somewhere 'a bit nicer' than Streatham, and how he was looking forward to getting started on the new album. And how much he loved writing music (who wouldn't?) and how much he loved touring and performing (a *real* day's work), and how much he disliked all the promo work. And how, with the tour finished, and a single due out, it would be one long round now of interviews and photo-shoots and TV and 'crap generally', and how he couldn't wait to get on with the next tour, the next album. Some peace from the spotlight, some space in which to write.

And as I watched his fingers move lovingly, fluidly, across his guitar, and his expression take on an intentness, a focus, that both took him away and yet brought him closer to me, I felt more privileged and special than I could ever recall feeling.

When he finished playing he leaned over his guitar to kiss me again.

Then smiled. 'That's yours now, okay?'

And I didn't know what was going to happen next in my life except that whatever it was it would not be able to compare with the exquisite beauty of this small taste of simple, perfect, uncluttered affection.

I wanted to cry.

I left the hotel before he was up.

Just beating the sun to its pink strip of horizon, I packed, checked out and was rattling along the breezy and deserted prom before six. The car felt cold and unfamiliar after its weekend underground, and I had to put the heater on to warm myself up.

What now?

I tried to focus on Max and Emma, to think sensible, meaningful, maternal thoughts. To think about buying new uniforms, Max starting High School, whether Emma was pining for Damon or not. Whether she'd sent him an illicit postcard, whether I (we) should let her continue to see him. About what sort of stand I (we) should take about sex. I thought about Lily, and the new life inside her, and whether she'd yet plucked up the courage to tell Malcolm. I thought about Time Of Your Life; that at this time tomorrow my alarm would go off, and I'd get up for work. And Howard. Would he and Nick keep things together? Was his mum okay? How would he cope with her death?

And each thought that I thought would be brushed to one side by the nagging and horrible consciousness that every single mile that I drove took me one mile further away from him.

As I waited at the traffic lights at Preston I spotted a familiar face. My constable: he of the cones and diversion, now striding the mean streets of Brighton at dawn. He was with a partner, engrossed in intense conversation, and I doubt they even noticed my car. Forty-eight hours and a lifetime had gone by. My VIP pass now said *Access Real Life.*

Chapter 25

WE HADN'T MADE ANY plans.

The last conversation we had (before the last – *wonderful*, *poignant* – sex we had) involved him asking if I was really sure I didn't want to go to Streatham with him on my way home (Kite were dispersing for a few days to see 'rellies etc.'), and me confirming again (agonisingly) that I had to get back and get organised and suchlike. I gave him my number; he gave me his; his mum's, his own, his mobile, his fax line, his email address. And ditto with Nigel's, all of which I duly deposited in my bag. We talked about when I might be next up in London, and whether we could meet up and do 'something' (huh?) then. We discussed the next month and Kite's busy itinerary, and whether he could drive down to Cardiff (come *on*) to see me. In the end I agreed that we'd fix something up just as soon as we knew how our schedules panned out. He would call me, he said, tomorrow.

But for what? To what end? What was going to be happening here? Would we meet up and make love on convenient tour dates? Would we send each other faxes? Exchange postcards? What?

What nothing. It was hopeless. We were going nowhere. Whatever we said, however we felt, there was simply no future for us. End of story. By the time I pulled off the M4 I had a such a hard, hot ball of unhappiness inside me that I thought I might die from the pain.

So, thank heavens for mayhem.

Sunday, late a.m. When I finally pull into our road, it is with the expectation of finding the house every bit as cold and empty as I am feeling. I am steeled for a whole day of Sunday-Evening-Work-Tomorrow melancholy. I am steeled, in fact, for a life of it. I am half writing a little speech in my head which begins 'if only…' (and ends, most probably, with a string of obscenities) when I turn into my drive and find that:

outside, I have:

A veldt

A telephone directory and copy of the Yellow Pages
A bouquet of flowers, propped on the doorstep
An unfamiliar car, with a man in it

As I have driven for three and a quarter hours without stopping for a wee, I digest the fact of these, but leave them all to their own devices and go on in. Whereupon I find that:

inside, I have:

A warm quiche
A cold, message-less ansafone. (Why had I hoped?)

And Lily. Who clatters down the stairs as soon as she hears me.

'Thank God,' she pants as I emerge from the cloakroom. 'Perhaps now you can go out and talk sense into him.'

Malcolm. I thought he looked strangely familiar.

'What is he doing parked outside?'

'He wants to talk to me.'

'Obviously.'

'But I don't want to talk to him. Ach! You can't imagine what it has been like...'

Lily has a key, and has been watering my houseplants. She tells me she came here, to escape, a couple of days back, but that he soon tracked her down. He has, she says, been sitting outside for an hour.

'So you told him, I take it?'

'I had to. I am the size of a house and throwing up all the time. He confronted me. He is silly, but not stupid.'

'So how did he react?'

'He wants to marry me. Oh, Julia, what am I going to do?'

I go into the kitchen and put the kettle on.

'What do you want to do, Lily? Really?'

She flops down on a chair and throws her hands into the air.

'That's just it! I can't decide. One minute I think, how can I do this? How can I stay with this man that I don't really love? And then I think, how can I not? He's a *good* man. He is the father of this baby. He is *pleased* about this baby. What right do I have to be so selfish? And then I think...'

But Lily clamps her mouth around her thought as the doorbell rings.

'Oh, *no*,' she cries. 'Again!'

185

*　　　*　　　*

Eventually, I persuade Lily to let Malcolm in, with his flowers and his apologies and his very patent distress. I finish making tea and then leave them to talk.

Everything Lily says strikes a new chord in me. How can I *this*, how can I not *that*. I consider the dilemma she now finds herself in. Such a difficult choice, at such a young age. At that time of my life it was all so simple. I was happily married, I wanted my babies. There was no choice to make, other than to cut back, miss a holiday, stop work for a while.

I try to imagine how it must feel to compromise on your heart so early on in your life. I think about Rani, and how she's told me, in an unguarded moment, that she knows that eventually she'll accept her parents wishes. Just *accept* them. And get on with it, whether she loves the man or not. No wonder she is so desperate to feel passion now. As if she needs to stoke up for a less heady future. Lily, I realise, doesn't even have that.

But it's all academic. She and Malcolm could be as deeply in love as it is possible to be and their future would be no more certain. There are no easy choices where children are involved. Just sacrifices, one way and another. There is a price to be paid for the joy they bring.

'But I don't see your problem. Why can't you carry on seeing him?'

We are sitting in Howard's flat, at either end of the sofa. There is something tinkly and soothing playing on the stereo and we've just finished sharing a (sex-free) kebab. Lily and Malcolm are long gone, in his car. Détente, for the moment at least.

I sip at my wine and shake my head.

'How can I? He's twenty-four, for God's sake! And he lives in London, and I live in Cardiff, and what about Max and Emma?'

'What about Max and Emma? Why are Max and Emma a problem?'

'Because it'll be awful for them.'

'But why?'

'Because it will. Because you didn't see Max's face when he thought I was going out with you.'

'But I am – was – his teacher. Of course he was embarrassed. This is completely different. I think you misjudge how much

186

importance children place on age. They probably couldn't care less. You're both ancient to Max, probably.'

'And then there's Richard...'

'What the hell's it got to do with him?'

'Well, nothing, but...'

'But he'll disapprove, right?'

'Not that it's any of his business...but...oh, I don't know. I just can't *see* it.'

'So why don't you try it on for size and find out?'

'Because I'm all done with trying things on for size. And because, as soon as I think about it with anything approaching a rational mind, I can't quite believe it. How can I feel so...so...*obsessed* about someone I have only met on two occasions? I'm thirty-*eight*...'

'As you are all too fond of saying...'

'But it's true! Far too old to be toying with notions of love at first sight or any of that nonsense...'

'Quite right. That *is* nonsense. But that doesn't mean you can't feel intensely attracted to someone, does it?'

'No. But I don't trust that feeling. It's just sex, isn't it?'

'I wouldn't say that. I mean, it can be...'

Sure can. I sigh.

'That's what Craig said, funnily enough.'

'About you?'

I shake my head and try not to look disingenuous. 'We were just talking. He said sex was just sex. No big deal on its own.'

'And you think that's how he maybe feels about you, right?'

'No. Yes. I don't know. That's what's so hard. I don't think so. But then...well, it's not unreasonable, is it? Listen, did you ever have a one night stand?'

'Once or twice.'

'Well, it's like, you know how if you do, then immediately after, or the next morning, or whatever, you think "what have I done?"'

'Or just *ugh!*'

'Yes! You realise straight away that you really don't like them at all, don't you? Or they you. Whatever.'

Howard nods.

'Well, after Craig and I...you know...the first time, we slept, and then when we woke up, I was *pleased* to be there. I wanted to do it all over again.'

'I think I realised that much…'

'No. But the point is, he obviously felt like that too, or he would have gone back to his room, wouldn't he? End of story. So what we've got here is not *just sex*, is it?'

'So, fine. Where's the problem? You really like each other. That's great.'

'But if that's the case, how can I keep this going? If I can't pretend it's just sex, then I can't help thinking about the future, can I? It's just what you *do*, isn't it?'

'Whoah! You've got to stop all this navel-gazing. You're running rings around yourself. What does it matter? Just see how things shape up. You're free, he's free, what's to stop you? It's nothing to do with anyone else, end of story. Julia, Who is going to get hurt?'

Do I really need to answer that?

And boy, will I get hurt. It's all very well zapping about the place pretending to be a walking sex manual, but it's actually a load of garbage. Doesn't matter how many times I tell myself sex is just sex, it isn't. Period. Not for *girls*. All this time I've spent feeling like a good shag would be just the ticket/give me back some self esteem/make me feel like I've got even with Richard/tone up my pelvic floor etc., and I've just been deluding myself. There is no such thing as having a satisfactory shag, then saying thank you very much and goodbye. You can either have an unsatisfactory shag (ta for nothing, I'm off) or you can have a very satisfactory shag, in which case you want to do it again. And again, and again, and again. Until such time as one of you goes off the idea, or you grow old, shrivel up and go to Bingo instead. It's called love. It's what happens.

If you're a girl. If you're male, on the other hand, while you are still as much prey to the pull of love as of lust, you can also, if you feel like it, sling your todger pretty much where ever you damn well fancy without compromising the integrity of your finer feelings one jot. Which is not to say that's what all men do. Just that they can. If they want to. I can't help thinking how nice it would be if men all got pregnant, like seahorses.

Similarly, I can't help feeling that I'm not very well.

'Howard,' I say (and the irony is not lost on me). 'I think I'm going to be sick.'

*   *   *

I'm in Howard's bed. At last!

If he wasn't so busy fetching iced flannels and washing up bowls for me to throw up in and such like, I'm sure we'd be having a really good, ironic-type giggle about it. And Nick's here now, of course, padding around being cringe-makingly helpful. So I can't help but enjoy a small nugget of satisfaction that he'll be getting none of *that* sort of thing in this bedroom tonight.

The general consensus is that the doner is the culprit. And that there's no way that I should be driving home. About which, if I didn't feel so awful, I'd be pleased. My home feels right now like there's nothing connecting me to it. No children, no food (bar Lily's quiche), no duelling stereos, no one stomping around bemoaning maternal ironing deficiencies, in short – no real life. So I'm going to spend the night here and abandon the idea of trying to drag myself into work tomorrow. Howard, he assures me, will take care of everything.

It is comforting to drift in and out of sleep, listening to muted conversation, picking out the odd word from the hum of white noise from the TV. Nick brings me water. Says 'how did the weekend shape up for you in the end?'

I tell him 'okay.'

He says he's glad he wasn't arrested. That Earth Patrol are very pleased with the way everything went. That Brighton looked bombed on Saturday. Did I see it? (Did I see *anything*?) We skirt around references to things that may involve references to the thing we seem to have a tacit agreement not to refer to. Plus I really can't be bothered. He knows what I think.

When I get home again, finally, on Monday evening, it is to a house that now not only feels empty and lonely, but that also contains the pungent and bitter aroma of a bacon-frying bonanza two days ago. I throw out the quiche (sorry, Lily. Nothing personal), take myself up to bed, and lie, sleepless yet exhausted, trying to re-connect to some semblance of sanity.

Of course, you can't carry on like this indefinitely. God alone knows how people with roller-coaster emotional lives ever get an iota of ordinary stuff done in their lives. I manage not the tiniest iota of sleep all night, and instead fill the hours with minute dissection of every thought, whim and emotion that floats into my mind. Statistics pop up to taunt me: his youth, my great age, my two children, our lifestyles, the roadworks on the M4, the availability of groupies, the fact that when he's forty-six I'll be sixty, etc. That I've known him for a total of about forty-nine hours, at least six of which we spent asleep, in my bed. (Come to think of it, it only takes forty-five hours of flying to get a private pilot's licence, doesn't it? That must count for something – though goodness knows what.) That I'm actually just stupid.

On Tuesday I'm feeling like I died and went to a pulper's, so I elect to allow myself another day in bed. Which is another thing. How many man-hours are lost due to this sort of rubbish?

When I arrive back at work on Wednesday (having taken only four days off sick in my *entire* employment with TOYL – these two, plus when Richard left, plus a septic laparoscopy scar) it is to be greeted not by Rani, but by the Area Manger, who seems to care little about the state of my health.

'Ah, Julia,' he trots out, 'glad you managed to join us. I wonder if you'd care to step into the office for a moment. I'd like a quick word before I move on to Bridgend.'

I do not care in the least for stepping anywhere with the fat git, but needs must, so I follow him in. He sprawls (sort of *spreads*) in the swivel chair.

One side-effect of my burgeoning career re-birth is a permanent, low-key, guilty undercurrent type feeling. Though what I have been doing for Colin can surely in no way affect the quality of my work for TOYL (apt acronym), it is almost as though my dissatisfaction and boredom might seep through my fingers, contaminate my equipment and freeze up my clients. At the very least affect relations with Milo and Doodles.

But it is relations with the now virtually recumbent AM that clearly need sorting, though at this point I've not the slightest idea why.

'I'm feeling much better now,' I say. (And thanks, toad face, for not asking.) 'No more kebabs for me for a while!'

'Kebabs?'

'The food poisoning...'

'Julia, the details are of no consequence. What is at issue...'

At issue? Of no consequence? What gives here?

'...is the fact that it simply isn't good enough. If you are unwell then you must telephone and let somebody know. We had a completely full appointment book – you *know* what it's like during

190

the school holidays – and only one photographer. We had to turn people *away* – and you *know* how I feel about *that*. Especially given that we're *completely* snowed under with enquiries about our *Captured for Christmas* media initiative.'

More crappy offers to stitch people up with.

'Hold on,' I said. 'You *were* telephoned. My friend called first thing on Monday morning…'

'There was no call. No message. Nobody had the slightest idea where you were. And given that you'd also just finished a week's leave, you could have been in Timbuktu for all we knew…'

'But he *did* call. Of course he called. Why would he tell me he was going to call and then not?'

'Hmmm. Well, whatever. I consider it *your* responsibility, and I am, frankly, disappointed.'

'Well, I'm sorry you feel like that. It won't happen again.'

(Too bloody right, it won't. Because you can shove your job up your fat behind, and stick a zoom up there as well.)

'Forget it,' says Rani. 'And don't take it personally. He's in a strop because he ended up having to get behind the camera himself for a change, instead of farting about on fact-finding missions and expense account lunches. And guess what?'

'What?'

'Not a single one of the pix he took Monday came out. We just found out.'

'Why?'

'Lens cover still on.'

When I get home Wednesday night I call Howard and tell him what happened.

'I did call,' he assures me. 'Though I did have to leave a message on their ansafone. Which might explain it.'

Ah.

'Well, I guess it never got there,' I say. 'But don't worry. They can't function without me, so there's not a lot the old sod can do.'

'Hang on, here it is.' He reads out the number. I don't recognise it.

'Where d'you get that?'

'Directory enquiries. I didn't want to rummage in your bag.'

Later, I call it myself, out of interest.

'Welcome!' it prattles, *'To Time Of Your Life. Is there someone special you'd like to capture for Christmas?'*

I stick out my tongue, purse my lips and blow.

And Craig, Craig, Craig, Craig, *Craig.*

Why haven't you rung me?

I have become so detached by now from normal circadian rhythms (in subconscious preparation for rock-wife lifestyle? no, no, NO!) that I elect to cut the grass on Thursday morning, before work.

The postman therefore finds me in shorts, vest and flip-flops when he comes to deliver such post as a sad, lonely person like me can expect. And it's paltry. A postcard of the channel tunnel, of all things.

'You know you're risking a toe, don't you?' the postman observes.

I glance down at my feet, wondering if he's mistaking my Calypso Blue nail polish for some sort of tropical infection.

'Erm…'

'One slip of that mower and you'll lose a digit. You mark my words.'

Oh, I see.

I said,

'I'm very careful.'

'Hmm. You can never be too careful where electricity's concerned. Got a power breaker, have you?'

'Erm…'

'Friend of mine's sister-in-law would have died if she'd not been in Wellingtons, you know. Hover mower slipped – just like that – swish! – and the cable was cut. Could've died. Just like that. Third degree burns right up her legs. Bad business…'

'Erm…'

'Still. Nice day for it. Bye.'

I turn over the postcard.

Julia!

The big news is a trip. We are driving to Bordeaux to meet my mother (with Malcolm) before next term begins. I couldn't get you on the phone and I couldn't find a time to come to you. Then I remembered on the journey here – I have switched your telephone

ringer off (you know why!!!!!). Oops! So now I know why you were
not at home! You were! Sorry! I will see you soon – and much fatter!
   Lily (and Malcolm). xxxx

Yes! So *that's* why Craig hasn't rung me! Or rather, why I haven't
realised that Craig *has* rung me. And he *has* rung me. Of that I am in
absolutely no doubt at all.

   I shower, go to work, hate work, take fifteen minutes for lunch
in which I do not eat, but instead stare absently out of a far-flung
toilet window (just off haberdashery), hate work some more, put the
Tweenies to bed (last client nauseating Mrs Worthington-type
Mother with offspring catatonic at concept of Bella being shoved in
old banana box), and, finally, stomp off to the multi-storey.

   It is there, among the exhaust fume and urine-scented air
pockets, that a new thought pops unexpectedly into my brain. *If* he
had phoned and it hadn't been answered, he would surely have left a
message on the answering machine. But he hasn't. *He hasn't.* I drive
home dejected.

   Once again, my house is empty and my fridge is empty, and as
soon as the word 'Pringle' springs to mind, it is joined by a rasping
sob, a pathetic flurry of tears and a bout of hand-wringing so intense
that I must force myself to watch *EastEnders*, to get affairs of the
heart into some sort of perspective. I wish my children were home.

Chapter 26

Fifteen minutes later, my wish is granted. I am trying to lose myself in yet another programme involving handsome young vets and cows' bottoms (what *is* it with the British that a conjunction of this kind is such a perennial favourite?) when there is not so much a knock as a clamour at the front door. And some ringing: ding dong ding dong ding dong ding dong!!!!!!!!!

'All right, I'm coming!' I call out, somewhat irritably. A woman in the throes of emotional distress does not want to get embroiled in conversations about novelty in-fridge air fresheners or flexible rubber drain covers. And then I open the door. It is not Mr Gadget.

'Mum, you're here!' (Max)

'Where else would I be?'

'In prison, of course!' (Emma)

'For what, exactly?'

'For drugs!' (Both)

Oh.

And then Richard comes trundling up the path, bearing backpacks, and we all go inside.

Where I am immediately subject to the kind of interrogation one would usually associate with an international money laundering and extortion type enterprises.

Richard sits wearily on a kitchen chair. It is, I'll allow, a long drive from Quimper.

'And we have been,' he assures me, 'worried *sick*.'

'But why?'

He rolls his eyes and tuts irritably. 'Because we thought you'd been banged up in jail somewhere.'

'In jail?'

'Yes. After that drugs bust.'

'You mean the one in Brighton? I wasn't even there.'

Richard chucks me a look of naked suspicion, then whips a piece of paper out of his trouser pocket, in the manner of someone who's serving a writ.

'We thought you'd been sent to prison, Mum,' says Max gravely.

I take it and unfold it. It is a newspaper cutting. Dated Monday. *The Herald.*

I read it, agog. It is an almost exact copy of the piece in the Saturday night *Brighton Reporter.* Except with one important addition. My name.

'Good God, someone did!' I said. 'Someone did what I said they would! Oh, this is awful! What will everyone think?'

'What do you mean? Did what?'

'Put my name in the paper. Nigel and Craig said they wouldn't. But how did this end up in here anyway? This is an almost word for word copy of the report in a local paper, in Brighton. Oh, this is awful! Suppose…'

Richard waves a hand to stop me. 'Julia, what are you talking about? Nigel who? And were you there or weren't you?'

'I *wasn't* there. Not by then, anyway. We were on the beach, doing a shoot. We saw the police cars and everything, and Nigel…'

'Craig?' asks Max. 'Craig *James*? Cool!'

Richard stabs a finger at the paper. 'It says here that you were.'

'But it didn't in the Reporter. And why would the *Herald* put this in anyway?'

'It happens all the time. Parliament's in recess, everyone's on holiday, there's no real news to report. And *Depth* is the *Herald's* supplement, isn't it?'

I nod. *Awful.*

'God knows how *your* name got in there, then. But the point is that we've been trying to get hold of you since Tuesday. Where on earth have you been?'

'I've been here.'

'Since when?'

'Since Sunday morning. When I got back from Brighton. Well, apart from spending Sunday night at Howard's…

'Howard's?' (Richard, Max, Emma. Close-part harmony.)

I can't even face *beginning* to explain.

'Howard. My friend. I was ill and I stayed at his place.'

'Ill?' asks Richard. 'What sort of ill?'

'Ill from a doner kebab – yes, I *know* – certainly not from ingesting any class A drugs.'

'So that's why you weren't at work. When I rang them they said they hadn't a clue where you were. They said they hadn't heard from you since before you went on holiday. But I left messages on the ansafone, here – half a dozen of them. Why didn't you answer them?'

'Because I didn't get them. There weren't any messages on the ansafone. There haven't been any messages on the ansafone at all.'

Richard stands up and then strides from the room. Moments later the air is filled with the tortured outpourings of a man with a lot on his mind. But it isn't Richard, and it certainly isn't Craig. It is Malcolm – and given how much of his soul he is bearing, he would probably pay me hard cash for the tape.

Then it stops. And a couple of clicks and whirrs later, Richard returns.

'The cassette's full,' he says.

Which is *why*......which is *why*...which is...*yes!*

'Well that's great! Thanks a lot, Mum,' says Emma, rising and snatching up her backpack from the floor.

'What?'

'You've just dragged us all the way back here for nothing, that's all.'

'But *I* didn't...'

'Oh, don't worry. Don't you worry about *ou*r holiday, will you?'

And off she goes.

'Name's Jerome, 'Richard mouths, 'from the village.'

Oh dear.

Max follows soon after, though in altogether better spirits, as he is to be re-united earlier than expected with his electricals cache.

Richard, on the other hand, shows no sign of leaving.

To show willing, at least, I make him a coffee. He looks tired under his tan.

'Didn't rain, then?' I comment.

'Not once.'

'It's been pretty hot here as well.'

'It sounds like everything in your life has been pretty hot just lately.'

I shrug.

'I've been busy...'

'So it's for real, then? All this high-flying Sunday Supplement stuff?'

I shrug again.

'Who knows? I mean, yes, it's for real in that I've had a couple of really good commissions. But it's freelance. It could all stop as of now.'

'I didn't realise, you know, that you were keen on getting into all that sort of thing again. I thought…'

'I didn't know it myself until it happened.'

'Hmmm.' Richard takes a sip of his coffee. Then says,

'We…I was really worried about you. I didn't tell the kids, but I didn't know what to think. I mean, you've been acting so strangely lately that I kept thinking…'

'Oh, Richard, come *on*. What do you take me for? I'm not some impressionable young girl, you know. I can look after myself.'

'I know that. But you read so much about that sort of thing. Rock Stars and TV people and such like. I should think it's a fairly seductive lifestyle…'

'Well, it's certainly exciting. And different. And for me, creatively, it is infinitely more enjoyable than taking crap pictures of snotty kids all day. But like I said, it could all end tomorrow.'

'Do you think it will?'

'I don't know. Features are features, but with the book coming out as well I suppose I'm hoping I might get asked to do more. Now the children are older it would certainly be easier for me to do jobs in London and so on. I haven't really thought about it. Except that I can't imagine spending the rest of my career in a Time Of Your Life photo studio.'

'I can see that. And look, I really am sorry about what I said before you went away. It wasn't fair. And it wasn't true. The kids…well, you know…'

I nod. I'm not angry about it any more. It seems like for ever ago.

'Forget it,' I say, as Richard drains his coffee and prepares to leave. He calls goodbyes up the stairs and taps the ansafone as I open the front door for him.

'Told you,' he says, grinning.

I hold my hand up in surrender.

Then he turns on the path and gives me a peculiar little smile.

'It's nice that we can have a conversation without rowing,' he says.

But now I know what he meant when he said rowing made him feel better. He knows, as do I, that an absence of rowing is not nice at all.

197

It is a clear night and the sky is sprinkled with stars. Instead of closing the door as I usually do, I stand and watch as Richard unlocks the car, climbs in and drives away. He is frightened, I realise, that he really has lost me.

I close the front door. At this moment, he has.

But it was not Craig but Colin who was first able to enjoy the luxury of free rein on an empty cassette.

'Are you still speaking to me?' he asked, when I called him back on Friday night.

'Of course I am. That article had nothing to do with you, surely?'

'Well, yes and no, sweet.'

Hmmm. 'In what way?'

'Well, only that the newsroom, casting about, as they do, for something other than Royal squabbles to rant about, called me and wanted to know the name of the *Depth* freelance I had covering the pix for the gig. So, naturally, I said you. It was only afterward that it occurred to me what the connection was. When I had a half-hour of earbending from Donna about it…'

'Donna Talbot? But she was there for some music mag.'

'Yep. But she does a lot for *Depth* – someone probably spotted her and put two and two together. You should be grateful for your current anonymity.'

'Of course! *She* must have been the one who got arrested. Hah! Was she charged?'

'Certainly was. Along with Heidi Harris, that Bunting bloke, and the entire line up of some hip-hop band. I bet you're glad you *weren't* there.'

'That's entirely thanks to you and that beach shoot you wanted. Though, mind you, it doesn't make much difference now, does it?'

'Don't fret. It's all yesterday's news. Now listen, sweet, I'm sitting in front of a whole pile of wonderful proofs here. It's not strictly necessary, but do you fancy a trip up to the smoke to have a run through? Obviously, the production team has last word, but I'm sure you'd like to have some input on this.'

'When though? The children are just back from holiday, and if I don't make it into work next week I won't have a work to make it into.'

'Well I was thinking Wednesday-ish. Couldn't you just take a day off?'

Sod it. I could.

'Don't worry, I'll sort it. I'll ring you on Monday.'

'Great. So how was it? I'm told Kite upstaged everyone.'

'They were good. It was great. Not a bit like doing a proper job. I could get used to the lifestyle.'

'Darling, you were born for it.'

I wish.

In fact, wishing was what I spent most of the weekend doing. Wishing I was twenty-four, wishing I was one hundred and four, wishing I could tell Mr Fat Chops Area Manager to fuck off, Craig-style, wishing Lily was around to talk to, wishing I could jolt myself out of this dreadful inertia, wishing the children were a little older, wishing the children were a lot younger. Wishing I could rewind. Or fast forward. Or just *feel* different.

On Sunday afternoon I sat in the garden for three whole hours listening to Craig, courtesy of Kite, on Emma's iPod.

'Are you ill still, Mum?' Max enquired when he emerged, blinking, from the house.

'I'm fine, darling, really.'

'Then why are you being so funny?'

'Funny?'

'Yeah. You've gone all peculiar. Like Dad said...'

'He said that?'

'He's been worried you're not well, but he doesn't like to ask.'

'Really?'

And then he called. Just like that. When I was least expecting it.

I was putting a pizza in the oven (couldn't even be fussed to make a roast).

Emma answered.

'Muuummm!' She bellowed. 'It's for you. Clive James or someone.' And then she squeaked. And clapped her hand over her mouth. And waved her free hand wildly about and did a strange little dance on the hall carpet. Then said, 'It's him!' she rasped, *sotto voce*, while I picked up the receiver. 'It's him, isn't it? It's him! It *is*, isn't it? It *is,* it *is!*'

I flapped her away and she belted up the stairs to get Max.

It was like trying to breathe normally when you are conscious of your breathing.

When I picked up the receiver it was with adrenaline schussing at great speed through my veins, my heartbeat at a canter and with a perceptible tremor in the hand that held the phone. It was, even at that instant, something of a revelation to me, that I could manage to produce a sound at all. Yet I did: a somewhat squeaky 'hello'.

Craig said 'hello' also. A strong voice. *His* voice. And all I could think of as response was, 'Hello.'

He then said 'hel-low' to which I said 'hel-low-ee,' to which he then replied 'Well, *hello*, Mrs P.'

I dare say we would have kept up this inane but merry banter indefinitely had I not become aware of the audience of two that were contained behind the stair rail, and that were quietly tittering.

'Hang on,' I said. 'Will you two please GO AWAY!!'

Which proved that some responses are completely instinctive.

'I'm sorry,' I went on, realising I must sound like a fishwife. Oh God. 'You know what they're like.'

Which proved likewise, and also my limited repertoire of repartee. He knew no such thing. Oh *God*.

'Where've you been?' he said next.

'I've been here. At home. Only my friend, who was staying, turned the phone ringer off, and then I found out on Thursday that the tape on the ansafone was full as well – her boyfriend prattling on at her – and well, here I am. How are you?'

'Tired. Pissed-off with all the promo stuff. Missing you. Why didn't *you* call *me*, then?''

Oh, oh, oh, *oh*!

I scanned the banisters.

'I wanted to. I've been missing you as well.'

I should be shot for understatement. And dismembered. And if they looked inside me they would find nothing but marshmallows and spun sugar confectionery.

'You should have called then. So, can we get together? Soon?'

'Well, I'm in London on Wednesday to go through the pictures for the book. Perhaps…'

'I know. Me too.'

'Are you? Really?'

'Nigel thought we should. Though it's all fucking crap of course. You know? I find it quite creepy, really. I mean, I know everyone wants to look like, *okay*, in photographs, but there comes a point when you realise what's portrayed isn't you. Just the way you looked at one moment when the light hit you right. You know? I have a whole life to live. I've got to grow up, grow older, do all that regular shit. I can't stand that I might lose my sense of self before I'm even together about who I am.'

'But you know who you are.'

'I know who I am right now. Who I am in ten years is something else. Blows you away, doesn't it?'

'I don't think I was sufficiently mature to question my identity when I was…'

I *could not* say 'your age'. I re-grouped. 'But it's been almost an obsession since my marriage broke up.'

'You seem sorted to me.'

'It's a lie. I just seem so.'

'You do. So you'll be able to come home with me after? Stay over?'

Uurrrgh.

'I hope so.' I know so.

'You'd better, Mrs P. You cannot let me down.'

'Or what?'

'Or I'll be really fucked off. Okay?'

Get your head together. *Now*. This is just:

A crush
An infatuation
A pre-menopausal hormone surge
A post-marital (not that again, *please*) response to a display of affection from a member (any member?) of the opposite sex
Selfish
Sex

I'm lovelorn. That's all it is really. I am a deserted woman and have fashioned this feeling out of old aches and pains that are nothing to do with the man I'm obsessed with, and everything to do with the one that left me. And, *yes,* I know that he didn't *actually* leave me, but in one sense, he did, in that he felt so little for me that he followed the pull of his loins and without due regard for the marital consequence, took his sex drive and drove it home somewhere else.

Isn't it amazing? You can read, literally, dozens of books telling you otherwise, but it still all comes down to rejection in the end. At least, *that's* what I keep telling myself. That's precisely what I told myself when I called Richard and asked him to have the children overnight on Wednesday. Even managed to invoke it (this is my *career*, Richard, I think you at least owe me that...) when he whinged about presentations and meetings with local MPs. Even ran it by Howard when he called to see how things were. But he was having none of it.

'Rubbish,' he said. 'You're in love, Julia. Face it.'

I snorted.

'I'm sorry? Did I hear you right?'

'Well, you must be. You're far too old to be infatuated with anyone...'

'Thanks a lot.'

'But it's true. And you have all the symptoms...'

'I have...oh, I don't know. He's just, so, so...oh, I just wish he was some egotistical fathead with nothing on his mind except the next shag. At least that way I would know where I stood...'

'Lay...'

'Exactly! At least then I could get on with feeling sorry for myself and regretful and cheap about shagging him and...'

'I thought 'shagging' was the whole point.'

'It *was*. But now I've accepted I'm not psychologically capable of strings-free casual sex, it would be so much better if he *was* a bastard and told me to sod off. Wouldn't it?'

'Would it?'

'Of course! Then I wouldn't have to waste another moment in fruitless daydreaming about some utterly ridiculous relationship, would I?'

'Utterly ridiculous only because you perceive it to be so. There was a time when I felt the same about me. Look, is this about you and him, or about Richard and the children and how they would feel? Because if you are really decided that there is no future in your marriage, then unless you elect to remain celibate forever, the problem is not going to go away. Only the person will change. The bottom line is that, whatever happens, you can take something positive out of what you have here.'

Which was sufficiently obscure a collection of concepts to ensure I maintained a total sensory deficit in relation to the repeat of *Inspector Morse* I'd been meaning to watch, and that I neglected to note that Max was still playing Sarcophagus Slammer on the Playstation a good hour after he'd been sent to bed. Parenting, I decided, would be a whole lot easier if the emotional temperature of the parent(s) in question was essentially tepid, with the occasional rumbling of lukewarm. Children needed the comfort and security of knowing that whatever maelstroms their own biological clocks had in store, their parents had nothing more pressing afoot than the odd skirmish about the football versus the BAFTA Awards. They didn't deserve this complete flake of a mother.

Howard telephoned again late that evening. His mother, he told me, had just passed away. And that he couldn't decide whether to go up to the hospice, or, as they'd advised, to wait until morning. He apologised for calling so late in the evening but said that as Nick was away overnight (an Earth Patrol Consciousness Raising Mini-Conference – *bastard*) he needed to talk to a friend.

He wouldn't drive over. He didn't want to be a nuisance. And alone with the children, I couldn't drive over to him. We talked for a while but I felt unable to comfort him. He needed a physical warmth, someone to hold him. But I couldn't persuade him. I wished I could have.

Chapter 27

BUTTERFLIES. BIG TIME.

I rang Rani. I told her I needed some time off and asked what she thought. She said 'you're living dangerously in the middle of August with the *Captured for Christmas* event in full flood. How much time?'

'Only two days. Wednesday and Thursday. I'm still owed some leave.'

The week I'd been saving for autumn half term. For a trip to my mum's. The kids would be ecstatic.

'Hmm,' she said. 'Well, I wouldn't rate your chances.'

'He can't stop me.'

'That's true. But he can make life hard for you. And he will if he can. He's as jealous as hell.'

The first of the series of Kite features came out in *Depth* on the Sunday. There was a flurry of phone calls, all complimentary, and an air of mild celebration in the house. Though Max and Emma strove to maintain a pubescent-appropriate rather grudging enthusiasm, they were, I realised, actually quite proud of me. And Richard called too. To let me know that he'd seen it.

'Your pictures are very good,' he said. 'You haven't lost your eye for composition.'

'I hope not. But you know, it was really so easy. They're all so photogenic – and not in the least camera shy, of course, and stadiums and crowds lend themselves so well to this sort of thing. And I was able to just follow them around and take what I wanted. I shot rolls and rolls of film...'

'Well, I'm sure you'll get lots more commissions now...'

'It's very nice of you to say so. I really hope I do. I'm getting so fed up at Time Of Your Life now. It's like I've been given a glimpse of what I could be doing and now I can't bear the thought that I might not get to do any more.'

'That Colin friend of yours (the contra of 'that dickhead husband') is clearly impressed by you. And he's come up with the goods, hasn't he? Now he knows you're interested in doing more freelance work, there's no reason why he shouldn't put some your way, is there?'

I agreed that there wasn't. Then he coughed and went quiet. And then suddenly said,

'Julia, look, you don't have to answer this. But, I don't know...I get the feeling you've...look, have you found someone? I mean, someone, something...you know, *serious?*'

Oh, God. But he was right. I didn't have to answer it. Wasn't sure how I felt about answering it. Wasn't even sure what it was that I'd found. I said, without hostility, 'What's it to you?'

'I need to know where I stand. The lease on my flat runs out in a month. And I don't want to renew it. I hate it here. I need to know what I should be planning. Plus I need to know if there's...'

I stopped him. I really couldn't handle one of these conversations right now.

'Yes. Yes, I have.'

'Oh. I thought so.'

I could hear him sigh, take a breath. Then a long, long silence. 'Okay. Good. As long as I know where we are at. So. Okay.'

When I put the phone down, I felt really, really, *really* guilty. But why? What did I have to feel guilty about? After supper I drove round to Howard's for an hour. We didn't talk much; just watched TV together. But when I left he said,

'Funny. You know what I keep thinking about?'

I shook my head.

'I keep thinking about how I'm the last. How I'm all alone now. You know? And how there won't be any more. My genes will die with me. D'you know, last night in bed I realised that there is absolutely no one else left. My only living relative now is a spinster aunt of eighty-odd who is completely demented. In a nursing home in Kent, somewhere. And my whole family is littered with childlessness and early death. It's almost as if natural selection decided that we weren't up to scratch. Look at me. I'm twenty-nine and I haven't got a soul in the world. And I'm gay, so I haven't got a stake in the future, either. It's going to take a lot of getting used to, I think.'

I drove home and considered the enormity of what he was saying. He had nothing and no one, except a guy who was cheating on him. It was so, so sad. And there wasn't a thing I could do about it. You can't fix other people's lives.

In the middle of the night I woke up in a panic, the depth of Howard's loneliness suddenly clear. Supposing he thought his own life wasn't worth hanging on to? I phoned him. Nick answered. Said, 'Who the hell's this?'

'I was worried about Howard. He seemed very low, and I…'

'For God's sake! We're asleep!'

Then his voice changed. 'Look, thanks for coming and that. But he's fine. Really. I'll let him know that you called. Everything's fine.'

Based on whose criteria?

Bastard. Thank heavens he isn't a female. Lest Howard expect us to become girly friends.

Butterflies. *Big* time.

Tuesday. Time Of Your Life. (I don't *think* so.) Big bad AM makes an unscheduled visit.

'It has come to my notice,' he says, without smiling (even nastily), 'that you've been involved in some sort of public order offence.'

Out comes the article, dog eared and smudgy. No more Mr Nice Guy. No more plaudits and praise.

'No I haven't,' I say. 'It was another photographer. Donna Talbot, her name is. Check with the *Herald* if you like.'

'Your name is what's written…'

'But it's not true. Like I told you…'

'The point is that we've got an *image* to think about. The *family* image of Time Of Your Life. It doesn't say much for our family ethos if our staff are involved in *criminal activities*, does it?'

'I have *not* been involved in any criminal activities, and I resent the implication that I have. I told you, if you would like to ring…'

'But the damage is done now, nevertheless.'

'But that isn't my fault.'

'It's your fault for being involved.'

'But I wasn't!'

'Are you trying to pretend that you haven't been working with musicians and the like?'

Musicians? As in international terrorists and all round scum bags? Oh, I *see*.

'Only tame ones.'

'Being flippant won't help you.'

'Being rude won't help *you*.'

206

Oops.

Butterflies, *big time*.

But, boy, am I glad it's Wednesday. What with feeling bad about Richard, and fretting about Howard, and then (of course) feeling bad about feeling like I needed to get away, it was all I could do to be nice to the children. And then I felt bad about feeling like that about *them*.

There's no doubt that the whole meet young, get married, have kids, stay married, men in fields, women home darning and suchlike lifestyle *serves a purpose*.

But not my purpose. Not at this time. At this time all I want to do is get to London, get the book sorted, get another commission (or, at least a bit of a sniff of one) get somewhere with Craig, get happy, get laid. I can't think beyond that. It all gets too complicated. My mind will crash if I think even a moment too far.

I fetch up at Paddington exactly on schedule and taxi it down (on flash bitch expenses) to Soho. The offices of the book publishing sector of the publishing empire Colin works for are just off a street of pornography vendors. Sex, it seems is everywhere today. It is just before lunchtime on a hot day and already I'm dizzy with desire. Now I'm here it's as if the previous ten days didn't exist: that I was dropped into a sitcom or comedy drama that turned out to be more of a play for today. And now I've slipped out, back to me-time, reality. Which is peculiar, as Brighton still seems like a dream.

There is a small knot of people outside the company's entrance and I have to 'pardon' and 'excuse me' and 'I'm sorry' continuously in order to make my way to the front. Once I am there though I am immediately admitted, because Colin has been waiting in the Foyer to meet me.

'Sweet! Look at you! You look such a *babe*! Let me pick up your bag for you. Journey okay? Look at you! – here, we'll take the lift up – are you hot? Can I get you a can of something?'

'I'm fine,' I say, pleased with my sartorial thinking. (The mauve, strappy, lace thing with a jacket on top.) 'Is everyone here?'

'All but Davey Dean, who's shopping for a new electric toothbrush, for reasons best known to himself. He's going to join us for lunch. Anyway, here we are.'

Butterflies. Big time.

And, finally, as if I've willed him into being by the power of longing alone, there he is again.

He is half-sitting, half-standing at the edge of an illuminated desk, upon which are arranged swathes of transparencies. He is wearing a khaki *Kite* T-shirt (why not? I recall him remarking. I get them free. And they're good quality), a pair of dark, baggy jeans with rolled over turn-ups, and green neon trainers that I recognise as being the ones Max would like. His fringe hangs in a flop over his brows, and the light from a sun shaft has painted a gilded stripe across it. The leg off the floor swings to and fro slowly, and one hand holds a pen, which he taps on his knee.

He is too, too beautiful. I almost find myself hoping I can sneak in unnoticed, because my heart's pumping blood round at such a great rate that I'm sure once our eyes meet, a log jam will happen, and I'll fall in an ungainly heap on the floor.

But I can't sneak in unnoticed, because Colin makes a big fuss about letting everyone know I've arrived, and Nigel comes up and hugs me like we were in Nursery school together, and the rest of Kite (bar Davey) mouth friendly hellos. I'm introduced to Ffion and Patrick and Andy, who are all very friendly and are in charge of production and whose names I immediately and completely forget. And all the while *he's* still in place on the desk edge and his eyes are focussed on me.

And then there is some sort of meeting.

Much of which I fail to take in. But unnoticeably so, it seems. It is only when everyone agrees 'lunch' and then move, that I re-focus my brain and move also.

The restaurant is one of those favoured by celebrities. The clientele are mostly people with familiar but un-nameable faces, and business types striving to look like they couldn't care less either way. Kite cause the smallest, politest of ripples then everyone gets back to not looking at each other.

There is a lot of cheerful, self-congratulatory chit-chat while orders are taken and drinks are dispensed. Craig is seated two down on our big circular table, so I have him in profile, but our eyes cannot meet unless we turn to achieve it. I concentrate hard while one of the publishing trio (Patrick or Andy?) fill me in on the next stage of the production of the book. He's talking about printing and paper coatings and covers, all of which floats straight up to the ceiling.

(Though I do not worry. I have motherhood neurones that I know will not fail me. I can cope with any number of different inputs at once. And my swoon state is simply a filter.) I choose some sort of warm salad, then excuse myself and set off for the loo.

Like many of its ilk, this toilet is themed. And the theme seems to be something like 'consider the twig'. Once I am able to find a stretch of mirror that isn't fronted by a spidery arrangement in a frosted-glass specimen bottle, I take heart from the fact that I don't, astonishingly, look in the least how I feel. By rights I should be flushed, a touch sweaty, with my pupils dilated and my hair stuck to my face. In fact I look fine. Sort of mauve and wispy and of a Cadbury's Flake-ad persuasion. But with the appropriate power line of the jacket in place. I touch up my lipstick – a tedious ritual – but my copy of *Female* was clear on the point. Women-who-win wouldn't dream of having bare lips – akin, it seems, to going to a meeting with your breasts hanging out. Or, horror, hair on your legs.

I emerge to continue my trial by endorphins (or *is* it pheromones, or is it estrogen, perhaps?) to find the chief executioner loitering outside.

'Gotcha,' he says – though quietly, and (thankfully) not sounding in the least like Noel Edmonds.

He takes both my hands in his and weaves our fingers together.

'How are you. How *are* you?'

'Actually, I'm trembling.'

'I can feel it.' He pulls our joined hands around his back so that our bodies are pressed closely together. He smells of soap powder and clean hair and some kind of deodorant. I want to *eat* him

'I can't stop it. I think I'm going to run out of adrenaline soon. Either that or die. Which wouldn't be very timely, as I haven't made a will or made love to you yet.'

He lets go of my hands and winds his own around my shoulders.

'Actually, I've done a recce. There's a cupboard right here, Mrs Potter, if you're desperate.'

'Aren't you?'

He presses me tighter against him.

'What do you think?'

'I think we're going to miss the champagne sorbet if we don't get back soon.'

'Fuck the champagne bloody sorbet.'

Then he looks down. 'Excellent choice of footwear. You're a good four inches taller. And as you have rather long legs in relation to your torso…yes. I think it might work. What do you think?'

'About my footwear?'

'About your *height*. In relation to…er…mine.'

'Supposing…'

'There's no lock. I've checked. That's the whole point. If *we're* standing against the door then it serves the same purpose, doesn't it?'

'What about the noise?'

'Don't worry, I'll sing. That should drown out your grunting.'

'So the plan is to have it in the bookshops late November, early December. The release date for the album is December 1st, right?'

We return separately to the table, to find that not only have our sorbets been and gone, but that our main courses have also been despatched back to the kitchen, to keep warm. Craig says, 'Sorry. Bumped into a friend in the cloakroom.'

A grinning Nigel calls the waiter to bring back our meals. Craig turns to me.

'God, what happened to *you*, Julia? Your neck's gone all red. Are you sickening for something?'

Okay. Smart ass. Ha, ha. I get redder.

But then I rally. 'Warm air hand-dryer. It's a genetic reaction. I'm told it's a little like prickly heat. My mum gets it.'

'But not as often as you must do, I'll bet. Ah, my T-bone. Top food here, eh, Nige?'

And so on and so forth, until three glasses of wine later I make a decision.

A decision not to make any further decisions about my life and rather, to go (again?) with fate's own ebb and flow and to take something positive from every encounter, and spread love and happiness wherever I go. Or something like that, just as Howard advised. You never know when you're number's up, do you? I say so.

'You're wasted,' remarks Craig as he heaves me into the car. Our publishing friends, apart from Colin, have gone now. He and Nigel look on benignly, like uncles.

I smile a happy little smile as the car sighs away.

'Not wasted,' I correct. 'Just euphoric.'

Craig tells the driver to take us to his place, then slides the glass partition across. I still can't get over the concept of having cars roll up whenever you a step out of a building. It seems so bizarre. So decadent.

I arrange myself decoratively against the black leather as we slide smoothly along. There is space enough in here to pose for an old master. Craig remembers my seat belt, and the brush of his forearm against the front of my thigh reminds me that I just made love, standing up, in a cupboard full of brooms and cash and carry loo rolls. Or did I dream it? So vast and diverse has been the range of my sexual fantasies about Craig over the last ten days that a cupboard scenario *must* have been among them. But none, as I can recall, involve me making much noise, bar the odd tuneful sigh of abandon. I nudge him.

'Do I grunt? Really?'

'Well, it's more of a low throaty moan, I suppose.'

'Then why do you say grunt? It makes me sound like a pig.'

'No, it doesn't. I find it really sexy.'

'*Oink, oink, oink*. You find *that* sexy?'

'That's not the noise you make. You do more of a ccrrraaaagch sound.'

'*Do* I? That's horrible.'

'Believe me, it isn't.'

'That turns you on then, does it?'

He slides a hand across my leg and traces a meandering route along the inside of my thigh.

'*Everything* about you turns me on. Ah, here we are.'

Craig speaks briefly to the driver and we clamber out. We are in Chelsea, in one of the wide, opulent, tree-lined streets that connect the King's Road to the ordinary world. There is a slight breeze which ripples the hem of my dress, and the bower of leaves sends a sprinkle of shade down. It forms charcoal puddles on the glittery pavement and the tops of the equally glittery cars.

All rather grand. I scan the row of regency buildings. They seem to reach up to touch the plane-trail patterned sky. They put me in mind of *Mary Poppins*, or *Oliver,* and stairwells for tradesmen – *God bless you, missus* – and carriages and nannies and long-legged dogs. They have tiers of tall windows: four or five floors of them, and every single one has got curtains to die for – all swags and tails and ruches and tassels, and held in elegant sweeps by tie-backs the size of koalas. No Ikea voile on a broom handle here. And no MDF either, I'll bet.

'This is all rather posh,' I say, wondering what sort of soft furnishing arrangements Craig goes in for. 'Some place to have a flat.'

I haven't up to now given much thought to Craig's living arrangements. I recall him telling me he lived alone in London, but I hadn't really thought beyond standard two bedrooms, South London most probably, with a futon perhaps, and a fridge full of beer.

He takes my hand and points to a glossy front door.

'Not a flat,' he says proudly. 'This is my house.'

Inside, of course, despite the stately home curtains and carpets so dense you could lose yourself between their creamy fronds, Craig's house, though obviously an order of magnitude bigger than many, is exactly what you'd expect the home of a twenty-four-year-old single man to be like. What appears to be the main living room could pass as a small branch of Dixon's. There is an enormous plasma screen TV, with the usual satellite paraphernalia, some sort of mega-stereo system, and speakers and amps and guitars and guitar stands and a necklace of cabling running round the walls. There is also a computer and printer, a fax, a scanner, and lots of other unidentifiable metal-ware with knobs on. It is functional, lived in. An organised muddle.

I take off my shoes and flop down on a sofa. 'How long have you lived here?'

'Just under a year. I was actually quite happy where I was, but I had a load of dosh sitting around in the bank and I was told I should invest some. I've got six bedrooms here and it's handy for everything. Ha. When I bought it I thought 'great, Chelsea, handy for the tube' but of course, it fucking isn't, and anyway, I can't use the tube these days, can I? But it's a nice house. There's plenty of room for my mum, and a family, I suppose, eventually. But it's empty half the time, as you can imagine.'

What I'm imagining is how big a load of dosh you need to have in the bank to buy somewhere like this. Then I remember what I keep forgetting: that Craig is (must be) a millionaire. Probably makes money every second of every day. Every time a Kite song gets played on the radio, each time a CD or download is sold. Every T-Shirt that's ordered, every poster and calendar. It is awesome to contemplate.

He puts on some music that I don't recognise.

'Truth is, I get dead bored sitting around here. I'd rather be round at Nige's, or my mum's. The neighbours are okay but mainly foreign, mainly old.'

'Isn't there a part of London where all the pop stars live, then?'

He kneels on the floor and starts flicking through a pile of papers. 'Not that I know of, and I'd steer well clear of it if there was. Like I told you, I don't like parties and all that crap, and I think I'd particularly hate having showbizzy neighbours. Couldn't stand all that in-crowd stuff. All that A-List celebrity crap.'

I recall what he'd said in Cardiff. 'Liggers and sycophants and slappers.'

'Dead right. Only worse, in some ways. Everyone wants to know you once you're successful in the music business. Everyone wants to be *seen* with you. And you get a bit twitched about people's motives, you know? At least, I do. I've never been that gregarious – apart from on stage, of course – I'm happiest with the mates I always had. And with girls...'

'They must queue up.'

'Exactly! It's fucking *awful*. I mean, I'm a bloke, right, so I make the most of the better than average pulling power Kite's given me. Course I do. We all do. But it gets mindless after a while. That's why with you it's so good. You know? You couldn't give a stuff who I was. I was just work, you know?'

'Not strictly true. I was very excited at having the opportunity to hob-nob with pop stars. But it never even *occurred* to me that I'd end up in bed with one.'

'Precisely. So when you realised you were attracted to me it was because it was me, an ordinary bloke. Not some Pop Idol. Trouble with most girls I've met is that they know so much about me before I know anything about them. It's creepy.'

'You're *not* ordinary. And I don't feel I really know anything about you. That's what makes it exciting.'

I kick off my shoes, then walk over to him. My feet feel like they're crossing a sea of mini-trampolines. I kneel down beside him. On a low chrome table just by where we are sitting, there is a cluster of photos in plastic frames. The face in one is familiar.

'Who's that?'

'My old man.' Craig stabs a finger at the photograph. 'He's another one. Couldn't give a damn when I was growing up. Treated us both like shit. And my mum just put up with it because she was worried about me not having a Dad around. Didn't throw him out until a couple of years back. He's all about now, though. Now his son's rich and famous. Surprise, surprise.'

'You've got his photo here. You can't hate him that much.'

'Oh, that's Mum. She's very sentimental about that sort of crap. Family really matters to her. Hence the little gallery. But no, I don't hate him. I'm just sad I can't have any sort of functional relationship with him. I tell you, when I have kids I'm going to make damn sure I'm around for them.'

'I'm sure you'll make a great dad.' Then I laugh. 'Listen to me! I sound like your mother!'

He leans across and says, 'Believe me, you are *nothing* like my mother.'

Then he kisses me, slowly and gently and softly, and the undergrowth carpet pile rises to meet us.

'So I'm going to play it for you again now. Plus lyrics.'

'These lyrics.'

'Those lyrics. I'm sorry it's not, you know, a love song or anything, but Jonathan can listen to exactly the same melody I do, and while I'm thinking angst, loss, depression or something, he could be just as likely to think 'seize the day'.'

He reaches for an acoustic guitar. His favourite, he says when he's playing with tunes. We are in his bedroom now. The sun is just setting and through the west-facing windows the treetops are burnished and the sky looks like it has been tipped upside down and dipped in blue ink.

I sit up, cross-legged, to read the hand-written lines.

'Ah, but *you* wrote this music. You probably had some sort of idea in your mind as you created it.'

'Not consciously. My thoughts are more along the lines of 'Yes! An A flat there's fucking brilliant!' Anyway. It's about war. Listen for the great chord change in the middle.'

So Craig begins playing and sings me my song.

Which is about an old man who lives on his own with a cat and a bunch of tarnished war medals and gets his tea from meals on wheels. And all the local kids call him names and terrorise the cat. The irony being, of course, that at their age he was fighting a war and killing Germans. And watching his friends being killed. Craig thought about calling it *Fin de siècle,* but then decided that *Fin de siècle* would make a brilliant title for their next album, so the song is called *Killing Games* instead.

It's hardly romantic, but particularly special. My grandad was killed at Ypres.

The sound of the guitar fills the lofty space above us, and seems suspended there for some minutes after he plays the last chord. I realise I'm in the presence of someone completely self-contained, and infinitely more complex that I'd ever have thought.

'There,' he says. 'Could make a single, you reckon?'

I nod. 'Without a doubt. It's brilliant. Well, in my opinion, anyway. But I'm not sure I'm really the best judge of such things.'

'Your opinion is good enough for me, Mrs Potter.' He grins. ' I need a beer. How about you?'

He gets up and places the guitar carefully back on its stand. 'Switch the telly on, will you?'

He throws me the remote and pads off down the stairs.

In my twenties, I once read a book called *The Dice Man*. By a man called Luke Rhinehart – a psychiatrist, I think I recall, rather appropriately – it was based on the concept of abdicating responsibility for your life and of having no control over choices and events. Its hero decides (though I can't recall why) that he will run his life according to the throw of a die. So for every decision he makes, from that moment, he must number six options and then roll for his choice. Both the concept and the book were so utterly fixating that having read it (in one marathon session, on holiday) I spent several weeks drawing up endless lists (nothing new there) concerning people and things I felt strongly about.

Switching on Craig James's television that evening is, I recognise immediately, a moment like that.

There's some sort of documentary about the completion of some sort of building project. I'm not really watching it until a coloured strip covers the base of the screen with the words *Peter Fielden – Fielden, Jones and Potter* on top. As he speaks, the camera pans around the familiar dirty grey of Cardiff Bay – I note the water level, pick out the church. The Pierhead Building. And then the hotel itself. Then the reporter thanks Peter Fielden, turns and smiles, and even before the new name comes on screen, I know what was coming next.

'Richard Potter,' he says, 'You must be breathing a sigh of relief. It's now been five years of delays and controversy. And you've taken your fair share of flak...'

Richard clears his throat and puts a slightly nervous hand to his chin. He's wearing his least favourite suit. The one with the mark on the side of the lapel. And the tie with Mickey Mouse on that Max had chosen for him the Christmas before last. I even recognise the shirt as being the one with the two bottom buttons missing and a small tear in the back. He wouldn't let me throw it away – being frugal, and also fond of it – but only wore it on days when he'd stay in his jacket.

'I'm extremely pleased,' he's saying. 'This is good news for the consortium. And validates the position we've always maintained.'

Craig returns at this point and sits down on the bed beside me. He hands me a bottle and gestures toward the screen.

'Good?'

'That's my husband.'

'You're kidding! But, Yeah, I see it. *Potter*. So. That's *Mr* P, eh?'

Richard's face looks lined and sallow. Like he's just stepped off a long haul flight. Which he can't have.

'What's this all about then?' asks Craig.

'It's a hotel they're building in the bay. Er…almost *have* built. Plus theatre, plus community arts centre. Richard is project manager. He's been living this for oh, over six years now, and there's been a lot of debate and argument over the cost, and whether Cardiff was even the right place for a five-star/ two thousand room hotel, let alone all the rest. That sort of thing.'

'Are there even that many *people* in Wales?' He laughs. 'No, you don't have to answer that.'

'But it's a valid point. It all presupposes a huge population growth, long-term, and in the short term that the area is going to become economically much more important than it is now. And some people feel something like this will become a sort of rich businessman's ghetto. Nothing to do with the community at all. But it will bring with it – has already brought with it – hundreds, if not thousands of jobs. And it's such an amazing building, and the concept…'

I point towards the screen.

'Every one of the two thousand rooms in the hotel is going to relate to a year – and will have a plaque detailing the important events of that year. And then there are ten separate conference areas – you know, rooms plus suites plus facilities etc., and those are going

216

to be themed to reflect each of the ten decades this century. It's an amazing place. I've seen all the plans. It's quite something.'

'Sounds like you took a degree in it! So they've just won something, have they?'

'I think they must have secured some more major funding. To finish it. There's been lots of delays because of money.'

The bar leaves the screen and the camera swings in an arc around the harbour. A knot of people are gathered. I recognise a local MP. Then:

'Good God, there's the kids!'

'What, *yours*?'

'Yes! There! That's Max, and just there – you see? Partly behind that guy with the hat? That's Emma!'

Craig leans closer to see.

'She looks like you, doesn't she?'

'She'd be mortified to hear that. Mind you, that *is* my jacket she's wearing.'

The camera moves back to the reporter it started with and then on to a report about lead pipes in some school. I feel strange.

Craig says,

'Hi-profile family, eh? Cardiff aristocracy almost. Bet you'll get a suite okay, once the place opens.' He smiles. He is not being flippant or sarcastic. He is, I realise, just quietly impressed. And why wouldn't he be?

Then he says,

'So that's the bastard, is it? Seems like an okay sort of a guy on the surface.'

I nod and take a sip of my beer. Then sigh.

'That's because he *is* okay. All the way through.'

Chapter 28

CLEAR HEADED
Decisive
Intuitive
Bright
Logical

All these attributes have been linked with the name Julia Potter at some point or other over the years. Which proves two important points. a) that you can put all sorts of rubbish on a CV and get away with it, and b) that other people (personnel officers and kindly GPs providing personal references etc., especially) either haven't the first clue what sort of person you are, or are completely taken in by the garbage your careers officer at school/college suggested you draw attention to in said CV. What I *actually* am (for the purposes of making manifestly *serious* life choices, at least) is muddle-headed, indecisive, devoid of insight, and stupid. If you par-boiled my brain it would probably work better. Which is great. Just great.

And I don't have any dice.

But there's no getting way from the truth. That I wish I was home, that I wish I had been there to support Richard, that I was with the kids, that I had sewed the buttons back on that shirt. That I suddenly feel horribly like I have slipped into someone else's life by accident. That I am experiencing all sorts of ambivalent feelings: about Craig (passion/empathy/*butterflies*, still, *big time*), about Richard (compassion/*some* kind of love still/regret), and about me (bloody *hell*/what's going on here?) That everything is simply *not fair*.

And I have developed a lurch. Bing! just like that. The sort of feeling that someone more poetic (or up themselves) than me would describe as a kind of tugging at one's heart strings. But it's really just a plain old lurch. I noticed it straight away.

Right after the piece on the hotel finished. Craig said, 'Did you never really consider forgiving him?' in such a level, measured, relatively light-hearted tone that it was impossible to get a handle on why he asked it. Was he just curious? Could he sense something had suddenly changed in my manner? Did he feel sorry for the guy? What?

I said (quite truthfully), 'I would have if he'd only done it once. But he did it twice. Which is a whole different ball game. Involving deceit and pre-meditation. Which were vastly more important than the sex itself.'

Then he said, 'Hmmm. Fair point. ' And my heart went *lurch*.

And has been doing so ever since. I now have in place a rather unsatisfactory flush/lurch combo. The sort of thing I recall someone describing once to me. Like a panic attack that got arrested mid-panic. Like the floor is rushing up to meet me even as I stand.

Except that I'm sitting. As if a three course meal involving veloutes, reductions, béarnaise and hollandaise and all that sort of food-to-expire-by wasn't enough, the plan was to go out for a curry with Nigel and Jacinta. So we duly, (him pensive, me busy flushing and lurching) got the car round and sped off to the Viceroy of Bengal (like the lunch place, a venue beloved of the stars and with men on the doors who would only admit you if you were famous, blue-blooded or on somebody's list). Not that I care.

But we're barely into the puris when Jacinta announces, 'Did Colin have a chance to run the book by you yet?'

'Book?'

'I've been commissioned to write a book for the noughties. A sort of post-millennial music and culture round up for the beginning of the new century. Some of the pix will be archive sourced, of course, but the bulk of it's going to be new stuff. I'm going to be doing a lot of interviews, gig reports and so on. I thought you might like to be involved and he said he'd ask you.'

It's like a bucket of warm custard to smooth over my turbulent feelings. Until Craig says, 'Great! That'll be really great, Julia. Keep you busy till I get back from the States.'

We made love again (*again*) when we got back from the restaurant, and afterwards Craig fell immediately asleep. I spent a good hour lying beside him, just looking. Not believing my luck. Not believing its end. When I did finally sleep, I dreamed a long, thoughtful dream. There were doors; doors ahead of Craig, opening before him, and doors after me, shutting softly behind. I kept running back and propping them all open with my mother's *faux*-vegetable doorstops, so I could still see where I came from. So I could still see an exit. Then the final door opened and Craig stepped on through it. Not

Disney this time, but impenetrable white light. Craig beckoned, but I didn't want to come with him, because this door was too heavy and it wouldn't stay open – even with a half-ton of clay propped against it. And there was a sign. It said 'one way only'. So if I went through, there would be no going back.

Laughable in the morning (we both laughed, of course). Chapter one in every volume of every dream book ever written. But that's because it's a universal feeling, I guess. But I found I still couldn't quite get a handle on the bottom line, decisions-wise, so I did the very best thing one can do in such circumstances. I didn't make a list, or make some dice out of sugar lumps. Instead, I arranged to meet my mother for lunch.

The deal is that we meet at the front of the Doc Shop. Even my mother cannot fail to find a shop that sells nothing but four floors of stout leather boots. But when I get there I find it isn't that any more. It's now a branch of a funky 'yoof' apparel emporium. But there's footwear in the window, and she's stepped inside anyway. I find her inspecting a pair of girls' biker boots with buckles, and wondering loudly why young women today don't appreciate how feminine a little peep toe always looks. With a lavvy-pan heel. And a nice pair of stockings. And a skirt that isn't trailing along in the gutter, or exposing their buttocks.

Richard, ironically, gets his name dropped into the conversation only moments after we sit down. Mother starts rustling. I'm used to my mother's rustling, of course. There cannot be a cinema in the South East that hasn't at some time projected its offerings to the low but insistent accompaniment of drink carton drainage, the opening of sweet wrappers or the search for the hankie she just *knows* she put somewhere. Today, however, her rustling is purposeful rather than an opinion on a film. She produces two items which she helpfully identifies as vases.

'When he came to pick the children up he admired several of my pieces, and I thought what a shame it was that he didn't have any for himself.' This last bit is accompanied by one of my mother's 'smiles' – the ones she uses in place of a 'you cow' suffix.

'So you made him these.'

'So I made him these. He told me his flat is mainly magnolia so I had complete artistic freedom with colour, which was nice.'

Listening to my mother throw expressions like artistic freedom into the conversation is deeply disconcerting. I fear she may be consorting with the man with the phallus.

'So you plumped for this pinky-greeny-magenta type combo. Very nice…'

'Doesn't it say 'Chinese rug' to you? I've always felt Richard appreciated a more traditional style.'

What?

'Hmmm. So what are you going to eat?'

'Do any of these dishes have a nice bit of steak in them? I can't make head nor tail of the menu.'

'There's a stroganoff here. That's got meat *and* gravy.'

'Or a pie. I've not had a pie for a while.'

'The only pie is a filo one with ricotta and truffles. I don't think you'd like that.'

'For pudding perhaps.'

Here we go then.

I leave my Mother at Victoria Station, with her rail-card, her rain hood and a round of tongue sandwiches, and promise to call just as soon as I'm back. Then I tube it to Paddington, grab a tea and a paper, and find my seat on the train for the long journey home.

I don't have the faintest idea what I'm going to do when I get there. I'm going to go to Richard's, of course, to make suitable noises about his exciting news, give him his vases (sic) and gather up the children, but that done I don't have any kind of a plan.

As we thrust smoothly westwards, I'm nurturing, I realise, a rather optimistic assumption that as soon as I clap eyes on him, it will all become clear. Why on earth should I think such a preposterous thing? In fact, why think at all? Has it helped me thus far? I should cocoa, it has. Why can't I just do a crossword or scrutinise the readers' husbands' bottoms in *Coffee Time!*, like everyone else does.

There is an awful lot of sky between Swindon and Bristol. Big sky, in that shade that is so beloved of travel agents and which it is impossible to describe without resorting to cliché. I ponder for ten minutes and come up with *Blue-Flush*. But it *is* luminous today. And criss-crossed with pale quilts of cirrus and mares' tails, and populated by high planes and solitary birds. Beneath these lie the soft curves of the Wiltshire fields. Like prairie, except they're not waving or nodding. Many are already shorn of their wheat and sport black plastic bales, like blackheads among the stubble. Which seems early to me. It is still only mid-August. Or have I missed some profound change in agri-technology? Do short stalks take less time to reach harvesting ripeness? I don't know any more. I only ever see sheep. I miss having arable farming nearby.

It is early evening when I finally pull up outside number seven Malachite Street. The sort of buzzy, scented, balmy early evening that makes you want to stuff your two boneless chicken breasts back in the freezer and go to a country pub with a garden, and sit at one of those picnic tables that have bird poo and ketchup splats on them, and say to yourselves 'ah! Summer at last!'. And guess what?

Butterflies. Small but robust.

Richard answers the door in jeans and a T-shirt. His feet are bare and his hair is slightly ruffled. Like he's been absently scratching an itch.

'Oh,' he says, not opening the door any wider. 'Didn't you get the message? The children aren't...'

'Here. I know. I came because I was driving by (Oh, *yeah*? Down a small residential street, off another residential street, off a road that leads to a community tip, a drop-in centre for the homeless and a place selling fireplaces and antique coal scuttles)...and I wanted to drop these off.'

I brandish my carrier.

'Oh.' His eyes narrow a little, but he opens the door a fraction more. The smell of Italian cooking wafts along the passage. Great heavens, he's not become another bloody pasta man, surely? I breathe in deeply. But no. It's only frozen pizza.

'So, can I come in?'

'Um.' Grudging. 'Yes, I suppose.'

For a moment I assume he must have a woman in. Rhiannon, perhaps? But then I realise the last conversation we had (bar arranging childcare logistics) involved him making a meaningful relationship declaration and me telling him in fairly unequivocal terms where he could shove it. No wonder there's condensation forming on the letter box. It will take him some moments to recover his equilibrium.

He stands aside politely and I move past him into the hall. My mother was right. It *is* mainly magnolia. With contrasting carpets. In a selection of colours to reflect bodily functions. Bile yellow, blood

222

red, a distressing shade of brown. I have never set foot in this place and don't know in which direction I should head. I am assuming (given the cooking aroma) that I should go kitchenwards. But there is carpet at every room threshold. So I hover with my plastic bag.

'Straight on,' he urges.

I'm reminded of the strangeness of our territorial conversations back in April, and how all the simple host/visitor exchanges stuck in my throat. And I keep spotting items that belong to the children: Max's baseball cap here, Emma's slippers there.

We enter the room at the end of the passage. The carpet had me fooled. This is the kitchen after all. Except it's the dining and living room too. God knows why, but I'm shocked by its smallness. It makes me want to blush. All I can think is that Richard went on the TV looking like a big noise in civil engineering and unknown to all the millions of people who saw it, he lives in a poky little hovel. Except it's not a hovel of course, because Richard is house-proud and tidy and good at minimising clutter (much enhanced, of course, by my lack of input), but it's bijou way beyond the point of being stylishly compact.

I sense he is studying my discomfort so I make a noisy fuss of busying myself with my bag. He glances at his watch. Me, or the pizza?

'So. What did you bring me?' he says, not sitting down.

'A present from Mum,' I say. 'She made them herself for you. Erm…'

I pull out the bubble wrapped shapes and unwrap them. 'They're, erm…erm…well, see for yourself.'

I laugh a little as he takes one. It's only a nervous/embarrassed type laugh (even though they *are* grotesque) but he wastes no time in upbraiding me for it.

'They're very nice *act*ually. It was a very kind gesture. You should try being a bit less…'

'I'm sorry?'

'A bit less critical of your mother. How do you think she would feel if she knew you were standing here tittering about these?'

He wields them aggressively.

'I wasn't tittering.'

'Yes you were. You were taking the piss.'

'I wasn't.'

'Yes, you were.'

He is quietly insistent. How dare he?

'I wasn't taking the piss, as you say. Not at all. And anyway, are you trying to tell me you didn't have a good laugh about the rotating hen egg holder?'

We are squared up like duelling toddlers across a kitchen table the size of a monopoly board. Do the three of them sit around this to eat? Richard's chin juts.

'That was different.'

'How?'

'Because it was funny.'

'Only because you painted nipples on two of the eggs. That's not taking the piss at all, I suppose?'

He carefully places the vases on the table. Like they were the crown jewels. And then looks at his watch again.

'It's not the same thing at all. Your mother has made a point of making these for me. Of letting me know that she's thinking of me. Of being kind. Of being *thoughtful*. And all you can do is pour scorn on her efforts and titter, like a...'

I intend to interrupt with something placatory and Mother-friendly, and to steer the conversation away from what is rapidly turning into an extended dip into the cess-pool of my character. But then he looks at his watch *again*, and irritated, instead I say, 'Spare me the pathos, *please*. And the lecture as well. And she's *my* mother, and just because I don't think she's Croydon's answer to Wedgwood, doesn't mean I don't love her. Okay?'

He picks up a tea towel. It is clean and has iron folds. Pizza time?

'I'm picking the children up from the cinema in an hour and a half. It would be easiest if I dropped them back to you, wouldn't it. All right?'

I am being dismissed. I am being *bloody dismissed*.

He doesn't even offer me pizza.

Bastard.

Making some sort of totally sleaze-ball comment about his catering arrangements I stomped out and down to the car.

I heard the front door shut only inches behind me, so there was little point in making a histrionic departure. So, instead, I sat in the car for a few moments and wondered where precisely, *precisely*, our bizarre conversation had taken a wrong turn and ended up where it had.

Then I did a new list, on the back of a Sainsbury's receipt. I wrote:

<u>Richard</u>
Bastard
Holier Than Thou (and then some)
Dismissive
Ungrateful (though did not know about me knowing about TV programme so slightly unfair)
Suspicious (so, above)
Unfriendly (so, above)
A bit *nasty*
? Motivation
Woman???

All in all, I decided, he had only himself to blame if I just told him to shove it.

By the time I got home I was so puffed up with righteous indignation that a stray pollen grain could have easily popped me. Just where did the toe-rag think he was coming from? There was I, all fired up to be friendly, even conciliatory, perhaps, and he threw it in my face with a barrage of sniper-fire. In fact, he may as well have gone the whole hog and just told me to sod off.

Which was why, when the doorbell rang fifteen minutes later, I found myself saying exactly that to him.

He blinked at me. 'Pardon?'

'You heard me. Where are the children?'

'I told you. I'm picking them up at eight-thirty. It's now only…'

'So why are you here?'

'Look. Can I come in or are we to conduct this conversation on the doorstep while Mrs Buckley deadheads her marigolds?'

I turned and glared but all credit to her. Though she had quite plainly heard she didn't even break snip. I moved the glare back. 'Which conversation would that be? I wasn't aware we were having one.'

'Oh, very droll. I'm coming in.'

Which he did. With a well-aimed left leg into the hallway. Followed by the rest of him.

'I don't…'

225

He exhaled. 'Can't you stop that for five minutes? I came to ask you precisely why you turned up at my flat half an hour ago knowing very well that the children were not there and that you could give me those vases when I brought them back here. I could think of no plausible explanation other than the one that occurred to me while you were standing in my kitchen, which was that it must have seemed like a good opportunity to have a nose at my shit-hole of a flat. Except that you could have found an excuse to have a nose round my flat any time in the last few months, so it's not a very plausible explanation at all. And I'm sick and tired of trying to work it out. So here I am. Well?'

He folded him arms.

'Wrong. For your information...'

'What's all this *for your information* tone about?'

'It's not a *tone*. For your information, I came round to your flat because I saw you and the children on TV yesterday evening and I hadn't realised that you'd got that backing you needed, and I wanted to let you know I saw it and to congratulate you on your success.'

Hah. Point to *moi*.

'You're kidding, of course.'

'I'm not kidding! Why should I be kidding? You must have been very excited about it.'

'So what?'

'So I thought I'd let you know I'd seen it.'

'So why didn't you just tell me when I dropped the kids off?'

'Because I didn't.'

'But *why*?'

'Because I *thought* it would be nice to come round and tell you face to face.'

'You could have told me face to face here.'

'I know, but...'

'But what?'

He sat down. Then stood up. Then said,

'Why do I get this horrible feeling in the pit of my stomach that you came round to tell me something else? You did, didn't you?'

I shook my head.

'Not as such, but...'

'You want a divorce now, don't you?'

What?

Which was the thing that did the trick for me really, because Richard's stomach's feeling hopped straight across to mine. Why bother being cerebral about affairs of the heart. Give me basic physiology any time you like.

I said, 'Richard, I did not come round to tell you I want a divorce. I came round because...well, because...because I was being nice. I saw you on TV and thought how you must be really proud and I thought how you had no one to share it with and so I thought I'd come round and let you know I'd...'

'You *what*?'

I didn't answer because I could see he was just pausing to gulp in another breath before saying, 'You *what*? You thought you'd come round to be *nice*? *Nice*?'

I tried a nod.

'I see. You thought you'd come round to be nice to me, did you? Well, let me tell you, you can take your nice and shove it, okay? The last – the *very* last – thing I need right now is to have you coming round and being *nice* to me. Got it?'

Did I imagine it, or was he shaking slightly?

'I didn't mean nice as in *nice*...'

'Oh.' He balled his fists. 'As in patronising, then, maybe? As in – don't tell me – *compassionate*, perhaps?'

Which was the thorny one *I'd* been tussling with. And had dismissed absolutely. 'No! None of those. I meant nice as in, well, as in... because *I* wanted to. I wanted to...'

He sat down again. 'Be Mother bloody Potter, patron saint of sad gits.'

'I'm sorry?'

'You heard.'

'You are not a sad git.'

'I'm well aware of that, thank you. But to *you*...'

'*Not* to me.'

I sat down as well. I felt faint. 'I came round because when I saw you on the TV it made me wish I'd been there as well. That's all. And because, well, you had that shirt on...'

'You see?' His hand slapped against the table. 'There you go again! Julia, my shirts are no longer your concern. I think we're both clear on that point, aren't we?'

'But that's the point. I watched it and I wished your shirts *were* my concern.'

Richard stared at me for some seconds. Then sighed, then began to look exasperated. Then angry...then was.

227

'Well they're not! You can't have it both ways! You can't just waft in dispensing pearls of benevolence, you know. You either wanted to stay with me or you didn't and you didn't. End of story.'

I noted the past tense. And Richard's behaviour at his flat became suddenly clear. I'd been so wrapped up in my own spin-cycle feelings that I'd entirely neglected to consider his.

'Richard, I don't want it both ways. I'm just trying to explain how I felt. What made me come round to your flat, and…'

He stood up again, and this time walked to the other end of the kitchen. Where he turned, and, arms folded across his chest, said quietly, 'I really couldn't give a stuff how you felt.'

'That's not true!'

'But it is. Don't you realise? I'm sick of considering your bloody feelings, and I'm sick of trying to fathom how you feel about me. I'm sick of feeling guilty, of feeling bad about the children. I'm sick of hearing the children bang on *endlessly* about all the exotic and exciting things you're apparently doing, and I'm sick of staring at my four crap walls every night. I'm sick, more than anything, of having to think about it at *all*.'

He crossed his legs at the ankle and put his head on one side. 'Got that?'

He seemed calmer, at least. I nodded. He uncrossed them.

'Good.'

Which amounted to a bit of a conversational cul-de-sac, because I couldn't think of a single constructive thing to say. It was obvious that anything short of a no-holds-barred declaration of absolute unconditional love and forgiveness would represent a gross insult to his intelligence. And I wasn't altogether sure I was ready to make one. I had been kind of hoping for a gentle slide into testing the water. Not to be chucked in the diving pool. While I silently cogitated, Richard uncrossed his arms and checked his watch.

'I suppose I should go and get the children,' he said.

'Shall I come?'

'There you go again!'

God, this was hard.

'I'm sorry. I just thought…'

'I could have built the bloody Forth Bridge single-handed in the time you've spent 'just thinking'. What useful thought could you possibly have had then?'

'I just thought we could go together. I thought…(deep breath, mantra: self helpinnerchildselfhelpinnerchild)…we could maybe discuss our, er…relationship on the way.'

'Our re-lay-shon-ship?' he said it in exactly that manner. 'Have we slipped into an episode of *Neighbours* suddenly?'

'How we're feeling about each other. You know, right now.' Where the hell did I read *that*?

'I can tell you how I'm feeling, Ju. Like you're beyond belief.'

Ju. He said '*Ju*'. I took a long, deep breath. 'No, but *really*. How do you *really* feel about me, Richard?'

'None of your business.'

'Don't retreat into sniffiness. You know you don't mean that.'

'Don't start.'

'But you don't.' I stood up. I had caught him on the squirm. Feeling empowered by this sudden shift in the dynamic, I said, 'Look, when I saw you on TV, I was completely floored by how I felt. But I wasn't sure if it was because of you, or me, or just rose-tinted glasses, or wanting my cake and all that, or just a residual effect of having spent the last fifteen years of my life married to you. All I knew was that I didn't expect to feel the way I did. So I thought if I saw you, spoke to you…then maybe I could sort out how I *did* feel and…'

Richard shook his head, picked up his car keys and began to walk out of the kitchen. So I followed. We left the house, and I locked it. Then we walked side by side up the path to the car. I stood by the passenger door while he pressed the alarm key. Our gazes met, as it clunked, over the warm, dusty roof. His eyes seemed to glitter in the last coppery rays of the setting sun. Or was I just being fanciful? Probably. He sounded every bit the long-married civil engineer when he said,

'Do you want to know how I *really*, as you put it, *feel* about you? Then think back a way to when we got married. Remember how I felt then? Well that's how I *still* feel. That's how I'll *always* feel. Boring, but there you have it. No blips, no changes, no crises of commitment. As you well know. Even if I did lose my senses for a while there. And even though you have become a bloody mad cow of late. Go on then, get in. And make sure you don't sit on my Millennium plans.'

I loved him for that. We got into the car.

The End

Almost…

Sunday

Me:
'Craig! Look, I can't talk at the moment.'
'You did it, then…'
'Erm…'
'I knew you would. Are you glad?'
'Erm…'
'I'm really fucked off…'
'Look, could I…'
'Give me a bell, yeah? Soon?'

Me:
'Oh, God, Craig, I wish I knew what to say to you. It was going to happen some time though, wasn't it? I mean, you knew that, didn't you? We both did, didn't we? I mean, not Richard necessarily, but you know, just you and me. You're going off to the States soon, and you're *so* much younger than me and – yes, okay, I *know* – but I would have been on a pension while you were still in a band, most probably – can you imagine it? – and I couldn't have given you any babies anyway, and…'
'Shut the fuck up, you dozy cow. I *know* all that. I just, you know – Christ, you've got me at it now – I'm finding it difficult to handle the idea of not seeing you again. You know?'
'Of course I know. But we will still *see* each other, won't we? When Jax and I catch up with you after you get back. They could hardly publish a book about Brit Pop and not put you in there, could they? Really?'
'I suppose. But it seems a long way off. And it's not like we'll be…'
'No. No, we won't. Craig, I'm sorry.'
'Bet I'm sorrier than you, Mrs Potter.'

Monday

Me:
'What's with this 'cow' business, anyway, Rani? That's twice now, in two days I've been called a cow. Richard called me a mad

230

one and Craig called me a dozy one. It's not really on, is it? I was kind of hoping I'd be able to exert a new authority on my relations with men now. You know, do away with all the passive/aggressive female thing and you know, just command respect. You know?'

'They'd never get away with it in Delhi. You could most probably be shackled up and dragged behind an ox for saying stuff like that.'

'But I thought women were so repressed in Indian society.'

'The *cow*, Jules, is sacred.'

Rani:

'What do you think? Here, take a dekko.'

'Bit under-exposed, focus slightly off. Lighting dodgy. Who's is it?'

'Not *who's* is it. *Who* is it. His name is Raul, he's studying accountancy in Bombay and I'm going out to meet him at Christmas.'

'Oh.'

'You said it.'

Tuesday

Lily:

'Alors! It is good to be back home at last! You must tell me every tiny detail of your love life. I am so fed up of hearing – on and on and *on* – about how my mother is going to knit me designer booties and stay for a month and cook endless quiches and potage. And Malcolm loves every minute! Can you imagine! He and my mother are going to drive me to a mother and baby home in despair. They are so in love with each other! You will have to rescue me at every opportunity – if, that is, you have time between dashing here and everywhere with your photographic jobs and so on. And please tell me if you would like to see the translations of Jerome's letters *before* I give them to Emma, which I think you should because they are more than a little rude. You know what French men are like! Bye!'

Wednesday

Howard:

'How's it going?'

'Okay.'

'Richard moved back now?'

'Yesterday. I have accepted the trouser press back into my life. How is Nick?'

'Oh, he's fine. Busy.'

'I'll bet.'

'You don't like Nick, do you?'

'Er...'

'Jules, I know what you saw.'

'Er...'

'Look. I know about Nick, and it's all right. Honest.'

'Don't tell me. Just sex?'

'It's not like what *we* have.'

'But couldn't he...'

'He tries...'

'Hard enough?'

'His best. Life's too short, Jules. So I don't want to know. I'm happy, he's happy. You happy?'

'I think so. Yes. Happy. I am.'

Thursday

Max:

'Mum, it says nothing in the prospectus about logos, honest. I've read it six times. There is nothing.'

'It says "outer coat to be black and *without* motifs", which means no *Nike* logos the size of a tea tray. Now, this one would do fine. It's black, and it's waterproof, and it's got lots of useful pockets...'

'Mum, it's total pants! I would look a complete derr-brain! Do you want the whole school to laugh at me?'

'Total what?'

'Total *pants*, Mum. Total.'

'Pants?'

'Mum, don't be such a saddo. I thought you were *cool*. Look, *K-Swiss* then. That one. The K's very small...'

Emma:

'I can't believe you are even *thinking* about it! Everyone knows the Bahamas are old hat now. Only sad people go to the Bahamas these days...'

232

'But your Dad and I thought you and Max would be thrilled! The Bahamas, Em, just think of it – white sand, palm trees, warm sea…'

'Mosquitoes. Tropical spiders. Snakes. *And* some naff teen-club for derr-brains as well, I suppose. Mum, why can't we just go somewhere cheaper and save the money? Buy a conservatory or something…'

'But I don't *want* a conservatory. I want an exotic foreign holiday. I want to drink cocktails out of pineapples and dance the night away with hibiscus blooms in my hair…'

'Ye-uch.'

'So where do *you* want to go then – the Siberian tundra?'

'No. Just France. *Please*?'

Friday

Richard:

'I don't know if I can live with this colour.'

'Too bad. It took me for ever to do.'

'What? Painting four walls?'

'You just don't get it, do you? This is a *paint effect*.'

'Quite. It's certainly affected. What was wrong with the cream?'

'Cream is yesterday's colour.'

'It's better than this. This looks like the inside of yesterday's take-away containers.'

'It's called Scorched Sienna.'

'Or a stomach upset.'

'Well it's staying. Since when will *you* get round to changing it?'

'I won't. Now you're almost rich we can get a man in.'

'What – *I* can?'

'*My* choice. Someone bald and retired.'

Saturday

Me:

'How many times then? *Really*.'

'*Okay*. Three times. Ju, Do we have to do this?'

'It says here "try to exorcise demons and unresolved resentments. It is vital that you are able to move on to a closer understanding of one another, and to achieve this you must learn to communicate more effectively" blah, blah, etc. Third time when exactly?'

'Isn't 'unresolved resentments' a bit of a tautology?'

'Come *on*.'

'Okay. Not when you thought. It was way after that. When you were away. I was really angry. And I thought, sod her, then. Look, Ju, don't you find it difficult to talk about this?'

'Yes and no. Yes, because I don't like to think of you between that *cow's* Egyptian cotton sheets, naturally, but no, because we're quits now, so we can discuss it as equals. Without any unresolved feelings of, well, inequality, I suppose. Which is important.'

'You make it sound very clinical.'

'I don't mean to. It's just that we've balanced the books now, haven't we? I honestly don't think I could have had you back, had I not, you know...'

'Slept with someone else as well?'

'You see? You *can* do it.'

'But unlike you I really don't want to know *anything* about it. Really, I don't. So please don't tell me. Except...'

'What?'

'Except, did you love him? When I asked you that day there was something in your eyes that...well, something. You know, I never really did feel anything for Rhiannon. Not like that. I actually felt really guilty about sleeping with her again. But you...'

'Of *course* I didn't love him. Let's just say I gave myself a bit of a shock. I thought I could just have no-strings sex with someone, like you did. But I found out I couldn't. For a woman – for me, at least – there really is no such thing. But then I also found out that you can't be happily married to the same man for fifteen years without a damn good reason. Extra-marital shagging notwithstanding, eh?'

'Ha, ha.'

'Ha, ha.'

'End of therapy session.'

So. We've drawn a line under the past and are moving forwards and upwards. Like Howard said, life's too short, isn't it? If you love someone – and have a stake in their lives and their happiness, then it would be sad to abandon all that because of one indiscretion. He knows what Nick's done, just like I know about Richard. And

234

Richard – well, Richard's just glad to be home. And all those books I've read didn't turn out to be pointless, because we've reached a new level of understanding now. The deal is that if Richard succumbs to his loins again (which I hope won't happen, and, frankly, I doubt) then it's *his* problem. His to deal with and his to cope with. The thing about marriage, the thing about *life*, is that guilt should be a strictly one-person affair. Richard knows that the night when he confessed about Rhiannon was simply a way of diluting his guilt.

We're more clued up now. Our marriage is important to both of us. If it happens again, he must keep it to himself.

Because what we don't know can't hurt us, can it?

Here's hoping. Wish us luck…xxx

Also by Lynne Barrett-Lee

Title	ISBN	Price
Out on A Limb	9781905170067	6.99
Barefoot in the Dark	9781905170371	6.99
Virtual Strangers	9781905170166	6.99
Straight On Till Morning	9781905170395	6.99
Secrets (A Quick Reads titles)	9781905170302	2.99

For more information about Lynne Barrett-Lee
and her writing please visit:

www.lynnebarrett-lee.com